# Private Party

# Private
# Party

## JAMI ALDEN

APHRODISIA

KENSINGTON BOOKS
http://www.kensingtonbooks.com

APHRODISIA BOOKS are published by

Kensington Publishing Corp.
850 Third Avenue
New York, NY 10022

ISBN-13: 978-0-7582-1986-2
ISBN-10: 0-7582-1986-5

First Kensington Trade Paperback Printing: November 2007

10  9  8  7  6  5  4  3  2  1

Printed in the United States of America

*To Gajus.*

*Thanks for loving me,*
*supporting me,*
*and always believing in me,*
*no matter what.*

# Acknowledgments

They say it takes a village to raise a child, but in my case it also takes one to write a book. As usual, I am indebted to my amazing friends and critique partners, Bella Andre and Monica McCarty. Thanks for reading this and giving me invaluable feedback even after the hundredth read. And thanks to the fabulous Fog City Divas—I always leave our gatherings inspired and ready to dive back in.

And I especially want to thank every single reader who has taken the time to write to tell me how much she enjoyed my books. When I'm sitting alone in front of my computer, literally pounding my head to get the words to come out right, it's feedback like that that keeps me going.

# 1

Julie Driscoll was, without a doubt, the most beautiful bride Chris Dennison had ever seen. Her strapless ivory gown left her arms bare, and, if he closed his eyes, he could imagine how silky her skin would feel against his fingertips. Though her veil obscured her face, he could vividly picture wide, long-lashed eyes the color of the Caribbean sea at sunrise; her small, slightly upturned nose; and full pink lips. Her breasts swelled tastefully against the bodice of her dress, though even that was enough to make his mouth dry and his palms sweat. With the wide, poofy skirt of her wedding gown nearly spanning the entire width of the aisle of San Francisco's Grace Cathedral, she reminded him of a luscious dollop of whipped cream, tempting him to lick her up with one lusty sweep of his tongue.

His chest got tight as she approached, his stomach twisting in knots as every step led her closer to the altar. She was really going to go through with this. He'd had eighteen months to mentally prepare himself, and still the realization hit him like a fist in the gut. He clenched his hands into fists, took a deep, calming breath, and willed himself not to turn tail and run from the church as fast as he possibly could. He'd made a promise, and unlike some men in his family, when he gave his word he kept it.

"Who gives this woman in marriage to this man?"

Chris watched, a sour ache building in his stomach, as her father, Grant, lifted her veil to reveal a nervous-looking smile that didn't quite reach her eyes.

"Her mother and I do," Grant replied, and Chris swallowed back the curse screaming in his brain as Julie's groom, Chris's older half brother, Brian, stepped forward to take her trembling hand.

"Where in the world is he? It's time to cut the cake."

"I'm sure he'll be here any minute," Julie Driscoll Dennison attempted to soothe the frazzled wedding planner. "Why don't you have one of the ushers check the bathroom, and I'll see if he's out in the lobby."

Honestly, you'd think Brian would know better than to disappear in the middle of the reception.

"Everything okay?" Wendy, Julie's maid of honor, sidled up alongside her and asked.

"I can't find Brian. He probably needed a moment to himself."

Wendy quirked a brow. "Right . . ."

Okay, so Brian wasn't exactly the introspective type, but still, it was his wedding day. God knew Julie was all but overwhelmed by it all. "I don't suppose you've seen him."

Wendy shook her head. "Where's his brother? I thought it was the best man's job to keep tabs on the groom."

"He left right after he did his toast," Julie said. She smiled a little when she thought of Chris's toast. So practiced, so polite. So unlike him. Chris wasn't the kind of guy who worried about what people thought of him, especially not the stuffy, overly self-important crowd attending her wedding. His easygoing, casual style made him stick out in this crowd, even as he tried to fit in.

Unlike Brian, who could have been a *GQ* cover model, Chris's dark brown hair was always a little shaggy, his big, muscular body always looking a little too big for his clothes. But he had looked absolutely delectable in his tux, the white shirt a seductive contrast to his skin, burnished from the strong Caribbean sun. Chris had always been gorgeous in a rough around the edges kind of way, and he'd only improved in the five years since she'd seen him last.

She closed her eyes, trying not to imagine the acres of tanned muscularity he had hidden under that tux. She'd thought she'd gotten over her silly teenage crush on Chris a long time ago, and her wedding day to his half brother was no time for her to resurrect it.

She mentally slapped herself. Today was her wedding day, for goodness' sake. All of her months of hard work and planning had finally come to fruition, and now was not the time to revisit her long-dead infatuation with her fabulous groom's black sheep of a younger brother.

She exited the ballroom and made her way down a hall, stopping to chat politely with guests along the way. As she neared a utility closet, a thump sounded from behind the door. Then a giggle. Then a moan.

A decidedly masculine moan.

Her stomach somewhere around her knees, Julie had an awful premonition of what she would find behind that door.

"You son of a bitch." Her voice sounded very far away, like it came from the end of a long, echoing tunnel.

She squeezed her eyes so tight her eyelids cramped. This could not be happening. It simply couldn't.

But there was no mistaking Brian, frozen mid-thrust as he

nailed another woman against the wall, who was gaping over his shoulder at her in a way that would have been comical under other circumstances.

She spared the other woman a quick glance. Ah, of course, the lovely Vanessa, Brian's newest assistant. She had suspected Vanessa's employment had more to do with her mile-high legs and oversized chest than her secretarial skills, and she kicked herself for stupidly giving Brian the benefit of the doubt. But the last time she'd caught him cheating he'd sworn to God, on his grandmother's grave, and the title of his prized Ferrari, that it would never, ever happen again. He'd promised that the next time he would have sex would be with Julie, on their wedding night. And with their wedding plans forcefully in motion, it had been easier to believe him than to admit she was about to make the biggest mistake of her life.

"Julie, it's nothing. It doesn't mean anything." Brian fumbled with his tuxedo pants, grabbing at his cummerbund as the trousers slid back down around his ankles. Vanessa had pulled her skirt down and made a dive to retrieve her underpants. The action sent Brian stumbling backward over a mop and bucket, and he landed on his ass in the middle of Vanessa's chest.

Julie had never been sucker punched, but she imagined this was what it might feel like. A sharp hit to the middle of her chest, a sensation of all the air leaving her lungs, leaving her gasping like a dying trout. Pain radiated through her, accompanied by the icy burn of humiliation. Still, she grasped for control, trying not to let Brian see that she was blowing apart from the inside out, into a thousand tiny fragments. Her mind worked frantically, searching for the appropriate thing to do or say in a situation like this. But there was no sweeping this under the rug with social niceties.

Taking a mop handle and shoving it somewhere extremely painful was probably not the best response, however appealing it was at the moment. "We're supposed to cut the cake now," she said stupidly.

In a daze, she made her way back to the ballroom. How could she have been so stupid? Allowing herself to be hauled to the altar like some sacrificial cow. Sweet Julie, perfect Julie, always doing the right thing for her parents, for her family, for the business. So determined to never make a fuss that she had refused to acknowledge the truth about her husband-to-be.

Barely conscious of her actions, she pushed open the door to the ballroom of the Winston hotel, the crown jewel in the D&D luxury hotel empire. Her father, Grant Driscoll, and Brian's father, David Dennison, had acquired the property just two years ago. Within a year, it was giving the Fairmont a run for its money as *the* luxury hotel in San Francisco.

But she didn't even see the beautifully redecorated ballroom with its elaborate chandeliers and silk wall coverings that conveyed an atmosphere of old-fashioned elegance and luxury. She didn't care about the tens of thousands of dollars' worth of white roses that adorned each of the seventy tables that had been set to accommodate the wedding guests. She didn't even care when she stumbled into a waiter and a glass of merlot splashed down the skirt of her custom-made Vera Wang wedding gown.

She moved through the crowd, seeing nothing but blurry flesh-colored shapes of guests as they tried to catch her hands, to kiss her cheeks and offer congratulations. Ignoring everyone, she made her way to the dais at the front of the room currently occupied by the band.

As she reached the first step, she felt a firm grip on her arm. She didn't even acknowledge Wendy as she shook off her grip.

Signaling the band to stop, she grasped the microphone and lowered it until it was at mouth level. It was then that she realized she was shaking. Not just a little tremble of the hand, but a full-body quake. She stared out into a crowd that represented a who's who of San Francisco society. Out of the corner of her eye she saw the mayor hitting on one of her cousins. Her father's business partners, city council members, and wealthy financiers and their spouses stared at her expectantly.

Julie licked her lips and grasped the microphone. Her knuckles were white as she clenched the microphone in a death grip. Glancing to her right, her stomach clenched as two waiters wheeled out the five-tier chocolate raspberry with vanilla fondant icing wedding cake, and positioned it next to her.

"Can I have everyone's attention please?"

The request was totally unnecessary—everyone was staring at her in slack-jawed astonishment.

"I appreciate that you have come here to celebrate what was supposed to be the most special day of my life." A vague, outer-body sensation overtook her, enabling her to see herself as though from across the room. What would the little psycho bride say next? "Unfortunately, my special day has been ruined by the fact that my husband," she gestured to the back of the ballroom, where Brian fought his way through the throng, "decided that his wedding reception was a perfect place to screw his new assistant."

A chorus of gasps and murmurs rippled through the crowd, snapping everything into sudden, vivid focus. Mouths gaped, eyes bulged as people craned their necks to catch a glimpse of the errant groom.

"So, while I encourage you to continue to enjoy the festivities, I'm going to call it a night." She gathered up her full skirts and had barely made it to the edge of the stage when Brian finally reached her.

"Julie, I'm sorry, please, you have to listen." Brian had combed his hair and straightened his tuxedo, and was once again the epitome of perfectly polished masculinity. Grasping her arms so tightly she knew she'd have marks, he said in a pleading voice, "I'm a sex addict. It's an illness. I can't help myself, Jules—"

She wrenched out of his grip, and a surge of rage violently snapped her out of her state of shock. It was exactly the sort of excuse Brian would come up with—one absolving him of all personal responsibility, eliciting sympathy rather than blame. Suddenly, so furious she feared her head might burst into flame, she yelled, "An addict? For an addict you sure haven't had a problem keeping your hands off me!"

Brian walked towards her determinedly, and she backed away and tried to skirt around him. "Can you blame me for trying to avoid a permanent case of frostbite?" he muttered so only she could hear. But for the crowd he said, "How can you turn away from me when I need your support?"

Every eye was riveted to the drama playing out on stage.

"Get out of my way, Brian." She had to get out of that room, away from everyone and everything that had forced her into this public humiliation.

He moved again to grab her, and she instinctively reached behind her, her fingers coming into contact with the smooth surface of the cake. Turning slightly, she grabbed the surprisingly heavy top tier. Using every ounce of strength in her body, she ground it into Brian's shocked face.

"You might want to zip up your fly," she sneered.

She straightened her shoulders, and raised her chin haughtily, as she, Julianna Driscoll, the perfectly poised princess of the D&D hotel empire, removed her wine-stained, cake-smeared, wholly enraged self from the ballroom.

# 2

"Damn him, damn him, damn him!"

Julie ripped the veil from her head, and cursed again as nearly half her hair detached from her scalp in the process. Hairpins sprang from her head like confetti as her perfectly smooth French twist was decimated, leaving her chin length blond bob sticking out in heavily sprayed clumps. She kicked off her custom-made Manolo Blahniks as she stomped to the bathroom to find a brush.

The reflection that greeted her was startling, to say the least. Her face was flushed with a combination of anger and the champagne she'd consumed. Her hair stood out, Medusa-like, in an approximation of the worst bed head she'd ever seen. A semi-insane laugh bubbled up from her throat.

Her gorgeous strapless dress, perfectly tailored to fit her petite frame, bore a giant wine stain on the bodice and a big black smudge on the skirt from where it had caught in the elevator doors in her frantic flight to her room.

*How could this possibly be happening?*

She wasn't normally the type to indulge in self-pity. How

could she when she had more than any woman had a right to ask for? Involved, if not particularly affectionate, parents and a handsome, successful fiancé—make that husband. A job she loved as the senior special events manager at the Winston, and a generous parental supplement to her income that allowed her an adorable two-bedroom flat in Pacific Heights.

But was it really asking too much that she be her husband's only sexual partner on their wedding night?

Suddenly her chest grew tight, her breath short. The bodice of the dress prevented any air from entering her lungs, and she frantically clawed at the buttons that ran down the length of her back.

She grunted and strained, but her trembling fingers couldn't negotiate the silk covered buttons. Her hyperventilating accelerated, and Julie knew she was moments from passing out. With her luck, she'd knock her head on the toilet and sustain massive brain damage.

"Stupid dress," she panted as she tried in vain to reach the buttons. Why did they have to make wedding dresses so hard to get in and out of? What kind of sadistic tradition was this to put a woman in a garment she couldn't put on or take off by herself in an emergency?

If she could find her nail scissors, she could cut her way out. She dumped the contents of her toiletry bag on the floor and was frantically clawing through the pile when a knock sounded on the door of her suite.

"Go away," she yelled as she sorted through the contents of her bag with shaking hands. Where were the damn scissors? Wendy had used them this morning to cut a stray thread from the hem of her skirt—maybe they were in the sitting room . . .

"Let me in." It was Wendy, her voice firm through the heavy wooden door.

Julie clenched her hands in the fabric of her skirt. "Go away. I don't want to talk to anyone right now."

"Jules, if you don't let me in, your mother will get the manager to give her a key."

Julie slumped to the bathroom floor, defeated. She had no doubt her mother would do precisely that, and Julie didn't have it in her to deal with Barbara Driscoll's hysterics right now. She had to let Wendy in, if for no other reason than to block the door.

"I'm coming." She came slowly to her feet, stepping on the hem of her skirt in the process. She heard a loud tearing sound and looked down to see a four-inch rip in the seam where the skirt of the dress met the bodice. Really, for twenty thousand dollars, you'd think a dress would be more durable.

She opened the door. Her best friend had a look of wary concern in her big brown eyes. Without a word, she stepped over the threshold and pulled Julie into her arms.

"Are you okay?"

Julie gently but firmly pulled out of her friend's embrace. While she appreciated the gesture, she feared she would fly apart at the slightest touch.

"You look like hell."

"Yes, I know."

She could well imagine the picture she made, especially in contrast to Wendy. Wendy looked glamorous and sexy, her tall figure and dark hair set off perfectly by the floor length lilac bridesmaid dress.

A fresh wave of anxiety swamped her as she remembered that over five hundred friends and relatives were no doubt still downstairs, wondering what the hell was going on. Her breathing accelerated, and she clawed at her dress again, desperate to rid herself of the cumbersome garment.

"Get this thing off of me!"

"Hold on, hold on." Wendy grasped her shoulders to still her frantic movements. Spinning her around, Wendy made quick work of the buttons, as well as the hooks of the French lace bustier underneath.

Julie sucked in several deep breaths, reveling in the ability to breathe freely as her dress fell in a frothy white puddle at her feet. She opened her eyes and angrily kicked it aside. Pulling the equally restrictive bustier from her torso, she went to the closet to retrieve her purple chenille bathrobe. Nearly ten years old, tattered and faded from too many washings, it was as comforting as a baby's security blanket.

"Brian hates this robe. He said it made me look like a grandma." Julie relished the sharp sense of satisfaction she got as she pulled the sash tight around her waist. "He made me stop wearing it in front of him, and I was going to get rid of it after tonight."

She sat down on the edge of the bed next to Wendy and put her face in her hands. Her favorite comfy robe seemed like a symbol for everything she'd been willing to give up in the course of her relationship with Brian. No longer hiking in the hills of Marin because Brian wanted her to exercise under the strict, regimented eye of her trainer at the Olympic Club. Never wearing cute, trendy clothes because she needed all the help she could get to look older and more sophisticated. Trading in her cute little VW bug for a BMW five series because it was "more appropriate for the image she needed to cultivate."

So many things, big and small, but all of them things she liked, things that were a part of her. She'd given them all up in her quest to be the perfect daughter, the perfect girlfriend, the perfect everything.

"I can't believe he did this to me," she said. "Can you believe he did this to me?" Julie stared at Wendy.

Wendy's raised eyebrow and consoling pat on Julie's knee were more than sufficient in conveying her utter lack of surprise.

"I feel so stupid. I really thought, after I caught him last spring, that he would be faithful. But I bet he never stopped cheating this whole time."

"Nope, he didn't." Wendy's conviction sent a prickle of irritation across Julie's shoulders.

"How do you know for sure?"

"Jules, I saw him all over the city." Unlike Julie, Wendy was an enthusiastic party girl, and loved to explore San Francisco's hottest restaurants and clubs. But despite her best efforts, it was a rare occasion that Julie joined her for a night on the town. "At least once a week, I'd see him with some woman at the Bubble Lounge or the Redwood Room. And if he didn't arrive with someone, he left with someone."

There were times when Julie really appreciated Wendy's bluntness. This wasn't one of them.

"Why didn't you say anything?" To be fair, Wendy wasn't to blame for Brian's behavior, but she couldn't believe that the woman who'd been her best friend for the past five years would ever keep this kind of information from her.

"I did tell you," Wendy said, exasperated. "More than once. And you took him back every time. You knew all along that he was never going to change. If you were willing to look past his affair, it wasn't my business to try to talk you out of it."

Julie's stomach knotted as she silently acknowledged the truth in Wendy's words. From the minute she'd met Brian, Wendy had disliked him. He was too much of a slickster, she said. He was too smooth, too polished, an Eddie Haskell in a better looking package. She had tried, sometimes subtly—but mostly not—to convince Julie that she should dump him. Once after a party, Wendy had even claimed that Brian had made a pass at her with Julie in the next room. The accusation had so enraged Julie that she didn't speak to Wendy for a full month.

The friends finally mended fences, but from that moment on, if Wendy disapproved of Brian, she kept it to herself.

But despite her strict "no comment" policy, she couldn't keep quiet earlier this spring. She'd seen Brian leaving the Clift hotel early one weekday morning when he was supposed to be in Seattle on business, with a sultry brunette practically glued to his side.

By that time, Julie was firmly entrenched in planning their fall wedding, racing full bore into her future as Mrs. Brian Dennison. She'd convinced herself that Brian had slipped up, just that once. And since Julie had been forced to admit, if only to herself, that their sex life was less than spectacular, part of her wondered if it wasn't partly her fault. After that she'd vowed to try harder to be the kind of lover he wanted to prevent any future lapses in judgment.

But in her heart she'd always known it hadn't been the first time, or the only time. Which was why her attempts at spicing up their love life had amounted to a huge pile of expensive lingerie and two rather lackluster encounters in the past six months. But she did like her sexy new undies, even if Brian hadn't seemed to appreciate them.

After that, she'd resigned herself to a comfortable, if not passionate, marriage. There were more important things in marriage than sex, after all. And by marrying Brian she would be instrumental in joining the two families, cementing their business relationship and raising the company's public profile. Even if she'd wanted to back out, she couldn't possibly do so without making a huge stinking mess.

Still, the mess had managed to find her.

"God, I am such a doormat," she groaned, flinging herself across the bed. Then she sat up, fists clenched, and said, "I want to go down there and kick him in his perfectly capped teeth."

Wendy laughed sharply. "Let's go. I'll hold him down. But don't forget to stomp his balls, too."

A knock sounded at the door. "Julie, let me in."

Julie winced at the quivery, slurring voice. Great, not only was her mother her usual emotional basket case self, she was also half in the bag. Usually it was Julie's job to calm her mom and talk her down from whatever emotional tree she'd gotten herself up, but tonight she just didn't have it in her. She grabbed Wendy's shoulders. "You have to get rid of her."

Wendy went to the door and motioned Julie to hide in the suite's kitchenette as she answered the door. She could hear Wendy's muffled voice, then her mother's shrill one.

"It's chaos down there," her mother sobbed. "Everyone keeps asking me what's going on, and I don't have any idea. Grant disappeared with Brian, and Julie needs to come downstairs to quiet everyone." Barbara's voice cracked, and Julie heard the muffled honking sound of her mother blowing into her hankie. "And all of the local media are here. What on earth am I going to tell them? There's no one around to tell me what to say."

"Mrs. Driscoll, why don't you go to your room and have a little coffee. I'll call the wedding coordinator and have her straighten everything out."

"But Julie—"

Julie peeked around the corner, and Wendy moved to physically block the doorway with her body. Luckily, Julie's mother shared her daughter's petite frame, so Wendy had no problem acting the bouncer. "Trust me, Mrs. Driscoll, it's best for her not to see anyone right now. Who knows what else she might do?"

Easily overwhelmed under normal circumstances, the stress of the evening had clearly drained her mother's meager reserves. With a small, pitiful sob and a plea for Julie to visit her when she felt up to it, Barbara agreed to retire to her room for the evening. Julie made a mental note to have a stiff martini sent up.

Julie breathed a sigh of relief when she heard Wendy close the door and slide the dead bolt. Wendy walked back into the suite and slipped her arm around Julie's shoulders.

"This is it. My mom's finally going to have a nervous breakdown, and it's all my fault."

"She'll be fine. First thing tomorrow all of her friends will call her and ooh and ahh over what a scandal you've created, and she'll get to wallow in all the sympathy and attention."

Julie snorted. "Think they'll spare a little sympathy for me?"

"You know you're better off, don't you?"

Julie shrugged and sat down on the bed. "I think we could have made it work. We've known each other forever. We move in the same circles. I've never had to worry that he was after my money."

"Or your body." Wendy went straight for the minibar, emerging with an armful of tiny bottles.

"For some people—"

"Sex isn't the most important thing," Wendy finished in a sing-song voice. "If you'd ever found a guy who knew what he was doing . . ."

Julie rolled her eyes. She'd slept with more than one guy before Brian—three to be exact—and the results had never been the transcendent thrill her girlfriends all described. It had never worried her all that much.

Wendy wouldn't let up. "And sex aside, what about trust, companionship, all that stuff? Admit it, Julie, the only reason you got involved with Brian in the first place was because it was the path of least resistance and a way to guarantee your dad's approval."

Julie groaned, unable to deny the truth. "That's so pathetic. I'm so pathetic."

"You said it, not me," Wendy said under her breath. Julie stuck her tongue out and ran her hands through her hair, grimacing as her fingers were impeded by the thick coating of hairspray. "Ugh, I need to take a shower. You make us some drinks."

She heard tiny bottles clinking as she stepped under the spray, and vigorously scrubbed away every bit of makeup, hairspray, wine, and cake, trying to erase this day from her life in the process. She was so tired of being polite, done with biting her tongue for the sake of appearances. Her backbone was twenty-six years overdue in making an appearance.

She emerged from the bathroom fifteen minutes later, hairspray and makeup free. She looked at the glass Wendy offered and shook her head.

Wendy's brow knit in confusion. "It's chardonnay, like you always drink."

"Give me that," Julie said, snatching a mini bottle of tequila off the side table.

"Uh, Jules, are you sure you want to drink that?"

"Chardonnay is for spineless debutantes. As of today, I am a strong independent woman." She uncapped the tiny bottle of Cuervo with a flourish. "I'd like to propose a toast to the new and improved Julie Driscoll. A new Julie who does what she wants, when she wants, and doesn't take shit from anyone. Especially her low-life, asshole husband who can't wait to cut the cake before having his first affair." She raised the bottle and tossed back the contents in a single gulp.

Her new tough girl persona was ruined as she collapsed into a fit of coughing and gagging. "Yuck. This stuff is terrible without the margarita mix." She reached for the wine to wash away the gasoline-like aftertaste. "Maybe I better work up to tequila."

Her eyes lit on a bottle of Veuve Clicquot chilling in a bucket along with two Baccarat crystal champagne flutes. "How romantic," she said snidely, grabbing the bottle in one hand and the glasses in the other.

Julie settled herself on the bed next to Wendy and made short work of the cork, spilling bubbly onto the carpet. She handed Wendy a glass of champagne.

"Let's try this again. A toast, to the new Julie Driscoll, former doormat, now bitch on wheels." She took a big swallow of champagne. The bubbles tickled their way down her throat and immediately warmed her belly.

Wendy's grin swallowed up the bottom half of her face. "It's about time!"

"I *know*. You've been telling me for years that I need to get away from my parents, get my own life, and get rid of Brian. I think this whole fiasco is the Universe's way of telling me it's time. It's a whole new world of possibilities, starting right now."

"Here, here." Wendy took a big gulp of her champagne, and Julie quickly refilled their glasses.

As the alcohol warmed her belly Julie got more enthusiastic about her new life. "I want to find someone wild, someone completely unsuitable."

"You should sleep with his brother," Wendy said, a champagne flush on her high cheekbones. "Six foot three, wide, muscular shoulders. I can only imagine what's hiding under that tux. And did you see his hands? Promising, very promising. I tell you, a good revenge fuck would really piss off Brian."

"I can't go after Chris." But even as the words left her mouth, Julie's brain was awash in images of Chris naked, over her, under her, moving inside her. "Besides, even if I wanted to, I'm totally not his type."

Wendy rolled her eyes, motioning Julie to unzip her so she could trade her bridesmaid dress for one of the suite's complimentary robes. "Bullshit. The only reason guys don't make a move on you is because of your butter-wouldn't-melt-in-my-mouth Little Miss Muffet routine. Believe me, given the slightest encouragement, there are plenty of guys who would love the opportunity to muss you up." She polished off her champagne and mixed herself a vodka tonic from the minibar. "Chris Dennison is no exception."

Julie clicked on the TV. Her inability to "work it" was a favorite, much discussed subject over the years, and it wasn't one she wanted to have now. Despite Wendy's vociferous arguments to the contrary, deep down, Julie didn't believe that she had a whole lot to work.

She was attractive enough, she supposed. But at 5'4", with her wavy blonde hair, big blue eyes, and modestly curved body, her looks were much more Sandra Dee than Marilyn Monroe. She might as well have had "future soccer mom" stamped on her forehead. Not exactly the type to inspire lust. And it had never really bothered before.

Okay, so it had bothered her the year she and Chris had overlapped at Berkeley, when she was the naïve freshman and he the overprotective senior. Since he'd been raised by his mother, Julie had only seen him a handful of times before in her life. She vaguely remembered the big, good-looking guy who was nice enough to her on those occasions. But when she'd run into him her first week on campus, twenty-two-year-old Chris had suddenly inspired all kinds of sexual feelings and fantasies the likes of which Julie had never known before. Or since.

"I'm like his adorable kid sister," she said glumly. "I always have been." She couldn't help smiling at the memory of Chris looming over many an unfortunate frat boy who sought to get her drunk on keg beer and trash barrel punch.

"I haven't seen him since he took off after that blowup with his father and Brian right after I graduated from Berkeley. God, he looks good." Julie had barely thought of Chris in the five years since he'd left. Or rather, she hadn't allowed herself to think of him, maybe because deep down she knew she'd find herself in exactly this situation. With her brain full of lustful images, her body itchy, tight, and throbbing in places it had no business throbbing, with no hope of relief from the gorgeous hunk of male flesh whose fault it all was.

An hour and a half later, Julie flicked through the channels for the hundredth time as she finished the last of the champagne. Wendy snored against the pillows, a half-empty bag of peanut butter M&Ms clutched in her fist.

Damn Wendy and her talk about revenge fucking and throwing herself at Chris. She couldn't stop thinking about him, tangled in his 600-thread count sheets, all muscles and tawny skin.

Lust pooled in her belly, mingled with indignation, as she took in every feature of the bridal suite. This was supposed to be her wedding night, damn it. She was supposed to be rolling around this bed and frolicking in the Jacuzzi with the man she had married.

Oddly, the thought wasn't so much painful as it was embarrassing. Now that the initial shock had worn off, she realized her anger was due to her pride talking, not to her heartbreak over Brian. She'd wanted to marry him, at least she thought she had. Still, she'd always known that their marriage had been one of compatibility rather than passion. And she'd been okay with that. But until today, she hadn't realized how little regard Brian actually had for her, that he would be willing to do something like this on their wedding day.

Looking back at the way she'd acted like such a doormat, was it really any wonder Brian thought he could walk all over her? But that was all about to change, starting now.

Maybe Wendy had a point. Maybe she really did just need to drop the Miss Goody Two-Shoes act and let men know that simmering under her apple pie looks was a sex goddess waiting to be released. There was only one way to find out.

She went to the dresser and pulled out a small pile of tissue paper, extracting the ivory silk La Perla negligee she had chosen for tonight. As she slipped it on, the cool silk soothed her heated skin. She smoothed the fabric over her hips and reached once again for the purple robe, then grabbed the intimacy pack so thoughtfully provided by the staff at the Winston.

The old Julie would never do anything like what she had planned. But the new Julie had been promised sex tonight, and she'd be damned if she didn't get it.

# 3

---

Chris stared into the minibar, pondering his next selection. He had to give it to his dad and Grant, they sure knew how to stock a minibar. He could stay drunk for a week if he wanted.

Which was probably what he would do if he didn't have to leave at the butt crack of dawn tomorrow morning to get back to Holley Cay.

He selected a single serving bottle of Jack Daniel's and cut it with the other half of the Coke left over from the rum and Coke he'd just polished off. He winced at the cost of the liquor on the minibar price sheet. Foolish, he knew, to hole up in his room drinking ridiculously priced liquor when he could be enjoying an open bar downstairs.

But he couldn't face it. He'd done his duty, showed up, acted the best man, acted like he was happy to see little Julie Driscoll tie herself to a stupid schmuck like Brian. Then he got the hell out of there as soon as he had choked out his canned, completely insincere toast.

Chris had no illusions about his older brother and what kind of husband he would make. Brian was exactly like their dad—

slick, scheming, always needing to be in power. It served them well in business, but it was hell on the women in their lives. Dad was already on his fourth marriage, and he was probably cheating on her. David Dennison couldn't give up the thrill of the chase, the satisfaction of the conquest. And Chris had no doubt that Brian was the same.

His grip tightened around his drink as he settled onto the plump pillows that graced the room's queen-size bed. He didn't know why he was so upset. It wasn't as though he'd spent the last five years pining for her. Much. But it had been nine months since he'd received the engagement announcement. Nine months to let go of any illusions he might still have of one day enjoying everything sweet Julie had to offer.

Nevertheless, images of her tormented him. Julie in her red gingham bikini the summer she'd turned sixteen. Plump little breasts pressing against the tight fabric, nipples beading hard against the cold water. Julie at the country club, looking all perfectly preppy in her sweater sets and pearls. She'd always been such a lady, even when she was a teenager, annoying him with her prissiness while inspiring lurid fantasies about peeling off her white cotton panties and showing her how fun being bad could be.

And finally the worst image of all. Julie, standing at the altar beside his brother, looking as fragile as a china doll as she pledged her life to Brian.

He sucked down the rest of his drink, as though it could drown out the voices in his head that berated him for not making a move on Julie when he'd had the chance. Oh no, somehow at the age of twenty-two he'd developed a noble streak when it came to her, knowing instinctively that getting involved with her would only hurt them both. So instead of indulging in his long running fantasy of teaching virginal Julie all about the joys of sex, he'd instead devoted himself to being her protector rather than her lover.

And while he was in the Caribbean killing himself to establish Holley Cay as a world-class luxury resort, his scumbag of a half brother had made his move.

A knock startled him out of his ruminations. A look through the peephole revealed the last person he would have expected. Julie Driscoll—make that Dennison, her features distorted by the fishbowl effect of the peephole—was pounding determinedly on his hotel door on what was supposed to be her wedding night.

He unlocked the dead bolt and opened the door. For a moment he thought he was hallucinating. Or maybe he'd mixed that last rum and Coke from the minibar a little too strong, had passed out, and was dreaming. This certainly wasn't the first time Julie had invaded his dreams, but most of the time she was wearing something a little more provocative than her ratty purple grandma robe she had back in college. She must be real, because if this were a dream, that robe would be on the ground and he'd be halfway inside her by now.

That didn't stop the blood rushing to his groin. That year they'd overlapped at Berkeley he'd arrived at her dorm room more times than he could count to find her fresh out of the shower wrapped in that robe. Thoughts of peeling back the soft worn fabric so he could run his tongue all over smooth, damp skin had made a mockery of his vow to keep his hands off her.

His cock thickened against his shorts, and he reminded himself savagely that she was a married woman, and to his brother to boot. Something must be really wrong for her to be here, and he had no business getting a boner when he needed all of his blood to remain in his brain.

"Is something wrong with Brian?" he asked when she didn't say anything. She was just staring, mouth slightly open. He could almost feel the heat of her gaze against his skin as it traveled, first across his chest, then down his flat abdomen, and lower, until her eyebrows quirked with interest.

Chris glanced down, face heating as he realized he wore nothing but his boxer briefs, and the bulge in the fly was growing as she stared.

Dragging her gaze back up to his face, Julie said, "Can I come in?"

Chris stepped back to let her in, and somewhere in the back of his minibar fogged brain a warning went off. Women didn't typically visit other men's rooms at two in the morning on their wedding nights.

She perched herself on the edge of the bed and clicked on the bedside lamp. The light cast her in a soft glow, illuminating her pale gold hair and baby smooth skin. She looked about fourteen years old with her big blue eyes and soft pink lips. She was staring again, her expression anything but innocent.

With his cock threatening to peek through the front of his boxer briefs, he casually reached for one of the spa robes hanging in his closet, grimacing when he realized that one-size fits all didn't apply to his frame. The robe pulled across his shoulders, exposing his chest, and he could barely straighten his arms. But at least if Mr. Happy decided to poke his head over the waistband, Julie wouldn't see.

"You left the reception early, didn't you?" she said, as though it was the most normal thing in the world for her to be in his room, when she should be enjoying her first night of marital sex. "You never did like any event that required a tie."

He nodded. "Yeah, and I have a really early flight." He sat down on the bed next to her, the mere scent of her was enough to drive him crazy. Just as in his dreams, Julie had shown up in his hotel room. And yet here they were making idle chitchat about the reception and his travel plans while he sported an erection hard enough to pound nails.

And even though every nerve sang with awareness and the need to lay her back on the bed and shove his tongue between her legs, he knew that wasn't what Julie came here for.

Or was it, he wondered as she shrugged, sending one sleeve of her robe sliding down her shoulder.

Chris's mouth went dry at the sight of the little strap of ivory satin resting against her smooth skin.

"I caught Brian having sex with his assistant in the utility closet."

Her revelation momentarily yanked him from his fantasy of taking the strap between his teeth and dragging it down the silky skin of her arm. "You what?"

"I went to find him to cut the cake, and I found him having sex with his new assistant, Vanessa, in the utility closet outside the ballroom."

She sounded surprisingly calm, considering the circumstances. But then Julie never did let her emotions get the best of her. If anyone could handle such a situation gracefully, it was Julie.

"So I got on the stage and explained to everyone what had happened, and then I smashed cake in his face."

It shouldn't have been funny, but Chris couldn't contain his burst of laughter. Perfectly poised Julie, smashing cake in Brian's oh-so-perfect face. In front of five hundred of his nearest and dearest friends and business associates, no less.

He couldn't control the low chuckle erupting from his chest. "Damn, I'm sorry I missed that," he paused, tried to regain his composure. "I'm sorry for laughing. I know it's not funny to you."

A mischievous little smile he'd never seen before crossed her face. "Actually, it was hilarious. Brian still had his fly down, too, the boob."

"I'm sorry." He scooted closer and wrapped a comforting arm around her shoulders. She snuggled close, and he buried his nose in the softness of her hair, breathing in her clean, fresh scent. He'd always loved how Julie smelled, like Ivory soap and white flowers. His cock grew what felt like another inch, and he firmly told it to settle down. This is what she had come for, to be comforted, not to be hit on.

But then she turned toward him and slid her hand down the front of his chest, inside his robe and around until it rested against the bare skin of his back. He almost purred when her fingers traced little patterns across the muscles of his shoulders.

"It's so good to see you again, Chris," she murmured, nestling even closer until the hot puff of her breath tickled his neck. "I've missed you."

"It's great to see you, too, Jules." He ran his hands soothingly down her back. He was simply comforting her. What was wrong with that? Nothing. His hand slid lower, testing the resilient curve of her hip, nobly bypassing her butt as he slid his hand back up her spine.

She pulled back a little, keeping her arms around him, hand still teasing the bare skin of his back. "This is supposed to be my wedding night." Her face was somber, but bore none of the grief he might have expected from a woman who had been betrayed by the man she loved. "Tonight I was supposed to spend the night making love to my new husband."

He could only nod in agreement. Where was she going with this?

"Do you know that I've spent my entire life trying to be perfect? I've done everything right, everything my parents ever wanted, and look at what it got me."

It was true. Unlike him, Julie had lived her life in pursuit of her parents'—her father's especially—approval. That was a big part of why he'd never made a move on Julie, because he knew Grant Driscoll would never approve of her running around with Dennison's wild son, the product of a brief, scandalous second marriage to a Las Vegas cocktail waitress. Whenever Chris had gone to visit his dad and run across Grant Driscoll's path, he'd made it clear he didn't like the idea of Chris so much as looking at his daughter. Julie had been so careful to keep their friendship a secret, he knew she would never take him home as her boyfriend. At the time he'd decided it was best to settle for friendship, afraid if he actually had sex with her he wouldn't be able to keep himself from shouting his claim to anyone within hearing range, and fuck the consequences. All the while he'd swallowed his resentment over hiding their innocent relationship like it was some kind of dirty little secret.

And when Chris had left the family fold to pursue his own dream of his own luxury resort, he'd known Julie would never consider leaving the security of her nest to join him. Not that he'd thought of asking her. Not more than a hundred times, anyway.

He hadn't had a chance of a future with her then, and he didn't now. But here she was, staring at him with those big blue eyes, showing off her sexy shoulders, filling him with an insane mixture of lust and tenderness, making him scheme to steal her away to his island paradise until she agreed she belonged to him. What the fuck was wrong with him? He'd had years to get over this bullshit. He'd had plenty of time—not to mention plenty of women—to help him get over the fact that his irrational crush on Julie would always go unfulfilled.

So what if she was in his hotel room in the middle of the night? He was too old to let Julie—who was so completely clueless about the tornado raging inside him—tie him up in knots. Though he knew it was a bad idea to keep touching her, he ran his thumb across the curve of her cheek, doing his best to ignore the sharp jolt shooting from his thumb to his balls.

"I wish I could have been more like you, had the courage to stand up for myself and what I wanted. Instead I let myself be talked into marrying a man who I knew would never make me happy."

He nodded. "I always thought you deserved better." He wrapped his arm around her and squeezed tight.

"As of today, I realize that, too. That's where you come in."

Chris's hand froze on her back. For a moment, it had felt like old times. How many times had he consoled Julie when a boy she liked broke up with her? Sure, part of him, the part throbbing insistently between his legs, was dying to get her naked, but he'd been able to suppress it as they fell into the old familiar rhythms of their friendship.

Now she had that look again. The look that said she wanted to lick him from head to toe, with special attention paid to the in-between parts.

As if. He really must be drunk or crazy. Probably both.

"Chris, I have a really big favor to ask you." Her expression lost the lusty glow and changed to one of polite expectation.

"Anything, Jules."

"I want you to have sex with me."

"What?" He had to have misunderstood her.

"Have sex with me, please," she repeated, her expression all earnest and polite as though she were asking for a refill on her Diet Coke. When he did nothing but stare with his mouth hanging open, she continued. "I'm serious. My whole life I let other people tell me what I wanted, because I was afraid of disapproval. After tonight, I don't care what anyone else thinks. For once, I want to go after something I really, really want. And that's you."

Her eyes went hot and liquid again, her hands delving under the lapels of his robe to stroke his chest. "I want you, Chris," she whispered again, leaning in to slide her lips along the skin of his collarbone. Still, he did his best to remember all the reasons why he shouldn't take her up on her offer. She was vulnerable, for one. She'd found her husband of less than a day banging someone else. That was enough to send anyone over the edge into irrational, inappropriate behavior. And he could smell champagne on her, and even as an asshole frat guy in college he'd never taken advantage of a drunk girl.

Her hand slid up the inside of his thigh, her fingers teasing their way under the leg band of his boxer briefs. He nearly came right then and there.

"I know you're upset," he half groaned, "but I don't think you really want to do this."

"Oh, I'm pretty sure I do." She stood up and pushed the purple robe to the floor and drew his hand to cup her breast through the creamy satin of her slip.

"I'm leaving tomorrow," he said, unable to resist whisking his thumb over the hard bead of her nipple, "and I don't know when I can make it back. All I can promise is one night." Jesus Christ, he had Julie Driscoll's tit in his hand. The mere thought sent a roaring through his head, so loud he almost didn't catch what she said next.

"I know what you're all about, Chris," she said in a sexy, throaty tone he'd never heard from her, throwing a leg over his thighs so she was straddling his lap. "That's the point."

He didn't have time to think about what she meant as she rose up on her knees and looped her arms around his neck. For all her bravado, her kiss was tentative, lips barely parted, seeking his mouth with the slightest of pressures. Her taste exploded into his mouth, sweet, spicy, shooting down his spine until his hands shook with want. He tongued her lips apart, needing more of her, needing the feel of her tongue tangling with his. Her hands fumbled with the belt of his robe, and he eagerly shrugged it off, groaning at the feel of her satin covered breasts against his chest.

He sucked and bit at her lips, quickly losing control as his hands slid eagerly up and down her back, lower to cup the lush curves of her ass. For all the fantasies he'd had about being with Julie, touching her, kissing her, tasting her, this was better than anything he could have ever imagined. He arched his hips up against the vee of her thighs, letting her feel how huge and hot she made him.

She let out a little squeak, stiffening ever so slightly against him. Fuck. He needed to get a grip or he was going to be the only one having any fun. "You're sure you want to do this," he asked again, praying she'd say yes, but needing to be sure all the same. Sure, he hadn't seen her in a long time, but the Julie he'd known had never been one for casual sex, and he seriously doubted that had changed.

"I do," she moaned, spreading her legs wider over his hips so he could feel the heat of her arousal through the thin cotton of his boxers. "I've always wanted you, Chris, and now I finally have the chance to have you." His thoughts were muddled with lust, but a tiny kernel of hope lodged somewhere in his gut. Despite what she'd said, was it possible that Julie wanted more? Maybe once this mess with Brian was cleared up, once his life calmed down enough, was there actually a chance they could be together? "Besides," she whispered between kisses, "I love the idea of how pissed everyone would be if they ever found out."

His hands froze in their exploration of her breasts. A revenge fuck. That was all this was about. He should have realized the second he saw her through the peephole. The realization did nothing to calm down his dick even as it stopped his vaguely forming fantasies of living happily ever after with Julie dead in their tracks.

Of course. He was the second son, the one no one took seriously. Good enough to fuck, but not much else.

His hands tightened on her hips as something dark and primitive rose up in him. If all Julie wanted was a meaningless fuck between friends, who was he to say no? He'd give her what she wanted. So good and hard the memories would torture her for the rest of her life, the way she'd tortured him. And with any luck, by finally having Julie exactly where and exactly how he wanted her, maybe he'd get her out of his system once and for all.

Switching their positions, he flipped her onto her back, securing her wrists in one hand above her head. His other hand slid down the firm plane of her belly, and lower. Wetness soaked through the material of her slip as he pressed his fingers into the heat between her thighs. He made a low sound of satisfaction, as he felt his cock become impossibly harder. Silk rasped against the pulsing bud of her clitoris as he increased the pressure, pressing his fingers into the drenched folds of her sweetly throbbing pussy.

He sucked her tongue into his mouth, swallowing her panting, breathy little moans. "I can't wait to get inside you." She quivered against him, so damn close to coming apart in his arms. He pulled his hand from between her thighs, smiling at her indignant sound of protest. He wanted her to come when he was inside her, wanted to look into her eyes and hear her scream his name as she pulsed and clenched around his cock.

He released her wrists and tugged her slip around her waist. For a long moment, he didn't touch her, just hovered over her, braced on his arms so he could stare at her perfect tits. Finally she began to squirm, her face flushed with embarrassment under his blatant stare.

He lay down on his side, propped up on an elbow as his other hand explored her almost lazily. "Do you know," he said, his big palm nearly covering the creamy flesh, "how many times I've imagined this?" Her skin was, impossibly, even softer than the fabric of her gown, her nipples small and pink, drawn tightly into hard little buds. For a moment his anger over being used faded as he reveled in the feel of her silky skin against his palm.

He bent to trace his tongue along the underside of her breast. "I used to watch you at the pool. You wore a red and white checked bikini." His tongue swirled around her nipple, flicking it with the slightest pressure. "The cold water made your nipples hard, like they are now." Her fingers threaded through his hair, holding his mouth tightly against her aching flesh. "I used to imagine you taking your bikini off for me so I could taste you." He followed with a slick slide of his tongue against one, and then the other nipple.

"Please," she whispered, her head rolling against the mattress as she arched into his mouth, begging for more than a teasing caress. He closed his lips firmly around one bud, tormenting her other nipple with the gentle pinch of his fingers. He opened his mouth wide, taking as much of her into his mouth as he could, then drew back and sucked hard.

He moved over her, settling between her legs as he continued to kiss, suck, lick her breasts in every way he'd ever imagined. Her legs wrapped around his torso and she ground against him. Her slip had ridden up her hips, and her bare, moist heat rubbed hotly against his abdomen. The scent of her arousal hung in the air, musky and sweet at the same time. She was killing him.

"God, you're beautiful."

Her eyes were bright and glassy with desire, her curls spread behind her head in a sexy tousle. Her slip twisted around her waist, baring her plump, perky breasts above and her lush tangle of dark golden curls below. Her parted legs offered him an unimpeded view of her pink, glistening flesh. The part of his brain still capable of thought marveled at the gorgeously sensual creature that lurked under Julie's wholesome exterior. Lying there across his bed, she looked sexy, eager, and hotter than any woman had a right to be.

His cock twitched, and he knew he couldn't wait much longer. He'd waited too many damn years for Julie. He had to get inside her. Now.

He stood up and quickly shucked his boxers.

"Oh my," she said in a tiny voice as his erection sprang free.

He couldn't suppress the purely masculine surge of pride when he saw the flash of admiration in her eyes. And behind that . . . nervousness. Leaning down, he braced his weight with his arms and caught her mouth in another scorching kiss. "This is going to be good. So good."

He grabbed a condom, and, with a quick motion, he sheathed himself and settled his weight between her thighs. Reaching down, he positioned himself against her opening and thrust inside.

"God, your pussy is so tight," he whispered, working his thick length inside of her. His eyes drifted closed as he felt the firm clasp of her sleek muscles gripping his cock. He thrust again, more firmly, and she let out a little mewl.

He may have been brainless with lust, but he would have to be blind not to notice the grimace of pain that crossed her face.

"Damn." Even that mild curse sounded strange coming from her lips. She smiled sheepishly and traced her fingers down his cheek. "It's been a long time." The soft chuckle that followed made her tighten around him unbearably, and his eyes nearly crossed as the hot silken heat of her gripped his cock.

He gritted his teeth, ruthlessly stifling the urge to thrust hard and deep. "How long?"

She sucked in a breath and tentatively thrust her hips. "One lackluster encounter nearly a year ago."

What the hell was wrong with his half brother? How in the hell could he have managed to keep his hands off her? Chris couldn't have made sense of it under the best of circumstances, and he certainly couldn't now when all of the blood had most definitely left his brain.

He tried desperately to form a coherent thought, not an easy task when he was nine inches deep in the tightest, wettest pussy he'd ever felt. He should have taken this more slowly, given her more time to get accustomed to his size . . . He attempted to pull out. She winced again, and the cold reality of her pain released some of the blood back to his brain. Fuck. In all of his eagerness to rock her world beyond anything she'd ever known, he'd ended up hurting her. Hurt though he may be at her using him to get back at his brother, it was important that she really, really enjoy this. Nothing like knowing you're causing a woman considerable discomfort to kill the mood.

But Julie had other ideas. "No," she said, clenching her legs tightly about his waist. "Don't you dare stop." She punctuated her command with a tiny upward thrust of her hips, and his balls tightened at the exquisite friction.

"You should have told me." He leaned down and kissed her tenderly on the forehead, wanting to soothe and comfort her now that he'd gone after her with all the finesse of a sixteen-year-old on prom night. "I would have gone a little easier on you."

"Somehow I didn't think this was the right place to talk about Brian and our disastrous sex life." Her hands ran up and down his spine, and it took all his willpower to resist the urge to thrust even deeper.

"Please, don't stop," she said again. "I want this. I've wanted you for a long time. I don't think I've ever wanted anyone like I want you."

Another little thrust of her hips, and Chris firmly grasped them in her hands to prevent any more movement. "Julie, stop moving. I don't want to hurt you."

She squeezed her inner muscles, clenching and releasing his cock in an unbearable caress. A crafty little smile crossed her lips, and she clenched again. He threw his head back, eyes squeezed tight. There was really only so much a man could take.

He reached his hand between their bodies, his thumb finding the plump bud of her clit. "Don't move," he said again, circling her in tight, firm strokes. Within seconds she was melting around him, hips rising in tiny, unconscious pulses as she grew slicker with every flick of his thumb.

The tight, tingling sensation started at the base of his spine, working its way to his balls. He wasn't going to last. She was so close, her breath coming in harsh pants, her nipples drawn into tight, cherry red peaks, her orgasm just over the horizon. But he couldn't stay inside her one second longer without coming, and he'd cut off his left nut before he let himself come before she did. Time for more drastic measures.

"No," Julie protested when Chris gently but firmly unwrapped her legs from around his waist and withdrew. Frustrated, tears sprang into her eyes. "You can't stop now." Not when she was so close to what she knew would be the most intense orgasm of her life. Not to mention the only orgasm she'd ever had at the hands—so to speak—of someone else.

He cut her off with another of his spine melting kisses. "I'm not stopping, Jules." He slid down a bit, so that his head was level with hers and his stomach pressed between her legs. His hand came up to cradle her jaw. She forgot what she was saying as his tongue leisurely explored her mouth. "I'm going to make everything a hell of a lot better."

Her arousal returned in full force. His eyes narrowed, the blue barely visible between the thick black lashes. He wore such a look of determination. Determined to give her pleasure.

His fingers and tongue lavished attention on her nipples, until she thought she'd go crazy if he didn't stop and kill him if he did. His hand trailed down to ease the moist flesh between her legs, caressing, soothing, and incredibly arousing all at the same time. She sat up in shock when his mouth followed. Not for the first time, she wondered at her impulsive decision to have sex with Chris. Not that she wasn't enjoying herself—she was, more than with any other man in her entire life. But it was all so much more intense, so much more overwhelming than she ever could have imagined.

Like now, she thought as she looked down, shocked at the sight of the dark waves of his hair contrasting with the pale skin of her thighs. She'd always been too embarrassed to let a man do this to her, but her self-consciousness fled at the first firm flick of his tongue across her already over-sensitized flesh. She moaned in delight as the sweet, hot pressure of his lips sent pulses of delight singing through every nerve ending. "I'm sorry I hurt you." The deep rumble of his voice tickled against her. "But now I'm gonna kiss it all better."

His tongue was magic, swirling and dipping into her aching core. Her fists clenched at the comforter, her head tossed back and forth. Never in her wildest fantasies could she have imagined anything feeling better. First one, then two fingers slid inside, stretching her wide, teasing against a bundle of nerves she'd never even known existed.

"Your pussy tastes so good," he murmured, his frank language sending a blush through her entire body. "You have no idea how many times I jerked off dreaming of fucking you with my tongue and my fingers." The image sent a jolt of pleasure through her, making her squirm against his hungry mouth. Her moans and squeals of pleasure melded with the hot wet sucking sounds of his loving. Tension knotted in her belly. The firm pressure of his fingers sliding slowly in and out, the gentle suction of his lips and tongue sent her spiraling. She couldn't have held back her orgasm if she'd wanted to. Her back arched off the bed, and she came on a seemingly endless wave, her harsh cries fading into soft sighs as the tremors eased.

It could have been seconds or hours that she lay there, slightly dazed. Her hands unclenched from the comforter and flopped, palm up on either side of her head. Slowly she became aware of Chris, kissing his way up her belly and rib cage. He stopped to tease her nipple with the barest flick of his tongue, as though realizing that the hyper-sensitive peak couldn't bear firm suction just now.

"Better?" he whispered, settling himself once again between her legs. She felt him, unbelievably thick and hard, pressing insistently against her inner thighs.

"Much, thanks," she said, and giggled in response to the wide grin that spread across his face.

"You sound like you're thanking me for tea," he teased, bending his head for a kiss. One hand reached up and threaded through her hair, while the other caught her leg and hitched it over his hip. He shifted, and she reveled in the stretch and slide as he pushed the very tip of his shaft inside of her.

"Ready to try this again?"

She tried to say yes, but instead all that came out was a garbled "yah" as the slick pressure and friction of him inside her sent renewed heat coursing through her.

A tendon stood out in sharp relief on his neck and sweat dripped from his temples as he struggled to maintain control. This time he didn't surge forward, but slowly squeezed inside, inch by tantalizing inch, until finally he was buried so deep tingles jolted up and down her spine.

"You okay?" His face was drawn in tight lines of concentration, and his arms trembled a little as they supported his weight.

He looked beautiful and savage as he held himself above her, his entire body rippling while he struggled to maintain control. Experimentally, she shifted her hips, gasping sharply as the movement brought the base of his cock against her clitoris. Mistaking it for a sound of pain, he swore and started to pull away. "I'm sorry—"

"No, please, don't stop. It doesn't hurt, I swear." Julie surged against him again, needing him to move. "It feels good, so unbelievably good." Sliding her hands down his back, she grasped his buttocks, pressing him even more deeply inside of her. "I think I can feel your heartbeat inside of me."

It was all the encouragement he needed. Finally he began to move, slowly sliding in and out, groaning as she squeezed around him, trying to pull him deeper with every stroke.

Instinctively she drew up her knees to open herself more

fully. He hooked his hands under her knees and pressed her thighs back against her chest, spreading her open so that she could feel his shaft slide against her clitoris on every stroke.

Vaguely she heard her moans, increasing in volume with every thrust. Her nails dug into the hard muscles of his buttocks, and her cries urged him on as he pumped in and out, until another orgasm hit her with such force she could swear she saw stars.

His head was thrown back and a guttural cry ripped from his throat as his own climax hit him. She milked him gently, feeling a delicious sense of power as he ground against her. When he collapsed on top of her, she cradled him with her arms and legs wrapped around him.

He was so much bigger than she, she should have felt smothered. But instead she burrowed her face into his neck, feeling an immense satisfaction. She, boring little Julie Driscoll, had the power to turn Chris Dennison into a quivering, helpless mass of male flesh.

# 4

Chris lay on top of her for several minutes, vaguely aware that he was probably crushing her but unable to move. He buried his nose in her neck, catching the sweet scent of her skin mingling with his own sweat. He was still trembling with the spine-melting intensity of his orgasm, but just the smell of himself on her was enough to make his dick go half hard inside her.

Finally he rolled to the side, hardly able to believe what just happened even as she snuggled into his chest. Julie Driscoll was lying naked in his bed, all but purring after a bout of the hottest, lustiest sex he'd ever had. Proving that reality was much, much better than any fantasy he could ever come up with.

He trailed his right hand over her silky blonde curls, over the curve of her shoulder, and down the smooth line of her arm. He covered her hand with his, wincing as reality intruded in the form of her giant engagement ring scraping against his palm.

"What happens now?" he asked.

Julie propped up on his chest and gave him a sleepy smile. "I was thinking I'd give you about five minutes or so to recover, and then maybe we could do it again?"

Blood pooled in his groin at her suggestion, but now that the edge had been taken off his hunger he wasn't so easily distracted. "I mean with Brian," he said, his thumb and forefinger closing over the massive rock on her finger for emphasis. "Are you getting a divorce?"

"I don't know." Julie tugged her hand away spreading her fingers and frowning at the offending piece of jewelry. But she didn't bother to remove it.

His jaw clenched as every muscle tensed. "You can't possibly stay with him. Not after what he did. Not after what *we* just did."

"I don't want to talk about it tonight." She feathered kisses across his chest. "Right now I don't want to think about anything but this." Her hand slid between his legs, capturing his burgeoning erection with a low murmur of satisfaction.

Chris closed his eyes, arching up into her hand. She was right. Why complicate things? Why dwell on the fact that less than twenty-four hours ago, she had married his brother? None of that mattered tonight. Tonight, it was Chris, not Brian, sinking his fingers into the hot, creamy clasp of her cunt. He was the one reaching down, covering her hand in his to show her exactly how he liked to be stroked. It was his cock she was pumping with fast, firm strokes until he was throbbing and twitching like he hadn't just come with enough force to make him lose consciousness.

He was the one watching her slide down his shaft, moaning as his cock disappeared inch by agonizing inch inside her sweet pussy. Tonight, he was watching her moan and squirm as she came all over him. Tonight she was his, and that was enough. It had to be.

Gray light was just touching the sky as Chris zipped up his suitcase. Julie was sprawled on her stomach, the sheet twisted so the whole of her smooth back and one creamy leg were exposed. His fingers itched to slide over her skin, his mouth watered with the urge to bury his tongue between her legs, have her wake up as she was coming against his mouth.

He resisted, in part because he'd already pushed his departure as far as he could. At this rate he'd be lucky to make his flight back to St. Thomas. But also because his emotions were a mess. Far from the pleasantly exhausted state he usually found himself in after a night like last night, this morning he was all simmering anger and old resentment.

What did he expect her to say if he woke her up to say goodbye? He knew what he wanted her to say—that she would announce her plans to dump Brian once and for all and run off with him. Fat chance of that happening, no matter what had happened last night.

And that was a good thing, he reminded himself as he quietly slipped on his shoes. Because he had no time whatsoever to devote to his personal life. The twisted, sour feeling in his stomach was just old wounds reopening. The long forgotten desire—for once—to be chosen first over his asshole brother. To not be chosen as second best, or in Julie's case, as a convenient and potent form of revenge. Chris thought he'd gotten over all of this in the years he'd spent building his own successful business away from the influence of his family. But watching Julie march down the aisle had brought it all bubbling back to the surface. And spending the night discovering all the secrets of her lush, sexy body hadn't helped matters any.

Best to leave quickly and quietly, not draw it out any further. Still, it seemed wrong to just leave her without a word, without some acknowledgement. As a nod to courtesy, he penned a quick note:

*Had to catch an early flight. It was great seeing you again. Thanks for a great night.*

He stared down at his own blocky print, biting the pen. It seemed a bit abrupt. He added:

*Come down whenever you need a break from the rat race.*

He almost scratched it out. What if she took him up on it? His stomach clenched with anxiety at the thought of her showing up at Holley Cay. A man could only stand so much emotional torture.

No, Julie didn't want anything more from him than for him to help even the score with Brian. She would see it for the meaningless invitation it was, but it kept the note from being a complete "thanks for the fuck" sort of brush off. He signed his name and indulged himself in one last look at her, golden, creamy, exhausted from his loving, before quietly closing the door behind him.

# 5

Julie closed her eyes and inhaled the salty Caribbean air, feeling her tensions melt under the warmth of the tropical sun. This was exactly what she needed, she thought as the low hum of the ferry's engine lulled her into a half dream state. A whole week of sun, sand, and umbrella drinks. And most importantly, a hot vacation fling to put the icing on the cake.

A curl of anticipation blossomed in her belly. It had been ten days since she'd woken up alone in Chris's hotel room. In less than ten minutes, she would see him again.

She sighed in pleasure as the light breeze caressed the skin of her shoulders, left bare by her gauzy white halter top. It was among the many purchases Wendy had insisted on in preparation for her trip to the Holley Cay resort.

As she settled back into the soft padded bench, she couldn't help but be impressed with the resort's service so far. She and several other passengers had been met by an SUV at Charlotte Amalie Airport in St. Thomas and whisked in air-conditioned comfort to the resort's private ferry. On board, they had been served delicious rum punch, shrimp cocktail, and a beautiful array of fresh tropical fruits as they awaited the arrival of additional guests.

If her greeting was any indication of the service she would receive, Julie could see why Holley Cay was quickly gaining a reputation as a favorite spot for the young and wealthy to rest, recuperate, and frolic. She couldn't help but admire Chris for realizing his dream. She remembered vividly back in college when Chris had talked about starting his own place, out from under the shadow of D&D. Chris had accomplished his dream and then some.

"It's nothing more than a sleazy swingers club," Brian and his father had grumbled after Holley Cay was described as "over the top, hedonistic luxury" by *Travel and Leisure* magazine. "I bet it's all orgies and people running around nude. It's an embarrassment to D&D to have Chris involved in something like that."

Julie had never bothered to point out that Holley Cay was in no way affiliated with D&D, that Chris had built the resort from the ground up and found his own investors. As far as she knew, he hadn't taken a penny from his considerable trust fund.

But Julie knew better than to argue. Grant Driscoll, Brian Dennison, and David Dennison all suffered greatly from "Not Invented Here" syndrome. If they didn't think of it first, it wasn't worth bothering with.

Nervous anticipation hummed through her. Coming down here had seemed like such a great idea when Wendy had suggested it two days ago.

"You need to get out of here," Wendy had said, surveying the piles of wedding gifts littering Julie's apartment a week after her disaster of a wedding.

"I wish," Julie groaned, threading her fingers through her hair. "But I have to return all the gifts, write apology notes to all the guests." She surveyed her normally immaculate living room.

"Apology cards? What are you supposed to say, sorry the groom was nailing someone else in the broom closet? Shouldn't Brian be doing this?"

"I don't know. Mother insisted," Julie said. "She's been such a mess lately, I couldn't argue with her."

"What happened to the new Julie? The Julie who doesn't let herself get pushed around?" Wendy asked as she settled herself into the high-backed wooden chair across from Julie.

"I think she's on my honeymoon."

"No, that would be Brian and Vanessa."

"Don't remind me." Julie let her head drop to the table.

Her phone let out a piercing ring. "Don't," Julie said when Wendy moved as though to answer. "It's probably one of those sleazebags." As if discovering her husband doing another woman at her wedding reception wasn't bad enough, somehow the national tabloids had latched onto Julie's story. In what must have been an incredibly slow celebrity news week, Julie had been featured in a piece called "Heiresses Gone Wild." A thoughtful wedding guest had furnished the tabloid with several candid photos, including one of Julie, veil askew, dress torn and stained with red wine, her face snarling with rage as she smashed cake into Brian's face. For the past several days she'd been plagued with phone calls, her every move dogged by photographers as the tabloid press tried to paint her—boring, dutiful Julie Driscoll—as the next Paris Hilton.

Thank God no one—except Wendy, of course—knew what had happened with Chris. She probably would have been disowned.

Which, admittedly, had its appeal right about now, with her mother calling her fifty times a day in hysterics, and her father nearly as many times, his manner much colder and biting as he castigated her for the PR disaster she had caused.

And Brian, who had caused the whole mess in the first place, wasn't suffering one bit as he drank umbrella drinks in Fiji while his new girlfriend rubbed him down with coconut oil. By the time he got back, the entire fiasco would have blown over.

Come to think of it, getting out of town until the world forgot about her wedding scandal did sound like a good strategy.

"Before I forget, I brought this, too." Wendy reached into her briefcase and pulled out a thick manila envelope. "It's the annulment papers. I ran it by one of the senior partners, and she says it looks fine. All you have to do is sign."

Julie did so, with such enthusiasm that her ballpoint pen left an imprint in the rustic wood finish of her kitchen table.

"And you made *US Weekly*," Wendy said, tossing the magazine on top of the pile of legal papers.

The magazine was open to a picture of Julie, free of makeup and dressed in running clothes as she went for her morning latte. It had been taken less than a block from her apartment. "You're right, I have to get out of here," Julie groaned.

"As usual, I'm one step ahead of you." Wendy pulled another envelope out of her briefcase and opened it with a flourish. "I have taken the liberty of booking you, the new and improved, complete with spine Julie Driscoll, a one week stay at the ultra luxurious Holley Cay resort, in the tropical paradise of the U.S. Virgin Islands."

Julie's head shot up. "You did what?"

"Don't worry, I used your credit card. You know I love you like a sister, but twenty thousand a week is pretty steep for a second year associate."

"I can't go there, that's Chris's resort. If I go there, and anyone finds out, the press will have a field day. This," she waved the issue of *US Weekly* under Wendy's nose, "will look like nothing in comparison to the chaos. Not to mention my parents will kill me."

"So what," Wendy scoffed. "If you ask me, if they'd been

more concerned with your happiness and less concerned with stock price and social status, you never would have married Brian in the first place. So, really, the whole mess is their fault. I don't see why you're so worried about protecting them."

While Wendy had grown up in a comfortable upper middle class neighborhood outside of New York City, she would never understand the pressure Julie was under to uphold a certain social standard. Nevertheless, Julie knew she had a valid point. No wonder Wendy was already on the fast track to making partner at her law firm.

"Besides," she continued, "who's going to find out? I'm certainly not going to tell anyone, and isn't Holley Cay renowned for its privacy? I mean, when Brad and Angelina went, no one even knew until a month after they left."

She had a point. One of Holley Cay's main selling points, especially to celebrities, was the fact that the press never seemed to be able to find people there. Maybe it would be possible to disappear, if only for a week.

With Chris.

A sly smile crossed Wendy's face. "Sounds pretty good, doesn't it?" She picked up the glossy brochure. "'We will go to any lengths to insure the pleasure and satisfaction of our guests.'" Wendy's eyebrows waggled. "And from the look on your face, you're remembering exactly what 'lengths' Chris will go to, aren't you?"

Julie felt herself redden at Wendy's knowing smirk. New Julie Driscoll or not, she still wasn't exactly proud of the fact that she'd slept with the best man on her wedding night, and said as much.

Wendy waved her hand dismissively. "If anyone deserved a good fuck from a hot guy, it's you. If anything you should be proud of yourself for taking initiative."

"I don't think a meaningless one night stand is something to be proud of," Julie grumbled. But she couldn't prevent a smile at the memory of that night. Okay, maybe she was a little proud of herself.

"Alright, wipe that ecstatic grin off your face. You don't have to rub your good sex in my face, especially when it's been ages since I've had any."

Julie highly doubted that, given Wendy's very active dating life. "Not good sex," she said, unable to resist the taunt, "Amazing sex. Perfect and amazing."

"Then I can't understand why you're not making a beeline to the airport right now."

Julie's smile faded as she remembered that morning, waking up alone in the rumpled bed that still smelled of Chris and sex. A single sheet of paper was folded up on the pillow next to her.

"*Had to catch an early flight. It was great seeing you again. Thanks for a great night. Come down whenever you need a break from the rat race—Chris*"

They might have gone out for coffee for all the emotion it contained. She was pretty confident that he'd enjoyed himself—she had three empty condom wrappers and the sore muscles to prove it. Okay, so he'd said she should come visit. But she was pretty sure he only said it because he was sure she'd never take him up on it. He certainly wouldn't expect her less than a month later.

"We had our one night," Julie said, "and neither of us intended it to go any farther. I don't want to push it." She wrinkled her nose at the potential for social awkwardness. "I don't want him to think that I'm like, stalking him, or something."

Wendy waved off her protests. Ever the optimist, she replied, "Hey, plans change. Do you or do you not want to see him again?"

"It would be great, but I'm in the process of getting an annulment. The last thing I need is to get involved again right away."

"Who said anything about getting involved? I'm talking about a week in a tropical paradise with a gorgeous guy. Why not indulge yourself a little? And by the time you come back, the annulment will be final, and the press will have moved on to the next skank of the week. Meanwhile, you'll be smug in the knowledge that the real scandal—you sleeping with Chris—will remain top secret."

Julie fiddled with the brochure, considering.

"You're offering sex with no strings—no guy refuses that," Wendy urged "And, from what I've read about this place, if Chris *is* crazy enough to refuse your offer, you'll have no trouble finding a very suitable substitute."

Julie crinkled her nose at that. Chris had been right about one thing. Casual sex was not her thing, and she hadn't thought of her night with Chris as such. It was one thing to have no-strings-attached sex with an old friend, and an entirely different one to do it with a complete stranger.

But . . . "It would be nice to have some time alone on a beach to figure things out," Julie conceded.

Wendy saw that she was caving, and a smile spread across her face. "Let's get you packed."

Since she had already been packed for her honeymoon, Julie figured she was pretty much ready to go. But Wendy had different ideas.

"Oh my God, what is this?" Wendy pulled out Julie's new black linen sheath dress and her khaki walking shorts. "Beach cruise with Ozzie and Harriet? And this?" She held out the offending garment, a tropical print camp shirt. "Please tell me this is not Tommy Bahama."

"What? Those clothes are fine."

"Yeah, fine if you want to fit in with the geriatric set." Wendy sniffed scornfully at the one-piece tank suit Julie had packed.

That afternoon, Wendy took her on a marathon shopping spree, interspersed with a full gamut of salon treatments at one of San Francisco's most exclusive day spas.

"Are you absolutely sure I need the Brazilian?" Julie had asked uncertainly after the aesthetician explained the procedure in graphic detail.

Wendy stood firm. "Absolutely. Even if you did insist on a full coverage bikini," Wendy rolled her eyes at Julie's lingering conservativeness, "It's better to be safe than sorry. It's easier to relax when you're not worrying about stray hair."

*No worries there*, Julie thought later as she winced out of the treatment room, denuded of all hair except for a tiny little patch on her mound.

Then it was off to Nordstrom, where Wendy had worked her way through college and law school as a personal shopper. She loved nothing more than to spend other people's money, and she had a ball breaking Julie out of her tasteful, elegant rut. By the end of the day Julie's vacation wardrobe was so well stocked, she would have to change outfits five times a day to get through everything.

Wendy had loaded Julie's Louis Vuitton luggage with flirty dresses from Chloe and Narciso Rodriguez, La Perla lingerie, sexy strappy sandals from Jimmy Choo, and what had to be the world's largest box of condoms. Earlier this morning, she'd dropped Julie off at San Francisco International with admonishments not to forget her sunscreen when she was having wild sex on the beach.

Julie closed her eyes, feeling the tension ease from her body as the ferry traveled through the calm blue waters. The murmur of the other guests increased in volume, and Julie opened her eyes to see that they were approaching the dock at Holley Cay.

One would think that having grown up visiting and working at some of the finest resorts in the world, Julie would be immune to the sight. Nevertheless, she let out a low whistle of admiration at her first view of Chris's domain.

It looked exactly like the brochure, and yet the brochure couldn't possibly convey the scent of the sea, the warmth of the sun, the soothing rhythm of waves gently lapping on the shore. A huge pale pink stucco main building sat perched on a hill above the beach. Bungalows ranging in size from small cottages to near-mansions nestled among the palms. The sugar sand beach stretched for hundreds of yards, and guests occupied lounge chairs and umbrellas set up to provide everyone with more than enough space and privacy. Julie knew that there were several smaller, more secluded beaches around the island, including the one that was right in front of the bungalow Wendy had reserved. She couldn't wait for her first swim in the warm, crystal clear sea.

She didn't see Chris until they were almost to the dock. Several yachts were moored nearby. Some must have belonged to guests, but most, she had learned from the brochure, belonged to the resort and were available for guests to reserve for private excursions.

"Chris, you have really outdone yourself," she said under her breath as the ferry pulled up to the dock.

He was there, waiting to meet the new arrivals, like a modern day Mr. Roarke from *Fantasy Island*. But instead of a white suit, Chris was the epitome of island casual. A loose blue-and-white tropical print shirt hung from his broad shoulders, untucked from the waistband of his wheat-colored shorts. His large, tanned feet sported flip-flops, and his eyes were hidden behind a pair of mirrored Oakleys.

Not to mention he was sexier than Mr. Roarke had ever been. His coffee colored hair was streaked through with auburn from the Caribbean sun, his body was tanned and hard. He exuded a masculine charisma that went beyond mere good looks.

And Julie already had firsthand knowledge that he could make all her fantasies come true.

"Oh my God," exclaimed a tall blonde to her group of three female friends. "Is that the owner? He's so hot."

Apparently she wasn't alone in her thoughts.

"Yes, that's Chris Dennison. He built this place from the ground up." Julie winced at her tone. She sounded like a proud parent.

"I heard that he came here with a few friends and returned home with a business plan," said the blonde with a friendly smile. "But with his connections his success isn't all that surprising."

"This place has no connection to D&D Resorts, if that's what you're thinking," Julie said. "He did all this on his own, no help or influence from his father."

"You sound like you know him pretty well," the blonde said. Now her three friends were looking at Julie as the group moved toward the front of the ferry.

Oh great, way to keep a low profile. "Our families know each other," she said, hoping they wouldn't press for details.

The blonde's eyes grew round. "Wait, I know who you are! You're Julie Driscoll! I'm Amy, by the way." The blonde offered her hand. "I read about you in the—the Chronicle. Your wedding, I mean. I saw the write-up in the Chronicle."

Julie appreciated the attempt at tact, but she was pretty sure Amy recognized her from a much less reputable publication than the San Francisco paper. "You're from San Francisco?"

"Napa, actually. My father owns a winery." She named a vineyard that Julie was familiar with. "I just want to say, I so admire you. Brian Dennison is a total male slut, and he deserved a lot worse than cake in his face."

Her friends nodded and murmured in agreement.

Julie's smile brightened. She may have been busted, but at

least these women seemed inclined to be allies. "Thanks. I'm sure you've seen some of the other stuff they've been writing about me." They grimaced sympathetically. "Part of the reason I'm here is to get away from all of that, so I'd really appreciate you not telling anyone back home that I'm here."

Amy looked almost offended at the suggestion. "Of course not. You totally deserve a break from all that crap. We won't say a word." She looked at her friends for their agreement, glaring particularly hard at a tall, sultry looking brunette who frankly looked bored by all the talk. Her face was vaguely familiar, but Julie couldn't place her.

"I'm getting married in a few weeks—this is my bachelorette party." Amy quickly introduced the rest of her group and continued. "I know how caught up you get in the wedding stuff. It takes a lot of balls to stand in front of everyone and just say screw it, you know?"

Julie couldn't help liking Amy and her blunt but friendly manner. She'd never been good at sticking up for herself, and it was nice to have someone, even a total stranger, back her up.

"You're here alone, aren't you?"

Julie nodded. "Yep, taking an escape from reality while I wait for my annulment to be finalized."

They all four alternately chuckled in understanding or nodded sympathetically.

Jennifer, an athletic looking redhead, patted Julie's shoulder amiably. "Well, if you decide you want company, come find us. Amy can't do anything," Jennifer slanted a look at the group of four good looking guys gathering up their bags behind them, "but I guarantee you the rest of us will be having lots of fun."

"I'll keep that in mind," Julie said with a grin.

Julie felt her breath hitch as she and the other guests proceeded down the dock, closer and closer to where Chris stood.

Chris's cousin, Carla, a pretty woman with dark, curly hair, stood next to him in a simple floral patterned sundress.

Quickly Julie stepped aside to check her appearance, allowing several more guests to pass her. She fluffed her hair and dabbed her nose with oil blotting papers. Sun or no, Julie didn't want Chris to see her sweaty. Well, not yet anyway.

What would he say? He would be happy to see her, wouldn't he? After all, like Wendy said, she was offering no-strings-attached sex, and what red-blooded man would say no to that? Especially when they both knew how absolutely awesome it would be?

Still, she wasn't able to rid herself of the tiny, nagging, uncertainty that gnawed at her belly. Taking a deep breath for courage, she slipped the strap of her Vuitton Murimaki "Eye Love You" bag over her shoulder and started down the dock.

Chris struggled to maintain his polite, friendly smile as he greeted the twenty-five new guests who had just arrived. He was grateful for the sunglasses that hid the dark circles under his bloodshot eyes. He was supposed to convey an image of relaxed luxury, and it wouldn't do for the guests to see him looking so haggard.

"Smile," Carla, his cousin and the resort's assistant manager, hissed through her own grin.

"I am," he hissed back.

"No, you're not. You're baring your teeth."

Chris pulled up the corners of his mouth.

"Better," she said.

Chris sighed and shook hands with a couple from London. The man was a musician or something. It didn't matter anyway. Part of the appeal of Holley Cay for the rich and famous was that the staff never let on if they were star struck.

Cowboy up, he told himself. It wasn't even the high season,

and already he was beat. But in the ten days since his return from San Francisco, he'd lost both his bookkeeper and his catering manager. All while trying to plan the top-secret, lavish wedding of one of television's most popular actresses. Both he and Carla had been pulling fourteen-hour days to try to keep up.

It didn't help that when he finally fell into bed, exhausted, he couldn't sleep. Not with images of Julie keeping him awake and frustrated.

It had been a real bonehead move, taking her to bed. Forget the fact that she had been the aggressor. He was more experienced, he was the one who should have known better. But Julie was so pretty, so sweet, and he'd wanted her for so long. Making love with her—and that was what it was, not doing, not nailing, not merely having sex with—had been one of the most incredible experiences of his life. He could remember everything about that night, the way she'd tasted, the way she smelled, every move of her beautiful body. Where all of his other lovers faded into an indistinct but pleasant blur, every moment with Julie stood out in brilliant, vivid clarity. Before, she'd existed vaguely in his subconscious, emerging to torment him through erotic dreams. Now memories of Julie invaded his consciousness like living things. Her sweet, salty taste, the buttery softness of the skin of her inner thighs, the hot little pants that burst between her lips when she came, all of it replaying incessantly in his head. Like an idiot, he'd thought one night with her could make up for all the years of unsatisfied lust. Instead, it had left him aching, hungry, and craving more.

But no matter how many times in the past ten days he'd considered calling her to invite her here or hopping a flight to San Francisco, he knew it was best to keep his distance. Nothing good could come of their being together, and he had too much going on right now to risk getting tangled up in Julie's pretty little web.

Dragging his thoughts back to the guests he was supposed to be greeting, he looked down the dock, scanning the rest of the group. A group of four women, all young and attractive, was making its way to him, and Chris tried to conjure up a spark of interest. In the past he had enjoyed brief affairs with female guests—discreetly, of course. As far as he was concerned, if a single, beautiful woman was looking for an island fling, and the interest was mutual, who was he to say no?

Maybe that was what he needed, scanning each woman in turn. Someone new to get the taste of Julie out of his mouth. But as he looked the women over, he found he couldn't muster up much enthusiasm. Jesus, what was wrong with him? One night with a woman was not supposed to ruin him for life. Admittedly, it was one wild, hot, insane night with the woman who embodied every adolescent and adult male fantasy he'd ever entertained, but still.

He was politely greeting the group of women when his gaze lit on the last passenger making her way down the dock. He felt like he'd been sucker punched. It couldn't be! It had to be an insomnia-induced hallucination. The petite blonde with the purple tinted Gucci glasses only *looked* like Julie. Her hair was loose and curly, falling an inch past her jaw. She wore a white cotton halter top and a matching, low slung skirt that gave him a nice view of her flat, tanned abdomen and a navel decorated with a tiny jewel.

Any more crazy fantasies that it might be Julie fled. Chris could claim intimate knowledge of Julie Driscoll's navel, and it was most definitely unadorned.

Chris's smile turned genuine as he felt the first stirrings of interest. He knew he couldn't have Julie, but there was nothing wrong with having fun with her sexy look-alike.

Finally she reached him, and he felt all the air escape from his lungs when she slipped off her sunglasses.

Something like joy exploded in his belly, followed almost immediately by a hard, cold knot of dread. It was a miracle. It was a disaster. He was completely, irrevocably fucked.

"Hi, Chris," she said, ignoring his outstretched hand and hugging him instead. "You have an amazing place here, and I know I'm going to have a great time."

Julie stepped back and tilted her head to look up at Chris's face. It wasn't easy. When she'd wrapped her arms around him it was all she could do not to nuzzle her face into the vee of skin exposed by his open-collared shirt.

Her smile faded as she saw the grim expression on his face. She'd been so encouraged by his wide, welcoming smile, convinced that he was as happy to see her as she him. But now he stared silently at her, his eyes hidden by his sunglasses, his full lips set in a tight line.

"What are you doing here?"

Not exactly the welcome she'd been hoping for. "It's great to see you, too, Chris."

Even through the sunglasses she could feel his gaze rake down her body, taking in her halter top, and exposed abdomen. She felt her nipples harden beneath the thin cotton, and, not for the first time, she questioned the wisdom of bowing blindly to Wendy's judgment.

"Trust me, Jules," Wendy had said when Julie had protested that she couldn't wear a bra with the halter top. "You are blessed with perfect breasts. They're big enough that you have a nice little rack, but not so big that they look sloppy when you go braless."

Julie had given in, but now she felt almost as exposed as if Chris's hands had peeled away the fabric.

"Hi, Carla, it's nice to see you again," she said, offering her hand in greeting.

Carla shot Chris a quizzical look and said, "Since Chris seems to have forgotten his hosting duties, let me help you get settled in." She gave Julie the key and map to her villa, assuring her that her luggage would be in her room when she arrived.

"If you want to wait a moment," Carla said, "we can give you a ride in the golf cart."

Julie politely refused, hoping that the walk would dispel the anger she felt coiling in her belly. Why was he being so cold? Her first instinct was to jump on the ferry and go back home. It wasn't in her nature to cause trouble or stay when she wasn't welcome.

Her spine stiffened. The old Julie might turn tail and run, but the new Julie needed to stand her ground. Chris didn't want her here? Fine. As Jennifer had pointed out on the ferry, there was plenty here to keep her entertained.

Chris watched Julie stalk away, mesmerized by the bounce of her luscious ass under her skirt. He resisted the urge to go after her and apologize. He'd seen the hurt in her eyes, the way it had overtaken her sweet, excited smile. He'd been unforgivably rude, a total ass, but she'd taken him by surprise, damn it, showing up unannounced like one of his ridiculous fantasies come to life. And Chris, who'd never had any sort of problem handling himself around women, found himself at a total loss. So rather than escort Julie to her villa, he stayed at Carla's side, trying to regroup and figure out his next move.

"What was up with that?" Carla asked Chris once Julie was out of earshot.

"A complication I really don't need right now."

"Weren't you just at her wedding? Where's her husband?"

"Drop it, Carla."

"Wait a minute—did you and she—at her wedding?" Carla might abstain from her own liaisons, but she loved to live vicariously through Chris.

"I said, drop it." Chris felt tension creep into the back of his neck, promising a killer headache if he didn't get some Tylenol and some sleep in the very near future.

"Oh, this is going to be a fun week."

# 6

Julie took one last look in the mirror, adjusting the straps of her pale pink camisole. The slightly gathered neckline prevented the silk from clinging too tightly, which was a good thing, since the top and the matching silk and chiffon skirt was yet another outfit that required the braless look. In fact, the way the skirt clung to her, it barely allowed underwear, but Wendy had assured her that one of her new pairs of thong panties would work fine underneath.

Which in itself was a new adventure. After spending most of her life trying to prevent her underwear from creeping up her behind, it was hard to get used to having a permanent wedgie.

But she had to admit, as she scrutinized her reflection, she looked nice. Sexy, but tastefully so. The pale pink of the silk flattered her skin, newly golden courtesy of the self tanner treatment she'd had after the rather invasive waxing procedure. The silky drape of the fabric flattered her less than impressive bust while miraculously diminishing what she had always considered her bubble butt.

One last swipe of her favorite MAC lip gloss, and she was ready to face Chris.

The short walk to her villa earlier this afternoon had done little to cool her irritation. But her tension began to fade the moment she stepped inside its air-conditioned coolness. The villa's sumptuous but comfortable wicker furnishings, the massive, king-size bed hung with mosquito netting, and most importantly, the beautiful white sand beach right off the villa's terrace went a long way towards calming her down. Why waste time dwelling on Chris's less than enthusiastic greeting when she had all this luxury at her disposal?

But after looking through the range of services offered by the resort, Julie couldn't help but wish Chris's response had been a little more enthusiastic. In addition to the usual range of spa services, Holley Cay also offered couples-only treatments where lovers could give each other massages and honey wraps or take private saunas and steam baths. And the room-service menu included an assortment of goodie baskets, with goodies ranging from condoms to flavored massage oils to handcuffs to cockrings.

Chris handcuffed to her bed, covered in coconut-flavored massage oil. The mere thought sent a rush of warmth between Julie's thighs.

After unpacking, she'd slipped on the most modest of her new bikinis and gone for a leisurely swim. How long had it been since she'd actually been on a real honest-to-God vacation? Sure, she'd seen the inside of more five-star resorts than she could count. But she was always working or scouting out the competition. She couldn't remember the last time she'd arrived at some beautiful spot and had nothing better to do than go for a swim and take a nap in the warm tropical sun.

But now it was time to face reality, in the form of Chris. Tonight was the welcoming cocktail party, taking place at the resort's beachside restaurant. Chris was sure to be there, since he was the official host.

Her belly tightened with a mixture of anticipation and apprehension. All she needed to do was get him alone for a few minutes, explain that she didn't want anything more from him than a relaxing two weeks, and everything would be fine.

In deference to the three-inch heels on her gold beaded sandals, Julie used the villa's complimentary golf cart to drive the short distance to the cocktail party.

The party was already in full swing, and it took her a minute to find Chris in the crowd of eighty or so guests who milled around the bar or occupied several tables.

She couldn't help but smile when she saw his attire. He still wore the same outfit he'd worn to the dock, a look echoed by most of the other male guests. The women, in contrast, were dressed in designer sundresses and skirts, and Julie gave a quick moment of thanks that she'd chosen one of her dressier outfits.

He gave her a quick smile and a nod of acknowledgement, but made no move to approach her. Hurt pricked at her like a mosquito, and she scolded herself for being paranoid and needy. His life might seem like one long vacation, but Chris was, in fact, working. He couldn't just drop everything to entertain her just because she'd decided to show up on his doorstep.

She wove her way through the crowd, trying to get to where Chris stood talking to a group of divers from the ferry, but her progress was halted when a cocktail waitress stopped to take her drink order.

"I'll have a white wine—" The woman looked at her expectantly. Hadn't she firmly put her white wine days behind her? "I'll have a Patrón Silver margarita on the rocks," she said.

When the waitress retreated, Julie took a bite-size crab cake from a passing waiter and once again looked for Chris. She had just found him when she heard a familiar voice to her left.

"Hey, Julie, over here!" Amy and her group of friends had pulled several little tables together, and they had been joined by the group of divers. "Come sit with us."

Julie was torn. They really did look like they were having a good time, but she still wanted to talk to Chris. She wanted reassurance that she hadn't really seen that shocked, hunted look in his eyes when she'd first stepped off the ferry.

Amy was busy shuffling people around, placing another chair in between herself and a tall, good looking blond guy whom Julie vaguely remembered as Mike. What the heck. Chris was deep in conversation with the couple from London. Maybe it was better to wait until the crowd had thinned out a little before trying to talk to him.

She collected her drink from the waitress and sat down in the proffered chair.

"Julie, you already know Jen, Kara, and Chrissy," she indicated her three friends. "And this is Mike, Dan, Greg, and Brad."

Julie politely shook hands with each, noting that none of them was subtle about checking her out. She took a sip of her drink, knowing that the warmth she was feeling had nothing to do with the tequila. Call her shallow, but it felt nice to be admired after spending most of her life feeling invisible.

The group made small talk, and Julie learned that the guys were all buddies from Harvard Business School. All were in their mid-thirties and had taken full advantage of the Internet boom of the late nineties. They reunited at least once a year to check out the world's best diving spots.

"So, Julie, do you dive?" Mike asked. His blond curls fell charmingly over his brow, and he had very pretty clear blue eyes.

"I have a couple of times, but it's not really my thing." She quickly related the story of her last disastrous scuba dive in Hawaii nearly two years ago. It had been her first—and last— vacation with Brian. He'd convinced her to go on a deepwater dive, despite her protests that she tended to panic when the water got too dark. A seal had brushed up against her. Julie, thinking it was a shark, had panicked and grabbed hold of Brian, and knocked out his mouthpiece in the process. Once they reached the dive boat he told her he wasn't going to dive with her again if she was going to be such a wimp. He'd spent the rest of their vacation diving with the sexy female Australian dive guide.

"Since I never really got over my fear of the deep water, it was a good excuse to stick to snorkeling." There were chuckles and nods of agreement from a few of the women.

But Mike was frowning. "That's totally uncool. If you were uncomfortable at that depth, he should have taken you on a shorter dive until you were more confident."

"Chivalry wasn't exactly Brian's strong suit," Julie said as she licked the salt from her glass and took another sip.

"All the more reason why you're lucky to be rid of that jerk," Jen said, raising her piña colada in the air. "Here's to Julie, and her well-deserved freedom from assholes."

Julie laughed and raised her glass. She really did feel free. And it felt great.

"You all sound like you're having a good time."

Julie jumped at the familiar voice behind her. She tilted her head back to look at Chris, surveying the group with a smile that looked a little strained around the corners.

"Your resort is fabulous," Amy gushed. "We're already having the best time."

Julie watched Chris as he moved around the table, greeting everyone in turn. Was it just in her mind, or was he checking out all of the women except for her? Julie reached up and tugged her earlobe, feeling suddenly self-conscious. Only five minutes ago she'd felt confident and sexy. But now she just felt like an awkward teenager among the glamorous group.

Kara, a Sophia Loren look-alike with bedroom eyes and a

rippling mane of dark brown hair, captured Chris's attention. His gorgeous midnight eyes gleamed down at her and his teeth flashed white as he laughed at something she said.

Julie took another gulp of her drink and quickly signaled a waitress for a refill. Just when she couldn't stand watching him flirt with Kara any longer, Chris made his way over to her chair. Capturing her hand, he brought it to his lips. Even that small contact was enough to send heat racing up her arm. His mouth quirked in a funny half smile. "And it's great to see you again, Jules. I'm glad to see you're recovering from your recent fiasco. I'm sure your new friends will help you forget all about it." Before Julie could respond, he straightened up and excused himself. "I should keep mingling," he said, "But I hope you all enjoy your evening and the rest of your stay."

It was all Julie could do to keep from running after him. What was that all about? He'd been friendly enough, and that kiss on her hand was—embarrassingly—enough to make her panties damp under her skirt. But what did he mean by "her new friends"? Was that his way of blowing her off so he wouldn't be around to entertain her?

Dimly she heard her new friends' conversation grow louder as empty drink glasses piled up. But Julie had a hard time following it, consumed as she was with Chris's cool behavior. She'd convinced herself that Wendy was right, that if she showed up and offered no-strings-attached sex, there was no way Chris would refuse. But now it looked like he was going to do just that. Hadn't they had a great time together? Had she done something so wrong, so inept, that Chris was now repulsed by the idea of sleeping with her again?

She tried to keep her emotions under control, trying to see things from his point of view. As far as he knew, she had traveled over three thousand miles to see him after only one night together. To be fair, that was a bit stalker-ish. The best thing to do would be to make her intentions crystal clear. As soon as he had a break in conversation, she'd march right over and tell him she wanted to rekindle their old friendship, but with a few fabulous benefits. Nothing more. Then he would have no reason to worry about any unrealistic expectations on her end.

"Is he still mad at you?"

"What?" Julie looked into Amy's concerned blue eyes. Oh God, had she somehow found out about her night with Chris?

"For dumping his brother?" Amy clarified.

"Oh, right. I just think the whole situation was difficult for him," Julie said. "Speaking of weddings, tell me what you have planned for yours." Amy eagerly embraced the change of subject. Like all brides, she enthusiastically described every detail of her upcoming nuptials, right down to the number of crystals that would adorn her silk bridal shoes.

Julie oohed and ahhed appropriately, all the while keeping an eye out for Chris to have a break. She polished off her drink with one last gulp, noting as she stood that her legs were a little bit wobbly. Two drinks on nothing but a crab cake in someone her size packed a powerful punch. She made a mental note to visit the cheese and cracker tray after she talked to Chris.

Chris was by one of the bars, casually leaning on one elbow as he sipped his drink. She raised her hand in greeting. His gaze flickered, so she knew he had seen her. But he couldn't seem to tear himself from conversation with a model Julie vaguely recognized. The model and her rock-star boyfriend were among the guests who had already been at the resort for several days, and it seemed that she and Chris were already fast friends.

Julie steeled herself and continued her approach, trying to ignore the uncomfortable clenching in her gut, the tightness in her throat. She'd never considered herself the jealous type—not even when Brian had given her more than ample reason to be. But if that woman tossed her hair and giggled just one more time, Julie was going to pull out every perfectly highlighted strand by the roots.

She worked her way through the crowd until she was standing next to Chris, who smiled at her but made no move to end his conversation with the model. Finally Julie ordered another margarita to make it look like she had a reason for being at the bar.

Finally Megan or Madeline or whatever her name was said, "Oh, there's Johnny. I'd better go cut him off before he decides to go skinny dipping."

"Chris," Julie grabbed his arm before he could find another reason to escape, "I need to talk to you."

"What's wrong? Is something wrong with your accommodations?" he asked, knowing damn well that wasn't the problem.

"No, the problem is that I'm getting the sense you don't want me here."

He resisted the urge to laugh. Not want her here? Hell yes, he wanted her here. Wanted to lift her up onto the bar and shove her skirt up around her waist to see what color her panties were. Then he wanted to peel those panties off with his teeth and spend about the next hour finding out if her pussy tasted as good as he remembered. Then he wanted to haul her off to his villa and keep her there, naked for the entire week. Fucking her every which way but sideways in the futile hope that maybe he'd work her out of his system, since one night clearly hadn't been enough.

But he had to keep working the party, mingling with guests. And when he was through doing that, he had to go back to his office to continue working on this stupid wedding happening in two weeks, the wedding that had initially seemed like such a great idea but now threatened to drive him insane.

Hell yeah, he wanted her. Too much. And that was precisely the problem. So rather than allow himself to be distracted by Julie and her considerable charms, he was determined to keep his distance. She wanted to run away to paradise for a week, fine, but he had too much riding on the next two weeks to get caught up in her little game of sticking it to Daddy.

"Of course I want you here. I want all of my guests to feel ·welcome."

Her eyes narrowed almost imperceptibly as her tongue scraped salt off the edge of her margarita glass. He swallowed hard, wishing he could chase that sweet little tongue with his own, suck it into his mouth. "I know I surprised you," she said. "But with everything going on, I just needed to get away to some place quiet, some place where I could lay low, you know?" She set her drink on the bar and took a step towards him. The scent of fresh flowers and warm skin nearly sent him to his knees. Somehow he remained standing, composed.

She placed her hand on his arm, her cool palm burning through his skin. "And I was hoping to . . . spend some more time with you." Oh, fuck, she couldn't make it easy for him, could she?

Though it nearly killed him to do so, he removed her hand from his arm. "I wish I could give you what you want, but I don't think I can."

Confusion furrowed her perfectly arched blond eyebrows. "I don't know what you think I want, but really, all I was hoping was to rekindle our friendship," she gave him a saucy smile, "with a few added benefits."

Exactly as he'd thought. He hadn't thought it was such a big deal, but somehow, having her say it out loud pissed him off all over again. "Friendship? Julie, I hadn't seen you in five years, and then you show up on your wedding night for a revenge fuck." The vitriol-laced words were out of his mouth before his brain could turn on the editor. "I don't see how that makes us friends."

Shock, hurt, and, finally, abject humiliation suffused Julie's face, and Chris felt his stomach free fall, stopping somewhere around his knees. Fuck. Now he'd gone and hurt her. Maybe she did want to use him for a little revenge against Brian and her father, but Julie was still the same sweet, wholesome girl who conjured up a whole host of protective instincts. Seeing her hurt made him feel like shit, and knowing he was the one hurting her made him feel like double shit. "I'm sorry." He reached out a hand, but she was already backing away.

"Thank you for making your feelings clear," she said, and to her credit, her voice only trembled a little. "Now, if you'll excuse me, I'm sure I can find quite a bit to keep myself busy, thank you very much." Darting from his hold, she wove her way quickly through the crowd. He started after her but was quickly waylaid by guests, forced to exchange polite greetings and small talk.

Pausing to refill his drink he half-heartedly engaged in a conversation with a software mogul from Silicon Valley. He wasn't particularly interested in how the next generation of software was going to revolutionize the corporate database, but Chris had perfected his interested smile over the past four years.

His gaze kept returning to Julie, who returned to her group of bachelorettes and divers, laughing and talking as though she didn't have a care in the world. He'd always admired her ability to so quickly regain her composure when rattled.

And he had definitely rattled her. He hated how harsh he'd been, but he couldn't help thinking maybe this was the best thing. If Julie thought he was a complete asshole, she'd do her part to keep her distance.

Besides, what he said was true. Sure, they'd been friends once, but they hadn't even been in touch until the day before her wedding to his half brother. Her recent behavior notwithstanding, Julie was obviously content in her safe, sheltered nest. A world where she always did what was expected of her, never questioned Mommy and Daddy, and in return she would always be very well taken care of.

He nodded in agreement at something the software CEO said, but his attention was focused squarely on Julie. She laughed at something that Mike guy said and put her hand flirtatiously on his arm.

Though his brain insisted that he keep his distance, that didn't stop the coil of jealousy knotting in his stomach. It was all he could do to fight off the primitive urge to walk over there, punch Mike in the face, and haul Julie off, caveman-style, to his lair.

Instead he tossed back the last of his drink and kneaded the back of his neck. His headache returned, creeping up the base of his skull, and it took all his strength to maintain a friendly smile.

It was one of the things that really sucked about his job. Most of the time he loved it. He was by nature a social creature, the kind of guy who made friends wherever he went and was always up for a party. Building the resort from nothing had been a dream come true, and he was well suited to the role of the dashing host. Meeting new people, feeling their genuine pleasure when he provided them with a uniquely luxurious environment that even the most spoiled of the fabulously wealthy could appreciate, gave him more satisfaction than just about anything he could think of.

And knowing that he had done it all by himself, without a lick of help from his father or his father's money—well, that was just a big fat cherry on top.

But sometimes, like now, he just wished he could have a break. Not only from the work itself, which had tripled in the last year with the resort's growing popularity, but also from the social burden he had to bear as owner and manager at Holley Cay.

He had no one but himself to blame. From the moment Holley Cay opened for business, Chris had populated the guest list with his friends and acquaintances, all other young, ridiculously wealthy people like himself. Holley Cay immediately took on an insider's club feel, and the burden was on Chris to make everyone feel like a member, even as the guest list grew to include fewer friends and more strangers. The result, which was part of Holley Cay's great appeal, was that guests felt like they were at one giant house party in the Caribbean, and Chris was the host of the century.

But tonight he just wanted to sink down on a lounge chair on his deck, crack open a beer, and maybe read a book. Or maybe just stare out at the turquoise sea until he felt drowsy enough to sleep.

Or, best of all, take Julie back to his villa and make love to her until he was too tired to move.

Instead he started up a new conversation with some minor member of British royalty, and watched as Julie walked to the railing overlooking the beach, Mike casually holding her arm.

At long last, the Lord whatever wandered off to find his girlfriend, and Chris leaned over the bar and retrieved a bottle of Caribe Lager and two Tylenol from the bartender.

"You shouldn't take those with alcohol, you know," Carla told him as he washed down the pills. "It's not good for your liver."

"Right now the pain in my head gets top priority, and the liver will just have to deal." Chris took another long drink of his beer.

"That bad, huh?" Carla eyed him speculatively.

"I'm just overtired." He yawned and cranked his neck side to side for emphasis.

"Um-hm." Carla looked past him, over his left shoulder toward the railing. A knowing smile crossed her full lips. "Why don't you go for it?"

Chris didn't bother to pretend he didn't know what Carla was talking about. "She's married to my brother, for one . . ."

"But she's getting an annulment," Carla interrupted.

"She is? How do you know?"

"Amy told me." Carla's curly brown head nodded in the direction of the bachelorette group. "I hung out with them by the pool earlier this afternoon."

"Even if she is getting an annulment," Chris said, ignoring the little pang of excitement and relief that ran through him, "that doesn't change anything. Julie's not the kind of woman I can just sleep with and leave."

"But what if she doesn't care? What if she just wants a little vacation fling to help her get over it?"

Chris didn't bother to explain that the problem wasn't on Julie's side. "Trust me, Carla. This can only end ugly, for both of us."

"You think it hasn't ended ugly before?"

Chris felt his temper heat. "Not like this." Not for me, anyway.

"Just because you're honest and try to keep things casual doesn't mean people don't get hurt. The difference is that you never cared before."

Maybe this was the Universe getting revenge on him. After all of his meaningless flings, all the women who'd left him with a wistful smile, now the one woman he wanted more than anything had showed up and only wanted a casual affair. And his cousin was laying out all the reasons he should take Julie up on it.

Chris didn't reply, and after a minute Carla continued. "Look, women make their own choices, bad and good, and if they tell you all they want is a casual thing too, you don't have any responsibility to look beyond for any hidden agenda. Some of them are telling the truth, some of them aren't, but it's not your responsibility to protect them from themselves."

"Julie's not like the other women," he said, " She's less experienced."

"So what? Once upon a time so were you."

Jesus, for once in his life he was trying to do the right thing—even if it was selfishly motivated—and all he got was grief.

"You might have missed your chance, anyway," she said, gesturing with her chin across the room. "I think someone else will be seeing to her entertainment."

Chris turned just in time to see Mike, his arm curved around Julie's waist, follow his friends and the bachelorette group off the patio and into the restaurant.

# 7

Chris hauled himself out of bed at five-thirty the next morning. Since he had been awake for two hours already, he might as well get up. After a quick five-mile run around the island, he showered and strolled over to the office.

He needed to go over the plans for the big celebrity wedding set to take place at the resort in ten days. It was the first time they would be hosting such an event, and Chris and Carla were twisting themselves in knots trying to make sure everything went perfectly. Complicating matters, the bride was one of the top-paid actresses in Hollywood, and she was determined to keep her wedding location top secret from the press. It was a huge challenge, even with Holley Cay's dedication to privacy. Carla and Chris were reduced to speaking in code with all the staff, the vendors, and anyone else who might leak to the press.

On the upside, if the wedding went well, Holley Cay would be known as the most exclusive place in the world to host a wedding.

Even better, once the news of his success hit, his father

would finally have to admit that even though Brian was the heir to the kingdom, it was Chris who really had what it took to rule an empire.

In the meantime, Chris thought as he dug his fingers into his nape, he was grateful for the work to take his mind off Julie. Visions of her tangled up with Mike the diver dude had been driving him insane all night.

Carla was already at the office waiting for him. "Thank God you're here. She's already called me five times this morning to go over the budget." Carla looked at her watch. "And it's like what, four A.M. on the west coast? That woman is psycho. Oh, and that security manager of hers . . ."

Chris poured himself a cup of coffee, only half listening as Carla went off on Jane Bowden's head bodyguard. "He thinks we're completely incompetent," she fumed. "He wants detailed background checks on every staff member, down to the last chambermaid!"

He took a seat behind the desk across from Carla's.

"What did Jane want?" Chris asked. Carla could complain about the bodyguard all she wanted. As far as Chris was concerned, Jane herself was the real thorn in their side.

"Is she bitching about the flowers again?"

The bride couldn't understand how flowers could cost so much when they were on a tropical island. She didn't seem to understand that the hydrangeas she wanted didn't grow in the Caribbean.

"No, this time it's the catering," Carla said. "She thinks we should be able to get a better deal on the champagne."

Chris fired up his computer and quickly found the cell phone number of the bride's personal assistant in his database.

"You'd think when someone's making a million dollars per episode, they wouldn't sweat this kind of thing."

This wasn't the first time Chris had questioned the wisdom of agreeing to host Jane Bowden's wedding. The money and the publicity would be fantastic, but after four weeks of negotiating every penny, he wasn't sure it was worth the headache.

"I know," Carla said. "I thought the whole point of this place was that if you were concerned about a budget, you shouldn't be here."

Chris managed a friendly tone when he left a message for Jane's assistant requesting that she call him about the catering.

"If she doesn't chill out she's going to end up with a special surprise in her wedding cake," Chris said.

"That's not a very customer-oriented attitude." Carla pulled out a file and handed Chris the latest version of the menu for Jane's wedding.

"I'm not exactly feeling the love today."

"Speaking of feeling the love, what's your little friend up to today?" Carla asked.

Chris scowled. "I wouldn't know. I'm sure she's keeping herself entertained."

"I'm sure she is. There's a lot of fun to be had at a place like this."

"Oh, like you would know," Chris snapped, "The woman who spends almost every night with Ben & Jerry."

"Are you saying I'm getting fat?" Carla half rose from her seat. She ran every day and worked out faithfully with one of the resort's trainers. Fat was definitely not an adjective Chris would use to describe her.

"No, I'm just saying you have no life."

"You need to get laid. You're starting to get cranky," Carla said.

"You're one to talk. What's it been? Four years?"

"Three."

"Bad enough. You've moved way beyond cranky into hostile. I think you're the one who needs some action."

"Nah, I can't afford to lose my edge. Therefore, I get to be the cranky one." She quirked her eyebrow at Chris. "You, on the other hand, have to be nice to all of the lovely people who come to visit you. I think you need to go find little miss Julie and get some relief."

"I already told you—"

"Oh, right, your whole nice girl hang-up. Well, someone else then. How about Kara DeMartinis?" she mentioned the brunette that came with the bachelorette party. "From what I hear she's the kind who'll hang from the chandeliers."

He wrinkled his nose in disgust. "Only if I want to catch something." Kara DeMartinis was a well-known party girl, the kind of girl who was famous for nothing really, other than her outrageous behavior and long line of wealthy boyfriends.

He clicked open the budget spreadsheet for the wedding and started through the pile of notes Sarah, Jane Bowden's assistant, had faxed over. He only wished he could follow Carla's suggestion and find Julie wherever she was and spend the rest of the week—how had she put it—"rekindling their friendship."

Oddly enough, despite what he'd said last night, the idea certainly had its appeal, even without the benefits she'd mentioned. Even though he hadn't seen her and had barely kept in touch for the past several years, he'd missed her. Missed watching stupid movies with her. Missed the way she blushed even as she laughed at the dirtiest joke he could think of. Missed the way her nose would wrinkle as she gamely drank her share of keg beer. Missed the way she would oh, so politely fend off her would-be suitors so that they wouldn't even realize they'd been dissed.

He'd left that friendship behind when he'd turned his back on the family and the business. And her hooking up with Brian was the final nail in the coffin. Not only was he unwilling to hear about her new life and new love, Chris also couldn't help feeling that if Julie was the kind of woman who could fall for Brian, maybe she wasn't the kind of person he thought she was. He had let their already infrequent correspondence die out. It had just been easier to cut the cord.

He was so lost in his musings that Carla had to physically walk over to his desk and wave her hand in front of his face to get his attention.

"Hello? Are the appetizer choices that interesting?"

Chris realized he'd been staring blankly at the first page of the catering menu for the better part of an hour.

Finally he focused on Carla's big brown eyes.

"I asked if you wanted anything for lunch."

Chris looked at his watch. Only eleven A.M., but since he hadn't had any breakfast, an early lunch sounded really good.

"Yeah, let's go over to the café," he said, referring to the small, casual restaurant next to one of the pools.

"Nah," Carla said. "Let's go to the beach bar. I think the view will be better."

Chris was still trying to figure out what she meant by that when his stomach, encouraged by the mention of food, rumbled loud enough to drown out any remaining thoughts in his head.

"Julie, do you want anything?"

Julie, half dozing in her lounger, turned her head towards Amy. "Hmm?"

Amy nodded her head to the cocktail waiter, waiting patiently in his uniform of tropical print shirt, baggy shorts, and no shoes. Julie couldn't contain a smile. If this were a D&D resort, the waiter would have been in a starched shirt, slacks, and dress shoes, no matter that he worked on the beach under the relentless Caribbean sun. His casual attire was one of the simple, but nonetheless important, differences that made Holley Cay seem so much more welcoming than other five-star places.

After all, how was a person supposed to relax and have fun if he or she was constantly waiting to make some social gaffe?

"I'd love a Pellegrino with lime, please," Julie told the waiter.

Amy rolled her eyes. "Oh, don't be so boring."

"Yeah," chimed in Jen. "I'm having a margarita, Amy's having a Bloody Mary, and Kara and Chrissy are sharing a pitcher of rum punch."

The other girls looked at her expectantly.

Julie glanced at her watch. "But it's only ten-thirty."

Kara rolled her eyes in what looked like sincere disgust. "Don't be so uptight," she said. Unlike Amy and Jen, her tone wasn't teasing. "You're allowed to loosen up a little."

"I—"

"Julie, we're just kidding. Order whatever you like," Amy said, shooting a glare at Kara.

Julie was glad her flush could be attributed to the hot sun. How typical. Goodie-goodie Julie orders water while the other girls cut loose. Kara was right. She was on vacation. She was allowed, no, she *deserved* to loosen up a little.

"I'd like the Pellegrino," she smiled at Amy, then shot Kara a sidelong glance, "and a Long Island iced tea." As long as she drank water along with her alcohol, she told herself, she would be just fine.

The waiter was back within minutes with their drinks. Julie settled back in the lounge chair and took a long sip. Something about the sweet drink and the accompanying bite of liquor made her smile. She felt decadent, like she was getting away with something, and told Amy so.

"That's a pretty sad state of affairs, Julie, if all it takes is a drink before noon to make you feel like a bad girl."

"It doesn't take much, I'll give you that," she said, taking another sip of her drink.

"Here's to being bad, or at least a little naughty," said Amy, and the girls all obligingly clinked glasses.

Julie smiled at the group, grateful once again that Amy had taken her under her wing. Otherwise she would have spent the week feeling like an outsider, lurking around waiting for someone to talk to her. Even though the resort had a reputation as a place for single people to have fun, Julie noted that all of the other single guests had come with friends.

She knew she would relish the solitude and downtime while she was here, but it was nice to know she'd have company when she wanted it. And Amy and her friends, not to mention Mike the diver guy, as Julie referred to him in her head, seemed willing and eager to make sure she had a good time.

Unlike Chris, the jerk. She still couldn't believe the things he had said to her. Did he really think she was some spoiled little rich girl? That all she wanted was to use him for some kind of revenge?

Okay, maybe he was right, at least a little bit. But she'd also slept with him because she'd really, really wanted to. And she really, really wanted to again, even though the admission—silent though it was—nearly choked her.

Well, there was nothing to be done for it. She'd had an incredible night with him, and she would leave it at that and try to focus on the good parts—of which there were many. But she would definitely steer clear of him for the rest of her stay, if only to prove to him that she didn't need his attention to have a good time.

But his easy rejection of her still rankled. How embarrassing! She'd made it clear that all she wanted was sex, and he couldn't even be bothered with that. He'd made that perfectly clear at the bar last night.

Good thing she hadn't told him the whole truth, about how she'd fantasized all the way down here about seeing him again. How he would pull her into his arms and kiss her in that toe-curling, blood-melting way he had. Then he'd spend the next week rubbing her down with coconut oil and making her come until she couldn't move.

Instead, he'd greeted her with panic, coldness, and finally outright hostility. *Come down whenever you need a break from the rat race.* Huh. If nothing else this whole fiasco would teach her not to impulsively accept an invitation that she knew damn well was only issued out of politeness.

Embarrassed or not, hurt or not, she was here now, and she was going to have fun even if it killed her.

She took another sip of her drink, surprised to see that she'd already finished half. *Better slow down*, she thought, and chased it with a sip of Pellegrino. The sun, combined with the alcohol lulled her into a dreamy, half-sleep state. Vaguely she heard the girls talking about some other guests who had just arrived on the beach.

"I thought we'd have this place all to ourselves," she heard Jen say.

The island had several beaches to choose from. Most guests, especially the couples, stayed close to their villas, where privacy was more easily found. Amy and her friends, in contrast, had chosen the main beach in front of the resort, preferring to be where the action was. So far the five of them were the only action to be found.

Julie cracked an eye open. Sure enough, it was the software mogul and his fiancée. They directed the attendant to pull their lounge chairs down the beach from the bachelorettes.

"So what's up with you and Mike?"

Julie was silent a moment until she realized Jen was talking to her.

"Yeah, he's hot," said Chrissy, a short blonde who could have passed for Julie's sister. "But so's Dan, and since Mike seems otherwise occupied . . ."

"I just met Mike yesterday," Julie said. "How could there be anything going on already?"

"Oh, give me a break," Amy chided. "One day at a place like this is plenty of time." She tilted her Versace shades down her nose and peered over the lenses at Jen. "Isn't it, Jen?"

Jen stretched luxuriously and said, "What can I say, time is short, resources are scarce, and I've gotta work fast."

"Jen hooked up with Greg last night," Kara said.

"He's the guy with the dark hair and green eyes, right?" Julie asked, and finished her drink in one last sip. Almost magically, the waiter reappeared, and Amy ordered another round for all of them.

"No, that's Dan," Jen clarified. "Greg's the one with blue eyes and dirty blond hair."

"And then the other one's Brad, right?" said Amy.

"You should know, you were sitting next to him at dinner," chided Jen.

"Oh, like I would remember. I was so bombed by then, I'm lucky I remembered my *own* name," Amy laughed. "Poor Brad, he probably thought he was going to get some bachelorette last-fling action." She sighed. "Unfortunately for him, I am much too in love with Will to ever even look at another man."

"Bullshit," Kara said bluntly.

"Okay, fine, I'll look, but I just won't do anything about it," Amy said.

Julie laughed and took her new drink from the waiter. She felt the slightest twinge of envy at the group's familiar banter. Except for Wendy, Julie had lost touch with most of her girl-friends over the past two years, having spent most of the time with Brian's friends and their wives. Although they were nice, they'd never stopped treating Julie with an unmistakable air of condescension, referring to her as Brian's child bride. As a result, Julie had always been on her best, most mature behavior in front of them.

The girls promptly started telling other vacation stories, teasing one another about past exploits. "Remember that guy in Jamaica, Amy—the one with the tongue piercing?" Jen asked.

Julie felt another stab of resentment. Thanks to Brian, she had missed out on making friends like this and having her own wild stories.

"Hey, I didn't know that was allowed."

Julie followed Jen's gaze down the beach. The software mogul's improbably endowed fiancée had taken off her top and was leisurely rubbing sunscreen over her breasts.

"Excellent," Kara said, and wasted no time ridding herself of her own top.

Julie could only watch, openmouthed, as the others removed their bikini tops with remarkable speed.

"Come on, Julie," Amy urged.

Julie shook her head. A drink in the morning she could do, but she definitely wasn't up for baring her breasts to a bunch of strangers.

"I forgot my sunscreen back in my villa." She took another sip of her drink.

Kara gave her a challenging look and tossed a bottle into Julie's lap. Startled, Julie sloshed her drink onto her stomach. "It's SPF 45."

Something in Kara's attitude rankled Julie, as though she could see through the breezy, fun-loving façade Julie was trying to put up, and knew that underneath she was so boring Kara would never bother speaking with her. Or maybe it was the way Kara had practically draped her boobs over Chris's arm last night at the cocktail party.

Whatever it was, after another fortifying drink of her Long Island iced tea, Julie took a deep breath, and untied the top of her bright coral bikini. The two small triangles covering her breasts immediately fell. Julie resisted the urge to cover herself, and instead reached around her back and untied the other string.

Immediately she felt her nipples pucker as the warm breeze brushed her skin. She quickly applied a generous coating of sunscreen and looked around sheepishly.

Jen laughed. "No one's looking," she said as she took the tube of sunscreen from Julie and applied it to her own breasts. Julie looked around. Sure enough, the software CEO was engrossed in the *Wall Street Journal*, oblivious to the breast fest.

Julie picked up her book, a thick historical featuring a brawny Highlander. What would Chris look like in a kilt, she wondered with a smile.

Her composure slipped a notch when she saw the cocktail waiter heading their way again. Unlike the other women, she just didn't have it in her to lie there on her back as though nothing was amiss. As casually as possible, Julie adjusted the back of her lounger so it lay flat, and flipped over onto her stomach.

"Jules, you want another?"

She knew she shouldn't. But then neither should she be exposing the virgin skin of her breasts to sun damage. What the hell.

"I will, but this time make it a banana daiquiri." True, it was the sort of sissy drink she'd been determined to avoid, but after two Long Island iced teas she was about to do a face plant in the sand.

She didn't realize the error of her ways until a few sips into the daiquiri. Here in the Virgin Islands, as well as in most of the Caribbean, the rum in a drink was cheaper than the mixer. In order to save money, bartenders were often overly generous with the rum. She remembered that she forgot to ask for a mainland pour.

*But where was the harm,* she thought as the words of her paperback started to swim together. She was on vacation after all.

The beach café wasn't crowded yet. Only a few tables were occupied, since most guests were either enjoying one of the many beaches, the pool, or on diving or snorkeling excursions.

While Carla waited for their lunch orders, Chris wandered out onto the front deck of the café, which overlooked the resort's main beach. It, too, was fairly empty, as were most of the lounge chairs.

What he wouldn't give to have an hour to flop down and

just stare out at the calming turquoise water. But that was the blessing and the curse of running a place like this. Chris lived in one of the most beautiful places on earth, but he had less and less time to enjoy it.

Chris watched a waiter as he scurried across the sand with a tray full of drinks. His gaze wandered over to the group the waiter was serving, and his breath caught.

It was a group of women—Amy and her bachelorette party. And on the lounge chair closest to him lay Julie.

Even though she was on her stomach, he could tell it was her. He recognized her profile as she propped herself up, and accepted her drink from the waiter. Her curly blond hair was caught up haphazardly in a clip, with damp tendrils coiling along her nape. The skin of her back gleamed gold in the bright sun, and he felt a rush of heat to his groin as his gaze traveled lower.

From his vantage point, he had a spectacular view of her ass, barely covered by the shiny coral fabric of her bikini. He'd always loved Julie's ass. Not fat, as she always called it, but mouthwateringly round. And—as he knew from firsthand experience—perfectly firm and smooth to the touch. He felt his fingers twitch as he imagined untying the string ties that held up the bikini bottoms and peeling away the fabric to reveal . . .

"Whoa, I hope they're wearing sunscreen."

Carla's voice startled him out of his daydream.

"What?" He said vaguely.

"Getting your boobs sunburned is just really painful," Carla said.

He wrinkled his brow and looked again at the group. Sure enough, all four of Julie's new friends were topless. And he hadn't even noticed. Topless sunbathing wasn't exactly a rarity at Holley Cay, but Chris was a man. Just because he saw bare breasts on the beach all the time didn't mean he didn't appreciate them.

But what the hell was wrong with him that he was so mesmerized by Julie's bikini clad ass that he didn't even notice four—and now that he looked, he noticed four very nice—pairs of bare breasts less than ten yards away from him?

This was getting ridiculous.

Just then, Julie flipped over, and Chris groaned. Of course, she was topless, too. Even as he scolded himself for ogling, he couldn't have stopped staring if someone held a gun to his head. Her breasts weren't the biggest of the group—Kara had that honor, he admitted objectively. But Julie's breasts were definitely the most appealing. Soft, creamy-skinned, with hard pink nipples that were pointing up at the clear blue sky. His mouth watered at the thought of tracing them with his tongue.

"Do you want a napkin?"

"A what?" Chris turned to Carla, who rolled her eyes at him.

"For the drool that's about to drip off your chin."

"Is our food ready yet?" He needed to get out of here. He started to walk back inside, but it was too late.

"Chris! Hey Chris!" Kara had spotted him on the deck and was now waving enthusiastically enough to send her D-cups bobbling.

He waved feebly and made to turn back inside.

"Come have a drink with us," Kara called. All the others, except Julie, he noted, joined in with an invitation.

"You better go on." He wanted to slap the smirk off of Carla's face. "Wouldn't want to spoil your reputation as the ever accommodating host." Carla turned and walked into the café.

Chris frowned but started toward the steps that led to the beach. How crazy was it that he was being invited to join five topless women and he felt like he would rather be standing in line at the DMV?

Reluctantly he pulled up a chair next to Julie's and did his best not to just stare at her like a complete letch. Under Julie's tan, her skin was flushed from the heat, and a faint sheen of perspiration glowed in the valley between her breasts.

In an attempt to distract himself from the urge to run his tongue along her damp skin, he found himself staring at her belly-button ring, the little diamond peeking out at him as it sparkled in the sun. Body jewelry, when taken too far, was a personal turn off for him. But Chris had always been a sucker for a belly-button ring, and the fact that it was Julie's navel made it all the more appealing.

"You know, if someone had told me that one day Julie Driscoll would have her navel pierced and would be sunbathing topless on a public beach, I would have thought they were insane."

Julie smiled, her eyes hidden by those purple tinted glasses. "Sometimes a girl has to shake things up a bit, you know, keep things interesting."

She took a sip of her daiquiri, but ruined her casual demeanor when the umbrella poked her in the cheek.

He forced his gaze away from Julie and focused on Amy and Kara's conversation. Judging from their own giggling and their voices just on the verge of being too loud, the women had spent the better part of the morning boozing under the sun.

"We're not busted or anything, are we?" Amy asked suddenly, "I mean for being topless? We saw what's-her-face—" Amy gestured sloppily to the woman down the beach, whose preternaturally perky boobs were sticking straight up like traffic cones, "and we figured it must be fine."

Chris forced a smile. "It's no problem with me." That was true when it came to the other women. But his fingers itched to wrap Julie's towel around her and secure it tightly. Maybe with duct tape. He supposed he should be grateful that there wasn't anyone else around to see her. The only other guy on the beach seemed more interested in monitoring his stock portfolio, and the staff at the beach café had seen so much in their time at Holley Cay that bare breasts were about as shocking as bare feet.

Up until about ten minutes ago, Chris would have sworn he'd felt the same way.

He glanced at Julie, who drained her daiquiri and waved the waiter over.

Chris caught her wrist in one hand. "Don't you think you should slow down?"

"What are you, my dad?" Julie snapped.

"Don't be a party pooper, Chris," Jen said. "Get yourself a drink, too."

Chris obligingly ordered a beer, and when Julie ordered another daiquiri, Chris cut in, "And make sure it's a mainland."

Julie sat up indignantly, and her breasts jiggled in a way that made his head spin. "You don't have to look out for me, Chris. It's not like I'm eighteen anymore."

"You're sure as hell acting like it," he snapped back.

Suddenly he realized that all conversation had stopped, and five bare-breasted women were staring at him in astonishment. Way to go. Way to make your guests feel comfortable and relaxed. But before he could backpedal and diffuse the situation, he saw something over Kara's shoulder that caused a knot to form in the pit of his stomach.

The diver boys were back from their excursion, and all four were heading their way.

# 8

Chris didn't care how bad it looked, but there was no way he was going to let Mike and company get a look at Julie on display. With no preamble, he stood up, grabbed Julie's cover-up in one hand and her arm in the other.

"We need to talk," he said, jerking her to her feet.

She staggered against him, and Chris let out a hiss as her breasts made contact with his forearm. He needed to get her clothed, and fast. He thrust her cover-up at her. "Put this on."

The other four women were just staring at him.

Julie ignored the cover-up and let it drop to the sand.

"Let go of me," she said. She tried to pull away, but Chris had his grip locked firmly on her forearm.

"What is your problem?" She jerked again, then staggered as she lost her footing. Chris stumbled as he took the full impact of her weight, but he managed to pull her up before they both fell.

"Oh, hey, Mike, hey, guys." Julie's attention was caught by the sight of the four guys walking up the beach, and she waved with her free arm. All four men were wearing sunglasses, but the shades couldn't hide the leering cast that came over all four smiles when they saw that the women were topless.

Jealousy twisted Chris's gut. He knew he shouldn't care. He had no claim on Julie. It shouldn't matter to him if she wanted to show her breasts to the world, but he couldn't stop the primitive, territorial urge that flared as these men lusted after a body he considered his.

*No, she's not yours, never was, never will be. And a reaction like this is prime example of why you need to stay far, far away from her.* Nevertheless, Chris couldn't sit idly by and let four other men ogle Julie. So he bent down, and, ignoring her shriek, caught her around the legs and threw her over his shoulder. One arm wrapped firmly around her thighs, he motioned for Amy to hand him Julie's cover-up and beach bag.

"Put me down, you ass," Julie yelled, pounding her fist into his back as he started down the path that led to her villa.

Chris smacked her firmly on her butt, then couldn't resist curling his palm around her buttock for a firm squeeze.

"Are you copping a feel?"

"Shut up, do you want everyone to hear us?" he scolded.

"I don't care who hears us, you're the one carrying off one of your guests like some Neanderthal. I'm sure that will go over really well."

"Hey, you're the one who's drunk before noon and running around with her top off." Chris turned the corner.

"I'm not drunk."

Chris snorted.

"I'm not. And as for being topless, I didn't hear you complain about any of the others. Oof."

Chris jostled her as he hunted through her bag for her key.

"What makes my breasts so particularly offensive?"

He took a moment to let his eyes adjust to the dimness of the villa. He passed through the kitchenette and the sitting room into the bedroom, where he unceremoniously flung Julie onto the king-size mattress. He threw her cover-up at her, but she ignored it as it slid down her body to fall to the floor.

"Brian always thought they were too small," she said, looking down at her naked chest.

She was still talking about her breasts. Chris almost moaned in frustration.

"Do you think I need implants?"

Chris swallowed hard in an attempt to get some moisture into a mouth gone suddenly bone-dry. She was screwing with him, right? But when he looked at her face, he saw that in her own tipsy way she was sincerely concerned. Her brow furrowed as she propped up on her elbows and tucked her chin for a better look.

"I think your breasts are perfect," Chris said finally, and the look of happiness that crossed her face was nearly enough to send him to his knees. How had he landed himself back in this situation, alone with a mostly naked Julie Driscoll, wanting her so much his cock was on the verge of bursting through his fly but knowing beyond a doubt that he should do absolutely nothing about it?

"Really?" Julie pressed.

Oh, God, she had to stop talking about her breasts and get some clothes on or he was going to go insane. He tried to look away, but even the smell of her, all warm skin and coconut-scented sunscreen, was enough make his groin tighten. "To quote one of our favorite movies, 'there is a shortage of perfect breasts in the world, and it would be a shame to lose yours.'"

Her smile brightened, if that was possible. "*Princess Bride*. I haven't seen that in years."

"Well, Buttercup, if you're a good girl and keep your top on, we can watch it at my place before you leave."

"I'd like that," she answered softly, but made no move to cover herself.

Unable to stand it any longer, Chris snatched the cover-up

from the floor and tucked it around her. But before he could straighten up, Julie's arm curved around his shoulder, and he felt her fingers twist in the slightly damp hair along his nape.

"Why do you care whether or not other men see me topless, Chris?" Her lips were pink and parted, and if he couldn't smell the faint sweetness of rum on her breath, he would have leaned down to taste her.

"Are you jealous?" she prodded.

It nearly caused him physical pain to reach up and gently untangle her hand from his hair. She was killing him, tying his gut in knots as his brain conjured a torrent of images of them, naked, spending the rest of the afternoon in a lusty tangle of limbs.

But she was drunk, and it was fueling her flirtatiousness. And like it or not, the same protectiveness and jealousy that made him want to conceal her from the eyes of other men was what prevented him from throwing all good sense to the wind and sinking down onto that bed with her. That, and the knowledge that taking her again, especially in her inebriated state, would only make his life more complicated.

"I just don't want you getting yourself into a situation you can't handle, Jules," he finally said. It was lame, but what else could he say? That the idea of another man seeing her naked made him want to put his fist through a wall? Or that the very notion that he was jealous had him more confused and pissed off than he'd ever been in his life?

Julie's bottom lip jutted out in a sulky pout. "I'm not a little kid." Her eyelids were heavy as she looked up at him from under her lashes.

"I know that. It's just . . . old habits die hard."

She rolled her eyes, looking exactly like the sullen teenager she claimed she wasn't. "Okay, Chris, I'll make a deal with you. I'll keep my top on and stay out of your way, if that's what you want. But you need to lay off and let me have a good time."

His brows snapped down over the bridge of his nose. "I never said I wanted you to stay out of my way."

"Bullshit."

Chris couldn't stop his grin. He didn't know if he'd ever get used to hearing Julie swear.

"God, you should have seen your face when I showed up. You looked so scared, like you expected me to whip out a boiling bunny or something."

Chris winced, but didn't try to defend himself.

"I had a great time with you, Chris, and I thought you did, too," she said softly. "But I know better than to confuse great sex with true love. Especially with you."

Now that hit him like the proverbial stake in the heart, making him suck in a sharp breath as her offhand comment hit home. Unfortunately for her, he wasn't willing to be her personal boy toy for the week. And even though the thought of it made him physically ill, he didn't have any right to stop her from finding herself a replacement.

"Okay, fine, I'll lay off. You just be careful." When she opened her mouth to protest he silenced her with a hand over her mouth. "Look, I know you're all grown up now and you want to have a good time, but that doesn't change the fact that you've led a pretty sheltered life up to this point. So don't go too crazy. Not all guys are nice like me."

"Okay, Dad," she said huffily. Then, in a friendlier tone, "Does that mean we're friends again?"

"Yeah, I guess it does."

She fell back against the pillows and closed her eyes. Chris leaned over and pressed a kiss to the smooth skin of her forehead.

Before he could react, Julie slid her arms around his shoulders and raised her head. Her soft lips parted over his, her tongue flicking out to tease the slick inner skin.

Sighing, Chris let himself fall into her kiss. She tasted so amazingly good, sweet and warm with a spicy undertone of rum. Even as his brain screamed at him to stop, step away, get out of her bed, Chris trailed his hand down her arm. His palm slid across the silky skin of her belly and up under where he had tucked the cover-up around her.

She let out a little moan when his hand enveloped her breast, and her hands slid down his back, her fingers sliding inside the waistband of his shorts. He groaned, savoring the feel of her in his hands, the taste of her in his mouth, the feel of her barely contained heat rubbing against the front of his shorts.

A sharp rap sounded at the door of the villa.

The sound jerked Chris abruptly back to his senses. He pushed away from her, sitting up so quickly his head swam.

"Go away," Julie called.

"Julie? It's Amy. I just wanted to see—"

"I'm fine, go away," Julie repeated. She got up on her knees and tried to pull Chris back down on top of her. "Now where were we?"

"Julie, I should go," Chris tried to gently pull her arms from around his neck, but she was wrapped around him like an octopus. "We can't do this," he said, wincing at his own lack of conviction.

"Why not? It's not like we haven't done it before. And it was so good," she murmured, torturing him with tiny, teasing nips at his neck and ears. "I haven't been able to stop thinking about how good you felt, fucking me so deep and hard."

He nearly came at that, shocked and unbearably turned on by her very un-Julie-like language. He closed his eyes, wanting so badly to give into her logic, but knowing that they would both hate him if he did.

"Just because we made a mistake once doesn't mean we should do it again."

Julie's arms fell away, and she lay back on the bed. "Fine. I guess I'll just have to take care of myself." With a sassy smirk, she spread her fingers and slid her palm down her bare stomach. As Chris watched her, paralyzed with lust, she slid her fingers beneath the waistband of her bikini bottoms, arching up into her fingers with a throaty groan.

He had a thousand reasons why he shouldn't give into his craving for Julie ever again. Right now he couldn't think of one as all the blood in his body fled to his groin. His cock throbbed as he watched her fingers move under the silky fabric of her bikini. His mouth went dry as she captured her own nipple between two fingers and gave it a little squeeze.

He had tried so hard to be good, to do the right thing. But a man could only endure so much.

Within seconds he was on the bed next to her, his hand covering hers as it stroked and massaged her breast. Her eyes flew open, lips parting in a surprised gasp at his touch. He took the opportunity to capture her mouth with his, dipping his tongue inside to taste and tease. His palm slid down the flat, tanned expanse of her belly, pausing to untie one side of her string bikini so he could peel back the shiny coral fabric.

He swallowed hard at the sight of her slender fingers buried in the slick folds of her pussy. Her clit was a perfect red berry, juicy with her own moisture as it poked eagerly through her smooth pussy lips. She stroked herself, fingers circling in a firm, steady rhythm. She moaned, the sound sending sizzles of heat straight to his balls, and Chris knew he couldn't last another second without touching her.

He traced two fingers along her juicy slit. Her fingers froze. "Don't stop," he whispered between the moist kisses he rained on her chest. "Show me how you make yourself come."

She let out a shuddery breath and resumed her stroking. He slid his fingers along her entrance, coaxing another wave of moisture, pressing inside. His eyes drifted closed, and he let out a groan at the slick, muscular feel of her surrounding him. She was melting all around him like warm honey, liquid sugar, bathing his hand in her sweet heat as she arched up and urged his fingers deeper.

Her own fingers moved faster, firmer, and Chris crossed his fingers, pumping in and out, twisting his fingers for maximum sensation. His tongue lapped up the beads of sweat that bloomed on her chest, licked its way up her breast to capture her pebble hard nipple. He sucked her hard, nearly coming as she stiffened against him with a high, keening cry. Her pussy rippled around him in waves, clenching his fingers in its tight, slick grip. He had to get inside her. Now.

He fumbled with the button of his shorts, grinning down at her as he pushed himself up and over her. Her eyes were closed, lips parted as her breath evened out. Then she made a soft sound that made him groan. But not in pleasure.

She was snoring. Passed out cold. He would have liked to give himself credit for making her come so hard she'd fainted, but he knew that the only guy responsible for her unconscious state was good old Captain Morgan.

The sound of her soft snores tortured him as he let himself out of the villa. He pressed his palm against his protesting cock, willing his painful hardness to subside. This was what he got for fooling around with drunk chicks.

Julie jerked awake. She lifted her head from the pillow, and she lifted crusty eyelids to peer around the room. What time was it, anyway? She looked at the sliver of light peeking through the curtains. Early evening, she guessed.

She swung her legs over the side of the bed, wincing a bit as her brain jostled against her skull. What had she been thinking? Drinking at ten in the morning, on no breakfast, to boot. Her mouth tasted like she'd been eating dirt sandwiches.

Somewhat unsteadily she stood, glancing down at the clock

radio on the bed stand. Five-thirty. She walked over to the French doors that led to the villa's patio and drew back the curtains. Odd. It was unusually dark for this early in the evening.

She flipped on the bathroom light, squinting as the brightness assaulted her eyes. She surveyed herself over the rim of a glass as she gulped down water. Nice. Her hair stood out in Medusa tangles, and there was a streak of dried drool on her cheek. Her stomach grumbled as the water hit it.

Room service. Then back to bed.

"Yes, I'd like to order some dinner," she said when the operator picked up.

"Dinner? Ma'am, we're just opening for breakfast."

"Breakfast?" Julie said stupidly.

"Yes, but we don't start delivering until six. But if you'd like to place an order now, we will be happy to bring you your meal as soon as possible."

Breakfast? Was it possible . . . Julie looked at her watch. Yes, indeed, according to the window that displayed the date, it was now Monday morning. Somehow she had managed to sleep for nearly eighteen hours.

"Ma'am?"

The attendant's voice startled her back to semiconsciousness.

"Yes, I mean, no, I don't need breakfast at this time."

*They must think I'm a complete idiot. Or a complete drunk.*

But then, the room service operator was the least of her worries, wasn't she? Based on yesterday's antics, several people probably thought she was an idiot.

Starting with Chris. "Oh, God," she moaned, vaguely remembering that he'd brought her back to her room. And then . . . oh God, the moments right up until she fell asleep. Chris's fingers on her and in her, making her come so hard she'd almost . . . No wait, she had passed out, no almost about it. She squeezed her eyes shut, embarrassment burning through her as she remembered what she had said, what she had done. Oh my God, she'd actually touched herself in front of him! Put her own hands down her pants and started to masturbate in an effort to taunt him.

Obviously, it had worked to a point, but to what point she wasn't entirely sure. She racked her brain, trying to remember what, if anything, had happened next. Had they had sex? Or had he left after he'd gotten her off?

Maybe if she was really careful, she could manage to avoid him for the next five days.

Her stomach knotted as more snippets of her behavior flashed through her brain like a poorly edited movie trailer. Taking off her top. That last banana daiquiri. Being thrown over Chris's shoulder and carried off.

She shook her head and made herself a cup of coffee. On her wedding night, she'd vowed to herself that the new Julie would shake things up. Unlike the biddable daughter she had always been, the new Julie wasn't afraid to cause a ruckus, to be the center of attention, to bring about a little scandal.

But getting drunk, stripping, and being carried off in front of her new friends wasn't precisely what she had in mind.

What would she possibly say to him? *Sorry I threw myself at you like a crazy chick from "Girls Gone Wild."* She'd been scolding herself for living such a boring life, but as boring, straight-and-narrow, never-break-the-rules Julie, she had never faced a situation like this.

And practically browbeating Chris into having sex with her when he clearly didn't want to renew their acquaintance was definitely not in her plans.

To make matters worse, she'd proven him right, hadn't she? After all of her protests that she hadn't come down here with any expectations, she'd latched onto him like a barnacle the first chance she got.

*Just because we made a mistake once doesn't mean we should do it again*. Though the rest of their conversation was a little murky, those words rang clear. A mistake. That's how he viewed sleeping with her. Not as a lark, not as a good time worth repeating, but as a mistake. So what if he'd finally given in yesterday? She'd been half naked—touching herself for God's sake!—practically begging him to do her. Julie didn't consider herself an expert on men by any means, but even she knew she'd given him an offer a single, straight man would have to practically be dead to resist. She remembered now, that before she'd pulled out the big ammo, he'd pulled away.

There was only one solution. To stay as far away from Chris as possible for the rest of her stay.

She looked at the clock again. Six A.M. Something niggled at the back of her brain. Something she was supposed to do today.

She grimaced again as she remembered. Diving. She was going diving with Mike this morning. She didn't really want to go, but Mike had seemed so sincere about wanting to help her overcome her aversion, she felt bad refusing.

If nothing else, it would give her a couple of hours where she was guaranteed not to run into Chris.

She looked outside at the sun, just now shedding its lemony yellow light across the beach. Her hangover was gone thanks to the water and coffee, and she felt restless energy course through her. No doubt one of the side benefits of sleeping for nearly a full day.

Deciding that a run was just the thing to kill some time and help her further rid herself of toxins, Julie pulled on her running clothes and headed out.

An hour later, she was refreshed and a tad lightheaded from running on an empty stomach. She made a detour by the poolside restaurant to order a smoothie.

As she waited for her peach protein power shake to blend, Julie's stare was riveted to the man swimming laps in the pool. She was surprised to see someone else up this early. Whoever he was, he was amazing to watch. His strong, tanned back gleamed under the surface of the water, his rippling arms pulling him sleekly through the water in a seemingly effortless stroke.

Then she groaned as she realized who it was. "Can't a girl get a break?"

"Pardon me, miss?" The waitress who was busy wiping down the bar asked.

"Oh, nothing," said Julie. "Just waiting for my smoothie." What, were they out harvesting the peaches? She glanced furtively back at Chris, still absorbed in his swim workout. Silently Julie prayed that she could get out of there without him noticing. She knew she would eventually have to face him, but right now she was afraid she'd die of embarrassment.

For a millisecond, she considered ditching her breakfast altogether and just ordering room service, but she was seriously afraid she'd pass out from low blood sugar before she got there.

She breathed a sigh of relief when finally, the waitress brought her a large plastic cup full of the thick shake.

Keep swimming. Please let him keep swimming.

Her breath expelled in a whoosh as she turned just in time to see Chris emerging from the pool. Water sluiced down his muscled chest as he levered himself out. He hadn't seen her yet—he was busy drying his face and hair. She could still make her escape.

Unfortunately, her feet wouldn't obey her commands to run. Instead she stood there, drool no doubt staining the front of her tank top, and drank him in. Even after a night of getting very up close and personal with Chris, the sight of his mostly bare body was enough to make her knees go all mushy.

Her eyes tracked droplets of water as they traced down his rippling abs, and she fought the urge to push him onto the pool deck and dry them with her tongue.

"Oh, hey, Jules. You're up early."

Julie's gaze snapped back to Chris's face, surprised to see

what could only be described as a welcoming smile on his face. Funny, after yesterday, she expected him to avoid her like the plague.

"How are you feeling?" he asked when she still didn't say anything.

"I'm fine. Why do you ask?" Julie took a long sip of her smoothie, savoring the icy sweetness sliding down her throat. It wasn't just her run that kept her body temperature elevated.

His shoulders rippled as he patted his arms and back with the towel. "I would have thought you'd have a little bit of a stinger."

Julie laughed nervously. For whatever reason, Chris was being nice this morning. She decided not to read too much into it. "Well, if I did have a hangover, I probably slept through it. I don't know what time I fell asleep, but I woke up about an hour and a half ago."

Chris let out a low whistle, walking over to join her at the bar. He thanked the waitress who immediately presented him with giant glasses each of water and orange juice. "You were even more gone than I thought."

Julie's hackles raised. "I wasn't *that* drunk." She avoided his gaze by pretending to adjust her straw before taking another drink.

"Yeah, that's why you passed out for eighteen hours—"

"I didn't pass out. I've been really sleep deprived—"

"Right after you tried to have your way with me," he finished with an annoyingly smug grin.

Julie didn't think she could possibly get any hotter, but the temperature of her face rose about ten degrees. Hah, if he thought she'd been totally hammered, why not just go with that? "I was so drunk, I don't even know what you're talking about." He'd handed her the perfect strategy—play it off like she couldn't remember a thing.

Chris laughed, but the mocking tone she suspected was absent. "Bull. You weren't that drunk."

"But you just said—"

"Yeah, because I knew it would piss you off, and you're so damn cute when you lose your cool. Did you just go running?"

The abrupt change in subject was too much for her still slightly foggy mind, and it took her a moment to answer. "Yeah. I wanted to go before it got too hot. And I'm not cute." Cute had dogged her for her entire life. Just once she wanted to be described as beautiful or sexy.

"You're adorable. And I know what you mean, I try to get my workouts in before the sun reaches the roasting point. Not to mention the fact that I don't necessarily need all of the guests seeing me like this," he gestured down at the close fitting Lycra shorts he wore as a swimsuit. "Unless you're Lance Armstrong, Lycra shorts aren't a look any man should attempt."

Julie stared down at the garment in question. The way they fit over his sleekly muscled thighs and ridiculously tight, gorgeous butt like a second skin, she had to disagree. Not to mention they did little to hide the very impressive goods Chris sported between his legs.

Chris cleared his throat.

Oh, God, she was staring at his crotch. Well, it wasn't her fault. He was the one who called attention to himself and the way the shorts lovingly clung to all of his . . . parts.

"I think you look . . . just fine," she said. She followed her statement with such a big sip of her smoothie that she immediately clenched her eyes and grabbed her head at the onset of brain freeze.

A low laugh rumbled from his chest. "God, Jules, you crack me up. Only you could sound so polite while you're ogling a guy's package."

Julie gasped, "I was not ogling your, your *package*."

"Hey, I'm not complaining. Listen, Julie, about yesterday."

"I really don't want to talk about it. I'm not entirely sure what all happened," *liar*, "but I'm not reading anything into it as far as your intentions or lack thereof. I know I acted inappropriately, and I'm really embarrassed, and I promise that I will not throw myself at you for the rest of the week, and if I do, you can send me home without a refund, okay?"

"Julie, I didn't mean—"

Why wouldn't he just drop it? "I can't help it if you're a really, really good looking guy, and I very much enjoyed having sex with you, but," she held up her hands as he opened his mouth to interrupt, "I also understand that you are not interested in having sex with me again and I will respect your wishes, regardless of how drunk I get."

He didn't say anything, just stood there, looking slightly confused.

"Now, if you'll excuse me, I have to go." She smiled ruefully up at him. "I'm going diving with Mike. You're no doubt relieved to know that I have someone to distract me from stalking you."

He caught her arm as she turned to go. "You don't need to be embarrassed. I'm not upset—"

She pulled her arm from his grasp. God only knew what she would do if he continued to touch her. Grasping for the composed façade that had always served her so well, she said, "I will endeavor not to cause you any more inconvenience for the rest of my stay."

She allowed herself one last discreet, covetous leer at his chest before she turned and walked away. Who knew when she'd be in such close proximity to his male perfection again?

*"I will endeavor not to cause you any more inconvenience for the rest of my stay."*

Who the hell talked like that? Chris thought as he finished his water and juice.

Julie, that was who. Julie, when she felt threatened or uncomfortable, always retreated behind the armor of polite
civility.

She was almost as cute carefully choosing all those SAT
words as she was when she got mad.

But while he had always loved teasing her, trying to get a
glimpse of her seemingly nonexistent temper, he didn't like to
see her embarrassed.

Blotting himself with his towel, he made his way back to his
house. Forget the fact that this was her vacation. Julie was paying what even he could admit was an obnoxious amount of
money to stay here. Regardless of her reasons for coming to
Holley Cay, she deserved to have a good time however she chose.

He frowned. But not if her idea of fun included getting
wasted and stripping off her top in front of anyone who wanted
to look at her perfect breasts.

This was such a fucking mess. He'd barely slept last night,
fighting the urge to break down her villa door and fuck her like
she so obviously wanted. He hadn't been able to get any work
done. All he'd been able to think about was the feel of her
sweet, hot pussy clenching around his fingers, how good it
would have felt to slide his cock against her smooth pussy lips.
Over and over until he'd had to go home and jerk off, just so he
could concentrate.

And now the sight of her, damp and flushed from her run,
made him so hard he had to wrap his towel around his waist so
as not to shock an unsuspecting staff member or guest.

All he could think about was getting inside her again, and
now she was going to spend the morning with Mike. Mike,
with his surfer good looks and good old boy earnestness, had
no doubt gotten quite an eyeful before Chris had managed to
cart Julie back to her villa.

Fan-fucking-tastic. Holley Cay's future success was riding
on his ability to pull off this stupid wedding, and thanks to one

small, blonde woman with perfect tits and a saucy little ass, he couldn't get his brain wrapped around it.

Just as he'd feared, Julie presented the world's biggest distraction, at a time in his life when he could least afford it. The question was, how in the hell was he supposed to deal with it? Sending her packing was the obvious answer. But even he wasn't that much of an asshole, and besides, it wouldn't do Holley Cay any good if he got a reputation for kicking guests out for no reason.

And though he was loath to admit it, he wasn't ready to say good-bye to her just yet.

Hours later, he still didn't know what to do. Carla was no help.

"What do you mean nothing happened?" Carla said when he filled her in on the details of what had ensued after he and Julie left the beach. "You carried her off like a mountain gorilla, and nothing happened? She was practically naked." Carla sat back in her chair and folded her arms indignantly.

"She was totally hammered—"

"And throwing herself at you, though I can't imagine why considering what a jerk you've been to her—"

"And I didn't want to take advantage of her."

"Oh, please, you've taken up hundreds of women on their drunken offers—"

"Not that many!"

"Okay, dozens."

Chris did some quick math in his head and didn't argue.

"Dozens of women," Carla continued, "and you've never had a single qualm about their states of inebriation." Carla paused, a frown puckering her forehead. "Well, that's not totally true—I've never seen you go off with someone in imminent danger of vomiting."

Carla spoke the truth, and damn, did it hurt. He'd never had any qualms about his behavior before.

"No one was ever so drunk she didn't know what she was doing." It was a weak argument, but for the first time in his life Chris was having a hard time justifying his own behavior.

"Was Julie?"

"Was Julie what?"

Carla's tone grew even more exasperated. "So drunk she didn't know what she was doing?"

Chris considered her words carefully. There was no question Julie had been inebriated. But if he were being truly honest with himself he would admit that it had been more of a case of inhibitions being lowered than Julie doing something she wouldn't otherwise do.

Like on her wedding night. Chris felt a familiar tightening in his gut when he remembered the hours he spent with her in that big bed at the Winston. He'd had her in every way he could think of, and still he'd been hard and aching for her as he boarded the plane back to Holley Cay.

Like he was now, remembering the feel of her perfect, bare breast under his palm.

But on her wedding night, taking advantage of her lack of inhibitions had been wrong, just as it would have been yesterday.

"After all of the crap you've given me about my past behavior, I would think you'd be proud of my restraint."

Carla rolled her eyes. "Fine, you kept it in your pants for once. You want a cookie?"

He tried to stifle her with a glare, with no effect whatsoever.

"All I'm saying is, it's obvious you want her. And even though she tries to keep her cool, it's obvious the feeling is mutual. I don't see why you're torturing yourself. Not to mention my torment, having to deal with your perpetual grumpiness."

"It's a bad idea, Carla."

"What's the big deal? What are you so afraid of?"

"Afraid?" he scoffed. "I'm not afraid of anything," he said, maybe a shade too vehemently because Carla leaned back in her chair, squinting at him in that way she had.

"You like her, don't you?" she said finally, eyes gleaming as though she'd discovered some deep dark secret.

"Of course I like her—"

"No, you *really* like her. You're still mooning after her, just like you were in college."

"I never—"

She continued, steamrolling over any protests he might have offered. "You had such a crush on her back then. In your e-mails it was always 'Julie and I did this, Julie and I did that."

"Yeah, and I was always dating somebody else."

"You were always *fucking* somebody else," she corrected. "But Julie was the one you really wanted."

"We were just friends."

"I still don't understand why you never made a move," Carla said, oblivious to the tension knotting every sinew of his body.

"Drop it," he said. It came out harsher than he'd meant, but at least she snapped her mouth shut with a surprised lift of her eyebrows.

He turned back to his computer, trying to put Julie out of his mind. But Carla's comments brought back all those old unpleasant memories of high school, when he'd gone to live with his father. He'd been out of control, drinking and partying and getting into trouble. Now, nearly fifteen years later, he could see his behavior for what it was. A cry for attention from a man who saw his brief marriage to his mother—not to mention Chris himself—as a mistake. David Dennison had barely stayed with Chris's mother—a cocktail waitress he'd met in Vegas— long enough to get her pregnant.

While he left her with a more than generous settlement, for most of his life his contact with Chris was limited to birthday and Christmas cards (always stuffed with a large check) and one, occasionally two, visits per year.

Then when Chris was seventeen and a senior in high school, his mother, at the end of her rope with Chris's increasingly bad behavior, had sent him to live with David. It was time, she said, for his father to do more as a parent than throw money at the problem.

Just because Chris had lived in the same house hadn't meant David or his then wife were involved. They, as well as Brian, who was five years older, had appeared in the giant Hillsborough mansion briefly between work and social obligations. Chris had still managed to make plenty of trouble, but he'd discovered that with no one to care, it wasn't nearly as much fun.

He'd instead tried actually focusing on school, winning his father's absentminded approval when he'd managed to pull straight A's without much effort. But even so, Chris had never felt like he belonged, never felt like his father and Brian were really family. And forget their family friends—they'd never known what to make of him.

Everyone had always been nice enough, but he'd heard enough of the whispers. They'd speculated about his mother, gossiped that she was a stripper, or worse, a prostitute who had somehow bamboozled David Dennison into marrying her and giving her millions.

He'd never bothered trying to convince them of the truth. That Gina Discala Dennison was a naïve twenty-two-year-old when David Dennison had swept her off her feet. That she'd really, truly loved David, and she would have given back the millions in a heartbeat for the opportunity to have a real family with him.

Only Julie had known the truth. She'd met Gina a few times when Gina had come to visit Chris in college. Julie had been the only person in his father's snooty social circle with enough courage to ask him outright about all the rumors. When he'd told her the truth about his parents' marriage, she'd just smiled and said, "I knew she had to be nice. Look how you turned out."

And yet for all her sweetness, Julie was never going to be his. That hadn't stopped him from wanting her. By the time he was twenty and Julie was sixteen, Chris had had more than his share of bad girls. But he'd taken one look at Julie with her creamy skin and fresh young curves and wondered what it might take to make a good girl like Julie go bad.

His musings must have been obvious, because Grant Driscoll had wasted no time in cornering him and disabusing him of any notions Chris might have about Julie. "You may be David's son," he'd growled, "but you're not one of us. Stay away from Julie."

Chris never knew if Grant had issued the same explicit warning to Julie, but it was obvious at Berkeley that she wanted to keep their deepening friendship quiet.

For a while, Chris had entertained the idea of seducing her for revenge, to get back at the people who, despite his father's halfhearted acceptance, would never accept him as one of their own. But all too soon he realized he liked Julie way too much to use her that way.

So Carla wanted to know why he'd never made a move? He'd never admit it to her, but he could admit it to himself. It was because he was a coward, plain and simple. Because he'd known that any relationship with Julie would come down to a choice: him or her family. And he'd always known he'd lose.

Idiot that he was, he'd tried for a while after graduating to gain acceptance into their world, working hard for his father and Grant at D&D, trying to prove he was one of them, worthy of a girl like Julie. He'd spent three years bashing his head against that wall before he'd finally wised up and gone off on his own to build Holley Cay.

"If she's offering it up, I don't see why you don't just get it out of your system," Carla said, breaking him out of his unpleasant trip down memory lane.

He rubbed at his eyes, hoping that would bring the numbers on the spreadsheet back into focus. "I asked you to drop it. Besides, we both know I can't afford to be distracted right now."

"Like you aren't distracted now?" Carla retorted. "You know, maybe if you just do it and get it out of your system, you could actually focus here."

He didn't bother telling Carla that he'd had Julie once, and it hadn't even put a dent in his hunger for her. "It's not that easy."

"What's the worst that could happen?" Damn, the woman was like a dog with a bone.

The worst? That Julie would leave and return to the bosom of her family, leaving him alone with all the pathetic yearning she'd reawakened. Basically, the inevitable. Fortunately the phone rang before Chris was forced to come up with a reply. As Carla had yet another tension-filled conversation with Jane Bowden's head security guard, Chris turned back to the ever increasing wedding budget.

But try as he might to concentrate, he couldn't get his mind off Julie, who, as Carla had pointed out, was already a huge distraction without his having slept with her again. Christ, at this point, he was suffering all the feared consequences without any of the benefit.

And when he really thought about it, all these years he'd been fixated on some idealized version of Julie. A Julie who never would have used him for revenge, who never would proposition a guy for a casual fling. In the five years since he'd seen her, she'd become a different sort of person. Maybe if he got a little dose of reality, of the real woman Julie had become, he could finally put this obsession with her to bed for good.

But first he was going to put her to bed. Starting tonight.

# 9

Or so he thought. Chris glared at Julie across the patio at the beach bar. Her white floral-print dress had a halter top, revealing the golden skin of her back to just below her waistline. Her blond, softly wavy hair glowed in the light cast by the torches. Chris's jaw tightened as she executed another turn, moving in perfect rhythm with the music of the salsa band playing several feet from the bar. The swing skirt of her dress twirled up her thighs. If she wasn't careful, her next move would reveal the cheeks of her perfect round ass.

But Mike pulled her back in, his long fingered hand splaying across the silky bare skin of Julie's back. Chris's white knuckles stood out against his tan as his fingers tightened around his drink. The knot in his gut tightened as Mike pulled Julie's hips against his, and they moved sensuously in perfect harmony.

She tossed her hair, a wide smile on her face as she laughed at something Mike said. Just then she stumbled, and Mike, the bastard, used it as an opportunity to grope her ass as he pretended to help steady her. He quickly moved his hand up her back as though it had been an accident, but Chris didn't miss the lascivious cast to Mike's features.

Nor did he miss the flush that crept up Julie's cheeks. Whether it was embarrassment or arousal, Chris didn't know, but he did notice she wasn't trying to pull away.

He couldn't take it. Watching another man touch her bare skin. Seeing her move her body against another man in a dance that all but simulated sex.

He'd come here this evening to take Julie up on her offer of no-strings-attached sex. He hadn't expected to see her laughing, flirting, *touching* another man with such obvious enjoyment. Nor had he expected the hot flash of rage and possessiveness that swept through him at the sight.

But he didn't stop to analyze it. He couldn't. One thought and one thought only reverberated through his brain. As long as she was on his island, Julie was his; she belonged to him.

Julie laughed at Mike, hoping her tension didn't leak through. "Maybe I should sit down. These shoes aren't exactly great for dancing."

To prove her point, at that exact moment the flimsy stiletto heel of her sandal caught in a crack. She stumbled into Mike's chest, who steadied her with a firm hand on her ass.

She stiffened and righted herself. He'd been doing that all day. This morning, under the pretense of checking her scuba tank, he'd managed to brush his hands against her breasts at least ten different times. Not to mention the dozens of other "casual" brushes of her legs, strokes up her arms, and touches of her hand.

She smiled determinedly as they resumed the rhythm of the dance. The problem was, she hadn't exactly discouraged him. After her earlier run-in with Chris, Julie had greeted Mike this morning with more than her usual friendliness. Truth be told, Julie had been outright flirtatious.

After being mocked for throwing herself at him, Julie had felt compelled to prove to herself that there were other men in the world besides Chris. And call her shallow, call her vain, but she had needed some masculine validation of her attractiveness, proof that she could get a man to like her without having to strip naked and carry on like an amateur porn star. Mike was perfect for her needs. He was extremely good looking in his own right, and could have availed himself to any of the single women here at Holley Cay. But he was paying attention to her, and Julie would have to be dead not to enjoy a little boost to her pride.

But now she was paying the consequences for giving him the wrong idea. It wasn't that she didn't like Mike. She did. He was funny, considerate, not to mention gorgeous.

But he just didn't do it for her. His touch didn't send prickles down her spine. Her nipples didn't tighten when his gaze caressed her breasts. And earlier today, when he'd tried to kiss her, instead of craving the taste of his mouth like a starving woman, she'd practically thrown herself off the boat trying to avoid it.

Now she was uncomfortably aware of his thumb drawing tiny circles around the small of her back, unsure of how to pull away gracefully without embarrassing them both. She looked over his shoulder, hoping to catch either Amy's or Jen's eyes. Maybe if Julie looked desperate enough one of them would see her and come to her rescue.

Her breath caught as she saw Chris, staring hard at her from his post at the bar. Her toes curled in her sandals, and she stumbled again as he pushed away from the bar and headed toward her with a leisurely but determined stride.

But halfway across the patio he was accosted by Kara, and as always Julie felt a surge of irritation at the sight of the gorgeous, leggy brunette. It was irrational, Julie knew, as Kara had been nothing but courteous to her. Still, she had a cynical, calculating air that rubbed Julie the wrong way.

Kara wrapped her arms around Chris's waist and moved her hips against his in a seductive movement that he willingly echoed. He draped his arms over her shoulders and smiled down at her, that lazy, charming smile that never failed to send a jolt down Julie's spine.

Pride and hurt warred as Julie struggled to keep her composure. It wasn't enough that he had practically laughed at her for her sexual antics, now she had to watch him drool all over another woman. A tall, curvaceous brunette. Not surprising. Chris had always displayed a preference for everything Julie wasn't.

All thoughts of giving Mike the brush-off disappeared. She'd show Chris that men—lots of men—found petite blondes like herself attractive, not to mention sexy and desirable. Julie closed the half-inch that separated her hips from Mike and executed an intricate swivel. His hand tightened on her waist and lust tinged his smile.

"Thanks again for taking me diving today," she said, her voice breathy. "I felt so safe with you down there."

His blue eyes twinkled at her. "I'm glad it was good for you. I hope I can make lots of things good for you."

Hoo-boy. He was not going to be pleased when Julie left him with nothing more than a kiss at her door. She supposed the right thing, the good thing to do would be to let Mike down gently before he went to the trouble of walking her back to her villa. But there was no way she was going to let Chris see her leaving alone.

A hand clamped down on her shoulder, and she didn't even have to turn to see who it was. Warmth radiated from the point of contact of his warm, broad palm all the way down to the pit of her belly.

"Mind if I cut in?" Though phrased as a question, both she and Mike recognized it as the demand that it was.

"Julie, are you okay with this?" Mike asked, concern replacing the flirtatious lust in his expression.

"It's fine," Julie said, turning to face Chris. As Mike started to walk away, she quickly grabbed his wrist. "I'll catch up with you later, okay?"

Mike smiled, nodded, and shot a venomous look at Chris.

"Don't count on it," Chris muttered when Mike was out of earshot. Instead of pulling her into his arms and leading her into another dance, he grabbed Julie's forearm and tugged her off the dance floor, towards a dark area of the patio devoid of guests.

Julie jerked at his grip, trying but failing to dig in the heels of her impractical shoes. "What is it with you and manhandling me?" she said as she stumbled after him.

Chris frowned at his hand wrapped around her arm, but didn't let go. "Are you trying to drive me crazy?" His blue eyes snapped with a fury she'd never seen before.

"What is it with you?" Julie snapped.

Even in the low light, Julie could see the tightening of Chris's mouth, the narrowing of his eyes. "You were practically humping him on the dance floor. I'm just keeping you from doing something stupid, and you know it."

"I have no idea why you even care," Julie replied, a nasty edge creeping into her tone. "You've made it abundantly clear that you're not interested."

"And if I'm not interested, you figure you'll throw it out to the first guy who is?"

Julie winced as Chris's fingers tightened, digging into the skin of her forearm. "Maybe." She had no intention of sleeping with Mike, but Chris didn't need to know that. "I don't see that it's any of your business."

"At least I have the consolation of knowing I was your first choice."

She tugged at her arm but he wouldn't release his grip. "It wasn't like that."

"What is it like?" he said, his voice low and menacing. "Because it looks to me like your wedding night was just the start of you getting back at Brian by banging anyone with a pulse."

Julie felt his words like a sucker punch in the gut. All the breath whooshed from her lungs and for a moment, she was actually dizzy.

"You know," she said, struggling to keep her voice steady, "I never regretted a second about that night I spent with you. Until now," she said, jerking out of his grasp. Her throat tightened, and she knew she was going to cry. Unable to bear that final humiliation, Julie turned and ran.

Chris couldn't believe what he'd just said. How could he have been so unbelievably crude? Especially to Julie, the only person who had ever acknowledged that he was more than a screwup, more than an intruder into polite society. She was the only one who ever took him seriously when he'd talked about creating a place like Holley Cay. And now, instead of executing his grand plan of seduction, he'd lashed out at her. His stomach clenched with guilt as her hurt, shocked expression replayed in his mind. Whatever her intentions might have been, she would never have set out to deliberately hurt him the way he'd just done.

He uttered filthy curses at himself as he took off down the beach after her. It didn't take him long to catch her. The moon was almost full, so he had a clear view of her running down the beach, and she couldn't move fast in those stupid shoes.

"Julie," he called as he ran up behind her, "I'm sorry. Please stop."

She didn't stop, but kept stumbling as quickly as she could with her spike heels sinking into the sand with every step. "Leave me alone."

"I'm sorry," he repeated as he fell into step beside her. "I didn't mean it, I was just so—"

"My wedding night wasn't all about revenge," she said. "Okay, maybe it was a little, but it was mostly about finally having something I really, really wanted. I'd denied myself for years, and finally I had my chance and I took it."

Chris felt like a fist was squeezing his heart when he saw the sheen of tears in her eyes. "And now," she continued, her voice threatening to break, "I feel like such an idiot, the way I keep throwing myself at someone who doesn't even want me."

He couldn't stand this. Pulling her roughly into his arms, he whispered, "You think I don't want you?"

She drew her arms up and pushed against his chest in an attempt to free herself. He wrapped his arms more tightly around her.

"The truth is I want you too much," he whispered, burying his nose in the softness of her hair. "I've been trying to be good, and stay away from you, but you drive me crazy."

She didn't respond, but she wasn't trying to push him away.

"And now that I know how good it feels to touch you," he thrust his fingers into her hair, "to fuck you," he whispered, tipping her head back so he could look at her beautiful, wide eyes, her sexy pink mouth, "it makes me insane to know what I'm missing."

Her arms slid around his neck, one hand clamping around his nape as she tugged his face down for her kiss.

The second his mouth touched hers, Chris felt like he was going to explode. His mouth opened over hers, his tongue thrust inside to mate with hers, and his hands tore at the tie that held up her dress.

They groaned simultaneously as his hand captured the weight of her breast and squeezed, kneading, pinching, with a fervor that precluded any gentleness.

"Tell me you want me," Chris gasped, dragging his lips down her throat.

"I want you," she moaned as her fingers dug into the muscles of his arms, "I want you more than anything."

He groaned as she boldly slid her hand along the bulge in his shorts, squeezing, stroking his cock to rock hardness. His hands slid up her skirt, moaning into her mouth when his hands met smooth flesh, left bare by her thong panties. He shoved a hand in between her legs, felt the hot moisture that soaked the thin scrap of fabric. "You're so wet, so ready for me," he murmured, sucking her tongue into his mouth. "I have to get inside you." He slipped his fingers under the flimsy fabric of her panties, groaning as a hot liquid rush soaked his hand. His cock twitched, demanding to take the place of his fingers. "C-condom," Julie stuttered, "I have a condom in my purse." She breathed and pulled away to locate the little bag that had fallen to the sand.

Chris was momentarily nonplussed. Julie was carrying condoms in her purse? What did that mean? What did that say about her plans for tonight? What—

Then he became incapable of rational thought as Julie's busy hands unzipped his fly and tugged his shorts around his knees. His knees threatened to buckle as she stroked his cock from root to tip, her gaze so admiring he felt like a fucking sex god. Then, in a move that made his eyes screw shut and his teeth clench, she leaned forward and sucked him into her mouth, her tongue swirling against the head. He quickly ran through the roster of the San Francisco Giants as he struggled not to come.

"Stop," he groaned as his brain refused to focus on baseball and remained fixated on the hot, wet suction of her mouth and teasing laps of her tongue. He cupped her head in his hands and gently pulled her away as he knelt on the sand beside her.

She wrapped herself around him, kissing and licking his neck, chest, shoulders as he quickly slid on the condom. He didn't even bother taking off her underwear, just snagged the material and pulled it aside as she settled on his lap.

She reached down and grasped his erection, positioned it against her core. And then, yes, God, yes, he was inside her, the wet warmth of her pussy gripping him like a fist as she took him all the way in.

He gripped her hips as she rode him hard and fast, his hips meeting her thrust for thrust. There was no grace, no finesse, as he recklessly pounded into her. He bent his head, tongued a nipple into his mouth and sucked, probably too hard. Julie squealed, throwing her head back as she ground her pelvis against him.

*Slow down,* he told himself harshly. This was too hard, too fast, she wouldn't—

"Chris, Chris, Chris," Julie chanted as she stiffened and jerked against him. Her mouth opened wide in a silent scream and her nails dug into his biceps as she gave one last shudder.

Chris didn't stop, just pushed her over onto her back and thrust, twice, three times, pummeling her into the sand with each drive of his hips. His orgasm hit him with blinding force, and he strove to get even deeper inside of her. He collapsed on top of her, trembling with every last pulse of his release.

"Ouch." Chris jumped as she nipped his neck, and not gently. "What was that for?"

"You've been really mean to me," Julie said.

Chris levered himself off of her and grinned. "I know, I'm sorry, honey." He leaned down and kissed the tip of her perfect little nose.

"You'll have to make it up to me." She slid her hands up under his shirt, lightly scraping her nails down his back.

"I thought I just did," he teased, savoring the taste of her as he trailed kisses across her cheek and eyelids.

"Mmm." She wriggled against him. "That was a good start, but you have a lot more work to do before I'm ready to forgive you."

"In that case," Chris said as he pushed himself to his knees and helped her sit up, "let's go back to my place, where I can wash you clean of every bit of sand and show you just how sorry I am."

They straightened their clothing as best they could, laughing as they attempted to brush the worst of the sand off each other.

"This would be a great spa treatment," Julie said as she presented her back to Chris. "Deep sand exfoliation. Here, you missed a spot." She glanced teasingly over her shoulder and raised her skirt.

Chris marveled. Just the sight of her round, sand-dappled ass was enough to make him hard again. He hadn't experienced this kind of rapid recovery since his college days. He pulled her back against him, rubbing his straining fly against her. "I have a great big shower at my place," he whispered, his tongue flicking out to taste the peachy flesh of her earlobe. "Big enough for two."

"That sounds," Julie paused, arching her neck to give him better access, "really great."

The sound of voices jerked them both to attention. Before they could be discovered, they took off running, pausing only so Julie could remove her sandals. Within minutes, they arrived, panting, at the door of his villa.

He ushered her in the door, trying to ignore the feeling that he was free-falling, hard and fast into something he'd never before experienced. He pinned her against the closed front door, kissing her like a starving man, already rock hard as though he hadn't come less than five minutes ago. There existed the very real and dangerous possibility that no matter how he indulged his fantasies, he might never stop wanting Julie. And that when she left, he'd be stuck with an ache that had nothing to do with sexual desire.

He forced the thoughts from his mind, choosing to focus instead on the hot, sweet taste of her mouth, the lush softness of her lips against his, the eager slide of her fingers over his skin.

For now, at least, she had chosen to be here, had chosen to be with him. She would leave, sure. But at least he could make damn sure she missed him when she did.

Chris wasted no time in pulling Julie into the bathroom and stripping her naked. "Now then," he said as he guided her into the marble-lined shower, "let's see if I can get you nice and clean again."

Chris's bathroom was a hedonist's delight, with its Jacuzzi tub the size of a small swimming pool and separate shower with multiple showerheads that seemed to hit her from every possible angle. But she had little time to admire the amenities as he grabbed the removable showerhead, twisted it to adjust the pressure, and ran it up the backs of her thighs. She shrieked when the spray hit her butt, the pulsating jets of water making her skin tingle. "Watch where you're sticking that thing," she laughed, trying to move out of the way. Wet skin slid against wet skin as she playfully squirmed past him, and she sputtered as one of the other shower heads caught her full in the face.

With a low chuckle, Chris caught her around the waist, pinning her back against him as he used the showerhead in his hand to teasingly circle her breasts. Her nipples tightened into achy little points. "I have to make sure I get all the sand off you." His low voice echoed off the walls of the shower, vibrating through her like a caress.

"I don't think I have any sand up there," she replied, saucily arching her back until her buttocks were pressing against his muscled thighs. His cock surged against her lower back, rock hard, insistent.

"How about here?" his voice was raspier now as he slid the showerhead lower, skimming the tops of her thighs with the spray. His other hand moved from her waist, and Julie watched, biting back a moan as he covered her mound. Liquid heat coursed through her, drenching his hand. Just like that she was primed again, ready to go off like a rocket at his slightest touch.

Slowly, deliberately he spread her wide with his fingers, exposing her fully to the shower's hot spray. At the first pass, she nearly jumped out of her skin. At the second, she let out a sharp cry and dug her nails into his forearm, a futile attempt to stay his hand. It was too much stimulation, her flesh already oversensitized from her earlier orgasm. Her stomach muscles clenched and the harsh sounds of her breath filled her head, blocking out everything else.

Without a word, without a sound, Chris replaced the showerhead in its stand. Holding her in place, he reached out for a bar of white soap. The rich smell of coconut filled the steamy chamber as he worked up a thick lather. Turning her to lean with her back against one wall, he ran slick hands over her in firm, sure strokes. Whereas before, his touch had been desperate, almost frantic, now he was slow, deliberate. His fingers rubbed, smoothed, massaged their way up and down her back, her legs, her arms.

Despite his almost lazy manner, there was no question he was as aroused as she. His cock stood straight out from his body, thick and veined, the swollen head deliciously dark red. She'd never been much of an admirer of penises, but she was struck by the primitive beauty of Chris's erection. Surging and straining, all for her.

His hands covered her breasts, his thumbs tracing slick circles around her nipples. She closed her eyes, head rolling against hard marble as she thought for a moment she might come with nothing more than the feel of his hands on her breasts. His fingers pinched and plucked, then soothed. "Please," she murmured, not sure if she was begging him to stop or to keep going.

He captured her plea with his mouth, his tongue thrusting and retreating in a rhythm that made her ache to feel him inside her again. Though compared to the beach, he was moving at a snail's pace, there was an intensity about him, in his touch. He raised his head, and the expression in his eyes made her breath catch in her chest. All traces of the charming playboy were gone. His eyes were dark with torment, desire, maybe even anger.

The look disappeared before she could analyze it further, and once again the taste of his mouth on hers, the feel of his hands on her body, drove all logical thought from her head until all she could do was feel.

Her fingers wound through thick, wet locks of hair as he kissed her, harder now, teasing her with soft nips of his teeth. She moaned and pressed herself harder against him, until her nipples were burrowing eagerly against his chest and his cock was sliding against the soap-slicked skin of her belly. Moving one hand between them, she closed her hand around him, her sex fluttering at the feel of him, so thick, so hot, rock hard in her hand.

He groaned, leaning down until his forehead rested against hers. His jaw clenched as she pumped her fist once, twice, before he stilled her hand. "I don't want to come again until I'm through with you."

There was just the smallest hint of menace in his voice. But instead of scaring her, it sent a bolt of heat to the place between her legs that already threatened to spontaneously combust. He captured her hands in his, raising them above her head and pinning them to the marble wall. With one hand easily holding both wrists, his other hand was free to roam her naked, wet torso. Eager to get her hands back on him, she tried to tug one hand free. He was having none of it. Though his grip on her wasn't painful, it was firm.

A shiver that had nothing to do with cold brought every nerve to screaming awareness. He rubbed his hand over her soap-slicked skin, chasing its path with his lips and tongue. He sucked and nipped at her neck, shoulders and breasts, so hard she worried she might have marks, but she couldn't bear to ask him to stop. Not that he would, even if she did ask. That thought, as much as the hot tug of his lips on her nipple, made her knees go watery.

He leaned into her. She was pinned, the slick marble at her back, the muscled wall of his chest pressing against her front. He hooked her leg over his hip, and using his hand, guided the tip of his cock to tease the wet mouth of her sex. She barely recognized the sounds escaping her throat as her own as she stretched up on tiptoe, straining for deeper contact. He was ruthless, pushing just the thick head of his erection inside, then slipping out to press hot, silky circles around her clit. Then back inside, sinking in another inch, but pulling out before giving her the deep penetration she craved.

She tugged against his grip on her wrists, to no avail. He grinned down at her, an almost evil glint in his eyes evident through the steam. His look said she was his to do with whatever he wished, and that he knew damn well she'd enjoy every bit of whatever he dished out.

Julie decided a more direct approach was in order. "Stop teasing me and fuck me again, already." His eyes widened in shocked delight at her graphic demand. Seizing her advantage, she slipped one hand free of his grip and wrapped her hand around his cock, pumping him in her fist as she positioned him to sink inside her. Hooking his elbow under her knee that was resting on his hip, he bent his knees and thrust high and hard inside her. A low groan rumbled from his chest as he held her there, hips pressed flush against hers as he pressed as deep as he could possibly go.

Her hands clawed at his shoulders as she squirmed against him, convinced she would kill him or go insane if he didn't start moving. But he just held her there, his eyes squeezed shut and his jaw tight, every muscle clenched in restraint. Then, unbelievably, he pulled out.

"No!" Her protest echoed around the marble and glass chamber.

He uttered only one word as he scooped her up in his arms. "Condom."

Even through her frustration Julie thanked God one of them still had a working brain cell. He carried her into the bedroom and with one hand whipped back the covers and laid her sideways across the wide mattress. He fished a condom out of the beside table drawer, and she watched him roll it on with lust-hazed eyes. He was such a gorgeous male animal, all hard muscle rippling under tanned, hair dusted skin. The scent of soap and male arousal radiated off him in waves, heightening her arousal to an almost painful degree. She didn't know it was possible to be so turned on, hovering on a precipice where the slightest touch threatened to send her over the edge.

He bent down and kissed her, surprisingly soft, his lips gently sucking at hers, his nose sliding alongside hers in a gentle caress. He knelt between her thighs, and Julie bit her lip in anticipation of the sensation of his penetration.

To her surprise he drew her legs over his shoulders, bending his head to bury his tongue in the folds of her sex. Her hands tangled in his hair, half pulling him away, half pressing him closer.

He made a slow foray up her slit, sending her hips off the bed as pleasure spiked down her spine. "You taste even better than I remembered," he whispered. "You're so sweet and juicy, like a wet little peach." Her breath was coming in gasping moans now as he ate her relentlessly, licking, sucking her into oblivion. "That's it, baby," she barely heard him murmur. "I love it when you come against my mouth."

That's exactly what she did, her whole body seizuring as waves of pleasure washed over her. She relaxed back into the mattress, fully expecting him to come inside her now. But he stayed where he was, showering her with gentle, soothing kisses until unbelievably, she felt another orgasm building at the base of her spine. He took her clit between his lips, suckling gently until she burst against his lips.

He thrust into her as the last wave was receding, her body clenching around him as he squeezed inside her. She was so swollen, so sensitive, she didn't know if she could take it, and her hands went to his hips in a halfhearted attempt to stay him. Chris brooked no resistance, grabbing her wrists and pinning them above her head, much as he had in the shower.

Helpless. She was helpless against him, what he was doing to her. Helpless against the pleasure that even now, when she thought she couldn't possibly take any more, built and built as he rocked against her in deep, almost imperceptible thrusts. He was everywhere, surrounding her, his chest hair rasping against her nipples as his kisses stole her breath. His movements were slow, languorous, like he could fuck her until she spontaneously combusted from sexual pleasure.

She was burning up. Her whole world became him, the taste of him in her mouth, the sound of his voice whispering things she couldn't even understand anymore. And most of all, beyond anything, the feel of him inside her, so deep and sweet she wanted to keep him there forever and never let go.

She was splintering, flying apart, breaking into a million tiny fragments. Vaguely she heard him moan, felt his fingers dig into the soft curves of her hips as his body shook and trembled. Her particles were finding their way back, settling into some semblance of order.

But as she opened her eyes and looked at his hard, beautiful face, Julie wondered if she would ever be the same. Through her exhaustion a kernel of unease took root. Sex with Chris had been intense before, but this time she felt like she'd unleashed something she hadn't bargained for.

He'd always had that bad boy, black sheep charm about him, but for the first time, Julie realized that Chris was dangerous. Not in a life-in-danger, physical peril, kind of way. But he was a definite threat to her emotional safety.

She'd been living in denial, thinking she felt nothing more for him than a lingering teenage crush. But he'd ripped away her blinders, revealing the depth of emotion he could unleash if she let down her guard again. If she wasn't careful he was going to seriously break her heart.

Julie woke up, disoriented at first. She looked around the master bedroom with its white paneled walls, high ceilings, and exposed rafters. Sunlight spilled through French doors, across the down comforter she'd pulled over herself to ward off the air-conditioner-chilled air.

She rolled over, frowning when she saw the empty pillow beside her. Where was Chris? Had he snuck out again while she slept? After last night, she wasn't sure she could take it if he'd left without a word.

A muffled clinking sounded over the air conditioner's hum. She slid out of bed, and wrinkling her nose at her crumpled and sand-encrusted sundress, opted to slip on Chris's discarded shirt. It was so big that the short sleeves ended just past her elbows, and the hem almost grazed her knees. She followed the sounds of activity to the open kitchen off the villa's living room.

Chris was busy chopping a small mountain of fruit. For a moment she didn't say anything, relishing the opportunity to admire the sleekly muscled lines of his back as he worked, shirtless, dressed only in a pair of fraying khaki shorts. The muscles of his shoulder and arm rippled as he chopped a pineapple into perfectly uniform, bite-sized chunks.

As though he felt her gaze, Chris paused in his chopping and turned, greeting Julie with a smile so warm and sexy she felt it down to her bare toes. She crossed the open living room to the kitchen and found herself enveloped in a paradise of warm skin and muscled arms. She nuzzled her face against the firm muscles of his chest, burying her nose in the soft whorls of hair. His scent washed over her, all soap and sex and man. Julie felt his contented sigh against her hair and squeezed him tighter in response.

"Good morning," she said, coming up on her tiptoes to receive his pineapple-flavored kiss. His hand cupped the back of her head, and she obligingly opened her mouth as he turned what had started as a soft peck into something deeper. She was just about to drag him back to bed when he raised his head.

"Come on, let's go out on the deck."

She reluctantly released him and grabbed the bowl of fruit Chris indicated while he carried a tray that held a carafe of coffee, cups, and plates.

Julie caught her breath as she walked through the French doors onto the patio. Situated above the rest of the resort, Chris's deck offered a two hundred seventy degree view of the bay. The turquoise water looked almost iridescent in the early morning light, and in the distance she could see the outline of Virgin Gorda, several miles away. "This place is amazing," she breathed as she set the bowl of fruit on the table.

Chris sat in one of the padded teak chairs. She poured herself a cup of coffee and started to sit in the chair next to him, but he caught her around the waist and pulled her onto his lap. "I think you're amazing," he murmured.

In about five seconds she was going to melt all over him like butter in the hot sun.

"Really, I mean it," she said, running her fingertips along the muscled forearm wrapped around her waist. "Holley Cay is fantastic." She tilted her head back onto his shoulder so she could meet his gaze. "I'm really proud of you, Chris."

He bent his head and kissed her softly on her cheek, her nose, and finally her mouth. "Thanks, Jules."

They were silent for several minutes, content to sip their coffee and enjoy the view. Then Julie said, "Your villa is great, too."

"Best view on the island," he murmured.

"It's much . . . smaller than I expected," Julie observed. In truth, when Chris said they were going to his place, Julie had expected him to lead her to one of the huge mansion-sized villas up the hill. Instead he had led her to a small but charming cottage. She hadn't explored much beyond the bathroom and the bedroom, but her impression was of an airy, comfortable place that perfectly suited Chris's casual, comfort-seeking personality.

"I live alone," he replied, reaching forward and selecting a chunk of pineapple to feed her. "It doesn't make sense for me to take over one of the larger buildings."

"But what about when you have . . . guests?" She forced the words around the tart-sweet bite of fruit. Julie hated the note of jealousy that tinged her voice, but suddenly she wondered exactly how many women had enjoyed Chris's expertise at wielding a massaging showerhead.

"I don't have them," Chris said simply, offering her a slice of mango.

The sweet juice bursting over her tongue momentarily distracted her. Was fruit ever this good at home? "What do you mean, you don't have them?"

"I mean no one ever stays over. Why should they, when I have guest rooms for one hundred people?"

"Never?" Julie craned her neck around so she could see his face. She found it hard to believe that Chris didn't host regular sleepovers.

"Not until last night," he whispered.

*Don't read anything into that,* she warned herself sternly. Last night, vulnerable after several intense orgasms, she'd started to confuse amazing sex with something more. But in the bright light of the morning, everything once again became clear. They were having fun. Satisfying a decade of mutual unrequited lust. Once they got it out of their systems, everything would go back to normal. She would go home, he would stay here, and life as they both knew it would continue, and they'd both have some very happy memories of her idyllic week at the Holley Cay resort.

Chris interrupted her silent self lecture, his mouth closing over hers and stopping all rational thought. Mango-flavored Chris. Too bad she was leaving in less than a week. She could really get used to this.

*I could really get used to this,* Chris thought as he slid his tongue into her mouth. He loved the soft weight of her in his lap, the scent of her, sweet and clean but branded with the smell of him, the scent of sex.

He'd never brought a woman here before. This was his place, his sanctuary. Even though he enjoyed the social elements of his job, it was important to know that he had a place where he could be alone and undisturbed.

When it came to women, he always went to their rooms, so he always had the option to leave if he wanted. More often than not he did. He rarely had the desire to wake up next to a woman. Mornings tended to take the polish off a woman, and Chris preferred to see them in all their well-groomed glory. He liked his privacy, enjoyed the solitude that the morning offered, and didn't relish the idea of making friendly chitchat with a virtual stranger right after he woke up.

But Julie wasn't a stranger. Somehow it felt right, falling asleep with her. So right it had made his stomach clench. She was leaving in just a few days, he'd reminded himself before he'd drifted off, and he had no business mooning over her and fantasizing about a thousand more nights, falling asleep next to her after loving her into exhaustion. But this morning he'd taken one look at her, warm and tousled, her face buried in a pillow as she slept, and instead of instinctively fleeing for the office, he'd made breakfast. He had tons of work to do, but he'd made breakfast, of all things, because he had no desire to leave her, and he wanted to give her an excuse to stay.

And as much as he'd wanted to make love to her, to continue to tap the newfound depths of her sensuality, he also just wanted to talk to her, to hang out like they used to. Not that they were getting much talking done now. He groaned as she turned to face him. He caught her legs behind her knees and pulled them across his lap.

She moaned in response as his hand slid up the smooth skin of her thigh. His palm moved higher still, until his thumb rested in the crease between her thigh and hip. She wasn't wearing any underwear beneath his shirt, his fingers encountering nothing but silky bare skin. He could *definitely* get used to this.

It was another hour before Julie got back to her villa. Chris walked with her and left her at the door with another one of his toe-curling kisses.

"If I come inside, I'll never leave," he said, tearing his mouth away from hers. "Have dinner with me tonight?"

Julie knew she probably had the dopiest, mooniest smile on her face, but she didn't care. "Of course."

Julie was so happy she was humming as she walked into the villa. She was tired, pleasantly sore, and yet full of an inexplicable energy.

She was on her way to the shower when she noticed the message light blinking on the phone beside her bed. The first message was from Amy. "Julie, it's Amy. I tried to reach you last night after you left." Julie's mouth curved up in a smile at the thought of why she'd been unreachable. If only Amy knew. "Anyway, I wanted to let you know we're all getting pedicures and massages this morning starting at nine. I went ahead and made you an appointment, so just meet us at the spa."

Julie glanced at the clock. Eight forty-five. She was going to have to hustle.

"Jules, it's me." Julie's stomach dropped when she heard Wendy's voice. Why would Wendy call if not for an absolute emergency? "I'm sorry to bug you—I wasn't going to call. But I didn't want it to come as a complete shock when you got home"—Julie rolled her eyes to the ceiling. Come on, Wendy, get to the point—"but Brian has been calling me nonstop, trying to find out where you are." Julie's hand tightened around the phone, then immediately relaxed as Wendy continued. "I didn't tell him, of course, but you should know he's looking for you. And there's one other thing." Julie sat down on the side of the bed, bending double as nausea roiled in her belly. "He's fighting the annulment. He won't sign the papers. Says it's not that simple. Anyway, I'm sorry to lay this on you when you're on vacation, but I just wanted you to be prepared for the shitstorm waiting for you. Call me if you need me."

Unbelievable! What did he think would happen? That if he refused, Julie would come running back? Knowing Brian and his ego, that was probably exactly what he thought. Part of her wanted to call him right now and tell him that she'd just had the most unbelievable sex anyone ever had, with his younger brother. Let's see if he wanted her back then.

She was actually reaching for the phone before she stopped herself. No. She was not going to taint this. She was going to enjoy her vacation, damn it, and if Brian wanted to stonewall her about the annulment, that was his business. She'd deal with him when she got home.

But the idea of rubbing her—whatever it was—with Chris in Brian's smug face was mighty tempting.

Julie did her best to put any thoughts of Brian and the real world out of her head. What better way to relax than with a little pampering? Half an hour later she and the four bachelorettes were wrapped in fluffy spa robes and having their feet rubbed, lotioned, and polished to perfection.

She succeeded in banishing thoughts of Brian, too, until Amy asked her if she was feeling okay.

"Of course," Julie said, jerking slightly as the woman pumicing the sole of her left foot hit a ticklish spot. "Why wouldn't I be?"

"Maybe I don't know you well enough to say this," Amy paused to nod in assent as her pedicurist held up a bottle of iridescent violet polish, "but you just don't seem your cheery self. It's like you're brooding about something."

Kara slanted a sly glance at Julie. "Is this about Chris? You two certainly left in a hurry."

As one, four pairs of eyes locked on Julie.

"N-no," Julie said, feeling a hot flush blaze up her cheeks. Even though it was true—Chris was the least of her worries right now—she still felt like she'd been caught doing something she shouldn't.

"The look on poor Mike's face when Chris led you away," Kara laughed. "It was like someone just ran over his puppy."

"Was Mike really upset?" Julie asked. She really did feel bad about leading Mike on.

"Don't worry about Mike," Chrissy grinned. "Mike was very well consoled."

"Lucky for you," Kara said with a nasty bite in her voice, "one little blonde was interchangeable with the next for Mike. Unlike Chris," Kara's hard stare turned back to Julie, "who only has eyes for you."

"Don't be such a bitch, Kara," Jen said, "just because he totally blew you off."

Julie glanced at Amy, whose smile grew more strained with every biting comment the women exchanged.

Maybe if she spilled the entire mess about Brian, she could prevent Jen and Kara from engaging in a full-blown catfight. In any case, these women, who had eons more experience than she, were bound to have some good advice.

"My best friend called me this morning," Julie said softly. "Brian's fighting the annulment."

"What a creep," Jen said with a roll of her eyes.

"I can't believe he has the nerve," Amy said. "Does he think you can work it out?

"I have no idea," said Julie. "Brian always gets his way, and somewhere in that fat head of his he probably thinks I'll come groveling back."

"What a jerk." Chrissy leaned over and patted Julie on the thigh. "I hope you don't let it ruin your vacation."

"I won't," Julie sighed, trying to convince herself as much as the others. "But it's more pressure I don't need right now, you know? I wish we could get it over and done with and move on." *And find someone who really loves me,* she added silently.

"Why don't you just tell him you're playing hide the salami with his brother?" Kara said. "That should change his mind about the annulment."

"It's not like that," Julie protested. But Kara's comment struck a nerve, boiling her affair with Chris down to its sordid essence. And hadn't Julie herself considered rubbing Brian's face in it just hours earlier? Julie could protest all she wanted, but it wasn't like she had any moral high ground to stand on.

Kara scoffed. "What, do you think you and Chris are going to ride off into the sunset together?"

Jen broke in before Julie could answer. "Don't pay any attention to her. Just because every guy gets sick of her after a couple of weeks, she thinks that happens to everyone."

Kara shot Jen an evil smirk. "But the two months I had with *your* guy were a hell of a lot of fun." She jerked the separators from between her toes and stalked off for her scrub and honey wrap. Jen flashed her middle finger at Kara's retreating back.

"Don't mind her," said Amy. "She gets bored easily, likes to stir up drama. If there aren't cameras following her constantly, she's not sure she really exists."

"Why are you even friends with her?" The question flew from her mouth before Julie could stop it. "I'm sorry, that was completely rude."

Amy sighed. "No, it's not. Kara and I grew up together. She used to be a lot different, before her parents got divorced. The whole bitchy party girl thing is a way for her to get her parents' attention."

"Oh, please," Jen snapped, "her parents got divorced over fifteen years ago. You can't keep excusing her behavior just because she was nice to you back when you were, like, five." Chrissy nodded in agreement. Obviously this wasn't the first time the women had had this conversation. "Ignore Kara and her poor-little-rich-girl, daddy-doesn't-love-me bullshit," Jen said, looking pointedly at Julie and Amy in turn.

Julie tried to relax, but she couldn't get Kara's comments out of her head.

"What do you think about Chris?" Julie asked as she and Amy lay on adjoining treatment tables for their facials.

"He's gorgeous, and seems like a nice enough guy," Amy said.

"But, what Kara said, he *is* Brian's brother." Julie turned slightly so she could see Amy's profile, covered in a green seaweed mask. "Don't you think me sleeping with him is, well, tacky?"

Amy emitted a short burst of laughter. "Julie, Brian was doing his secretary in the utility closet at your wedding reception, and you're worried about being tacky?"

The aesthetician giggled and gently held Amy's head in place. Julie was grateful that her own mask hid her embarrassment. New Julie or not, she really didn't appreciate having her personal life so much part of the public record.

# 10

An exfoliating rub, herbal wrap, and full-body massage still weren't enough to ease Julie's mind. All of the doubts and misgivings she'd shoved aside had come rushing back with Kara's snide comments. *What the hell did she think she was doing?* she thought as she showered off the residue left by countless coats of oil and lotion.

Oh yeah, that's right, she was sleeping with her husband's younger, wilder half brother. If her parents ever found out they would kill her. Her father was always despairing of David Dennison's behavior, his affairs that were ripe fodder for the gossip pages. If the press ever got wind of where Julie was and what she was doing, there would be absolute hell to pay.

She wasn't a complete idiot. She'd known her impulsiveness could lead to disaster. But she was so sick of worrying about what everyone thought and about doing the right thing, that for a while, at least, she'd been able to ignore reality in pursuit of a little fun.

No one could ever find out that she was here. And no one could ever find out about Chris. She chewed a thumbnail, praying that none of the girls would say anything when they got home. Especially Kara. She definitely seemed the type to blab out of spite. On the other hand, she and Julie didn't run in the same social circles. She might not even realize Julie would be a target of the press.

She looked at the clock. Four-thirty. She still had an hour and a half before she was supposed to meet Chris for dinner. An hour and a half to call him and cancel. Because that would be the smart thing to do. End things now before they gave anyone anything more to talk about. And before her feelings got any more complicated. Really, who was she trying to fool?

Despite Wendy's pep talks, regardless of all of her own resolve this morning to keep things casual and uncomplicated, there was nothing casual about the way he made her feel, nothing casual about the way his hands and lips felt on her body. But even if there was a chance in hell they made this last beyond her short time here, could she really face her parents and tell them she was in love with Chris?

Good one. Like it or not she still had obligations to her family and the business. Once she got home, she had enough of a mess to clean up without adding a hot romance with her ex-husband's brother to the mix.

She should really nip this thing in the bud now before too many feelings—namely hers—got ground into the dust.

But before she could pick up the phone, a knock sounded at the door.

Gathering her white cotton robe more closely around her, she flung open the door to find Chris leaning casually against the doorframe. His coffee brown hair gleamed with auburn lights and his gorgeous blue eyes crinkled in a self-deprecating grin.

"I know we're not supposed to meet for another hour," he said, pushing away from the doorframe and wrapping his arms around her waist, "but I couldn't wait to see you again."

He lifted her off the ground to meet his kiss, and all thoughts of canceling their date and ending this melted at the first taste of his mouth. She wasn't about to deny him—or herself—a damn thing.

"I've been thinking about you all day," he said, his tone almost accusing. He carried her into the sitting room and settled her on his lap on the padded wicker sofa. "I've been staring at spreadsheets for six hours, and I can't concentrate because all I can think about is this." He untied the knot at her waist and slowly spread the lapels, licking his lips as her breasts were bared to his gaze.

The hot, hungry glint in his eyes made Julie feel like the most beautiful, desirable woman in the universe. When he covered her breasts with his large, callused palms Julie couldn't hold herself back. She plunged her fingers into the thick silk of his hair and pulled his mouth to hers, thrusting her tongue between his soft lips. She wanted him, wanted him so much.

At that moment, it didn't matter that this couldn't go anywhere, that once she left Holley Cay, she and Chris would go their separate ways, no looking back. Didn't matter that if the world found out, the scandal would be bigger than when David Dennison had left Brian's mother for Chris's. There was no way she could give this up. She would take whatever he could give, and relish the time they had together.

And if, as she feared, she was left with a broken heart? She'd jump off that bridge when she got to it.

He couldn't get enough of her. That was all there was to it. Julie lay back against the pillows of her king-size bed, a well satisfied smile on her lips.

Chris couldn't resist the urge to lean down and taste it.

"Mmm," Julie moaned. "You are the most amazing lover in the world," she purred.

The soft, husky rasp of her voice was enough to bring him back to semi-hardness.

"You're going to be the death of me," he sighed.

Julie wriggled against him with a sleepy, naughty smile. "Really? Because I feel like I need more practice." She raked her nails lightly down his back, sending shivers all the way to the soles of his feet. "This whole wild, uninhibited sex thing is new for me. I have a lot of catching up to do." She was nipping at his neck, following the soft bites with flicks of her tongue, just the way he loved.

"Trust me," he said, smoothing his hand up her thigh, "you're a natural."

Unbelievably, he was already hard again. But just as he slid her underneath him for round two, both of their stomachs growled. Loudly. In stereo.

Julie practically shook the bed, she was laughing so hard.

"Jesus, for a little girl you have a very loud belly," Chris said as he rolled off her.

"You should talk! You sound like the lion pit at feeding time."

They both dissolved into fits of laughter, tears streaming down their faces. Even as another wave of laughter hit him, Chris acknowledged that it wasn't even that funny. But he felt so damn good, what else could he do but laugh?

Apparently she felt the same way. His amusement faded as he noticed how her sweet little tits jiggled while she laughed. With a mock growl, he pulled her back down to the bed, enveloping her breasts in his hands while he snarled and bit at her neck.

"No," she gasped, trying her best to squirm away, pausing when she felt him pressing hard and hot against her ass. For a moment she leaned back into him. "No," she repeated. "I'm starving. We have to eat." She pulled on his wrists and he reluctantly released her breasts.

"I suppose we need to keep our strength up," Chris said, watching regretfully as Julie slipped on her robe.

Julie stood up and walked to the bathroom, and Chris heard her turn on the shower.

"Do you just want to go down to the beach bar?" Julie called over the sound of the spray.

Chris thought about it for a moment. He'd never been much for long, romantic candlelit dinners. Truth be told, after a couple of hours alone with a woman, he usually found himself bored, craving additional company to liven things up.

Plus, he knew he should be out and about, mingling with the other guests. But strangely—frighteningly, if he was honest—the idea of sharing Julie with anyone tonight was completely unappealing. He didn't want to see or talk to anyone else. He just wanted her all to himself.

A notion that would have scared the crap out of him if he'd taken any time to think about it.

So he didn't.

Instead, he walked to the shower, stepped in, and took the bar of soap from Julie's unresisting hand. "I have a better idea," he said, gently massaging her with the coconut-scented lather. "Why don't we order room service and have a picnic on the beach so I can have you all to myself?"

Julie pulled his mouth down to hers and hooked a leg around his waist. He took that as a yes.

By the time dinner arrived, they were so ravenous they fell on the food like a couple of hyenas. Needless to say, they didn't make it out to the beach, but barked at the waiter to leave the tray on the coffee table. After inhaling half of her burger in about two point five seconds, Julie leaned back with a groan. "Oh, I need to slow down or I'll make myself sick."

She covered her mouth, and Chris couldn't believe what he heard next, delicate and soft though it was.

"Was that a burp?" Surprised laughter exploded from his chest.

"Shut up!" Julie threw her napkin at him, the gesture followed by another louder belch. "It's not that big of a deal," she yelled, turning red to the roots of her hair. "I'm human and I ate too fast, so I burped. Like you don't do it all the time."

Chris wiped another tear from the corner of his eye. "I know, I know, it's just"—he started laughing again—"it's just that you're—"

"I know," Julie said, rolling her eyes, "I'm perfect. I never burp, never fart, never smell, never say the wrong thing, never do anything wrong, and I'm sick of it." She sat back against the back of the couch, arms folded belligerently across her chest. "I'm sick of trying to be perfect all the time."

Chris realized he had struck a nerve. "Hey," he said, wiping his mouth and leaning back next to her, his arm around her shoulders. He tilted her face up to meet his gaze. "I know you're not perfect." Her dark golden brows slanted and she looked away. He cupped her cheek, bringing her face back to his. "But I don't care. In fact, I like you better this way. You forget, I knew you when you were a dorky teenager, before you got all perfect and polished. It's the real Julie I want to be with. The one who occasionally burps."

She gave a watery giggle.

He kissed her forehead. "The one who sometimes says the wrong thing." He kissed her cheek. "And I really like the girl who hangs out with inappropriate men." He ran his tongue along the slick surface of her teeth. "But I draw the line at farting in bed."

She let out a shriek and clobbered him with a pillow. The resulting wrestling match ended up with them both half naked, panting on the floor and completely turned on again.

She bit her lip coyly and ground herself against his burgeoning erection. "Mmm, looks like you've got your strength back."

Chris slid his hand inside the lapel of her robe and rolled a nipple between his thumb and forefinger. He bent down and trailed his tongue down the velvety side of her neck. "Just about. But first I need dessert." He levered himself off of her and picked up the basket that he'd stashed next to the sitting room sofa.

"What's that?" Julie asked. But he could tell from the eager glint in her eyes that she already knew what it was. When he'd ordered dinner, he'd slipped in a request for one of Holley Cay's special "couples" baskets. From the look on her face, Julie was eager to give the goodies a try.

"Let's see what we have here," he said, motioning for her to join him on the couch. He pulled out the items one at a time. "Cinnamon massage oil." He grinned approvingly as Julie snatched it up and rubbed some on her hands, sniffing appreciatively at the spicy scent. "Hmm, won't be needing this." He threw a tube of lubricant over his shoulder. "But these—"

Julie grabbed the faux fur-lined wrist restraints, a flush staining her cheeks. "You want to tie me up?"

"That was the idea," he grinned.

"I've got a better one," she said. She led him to the bedroom and gently pushed on his chest until he fell back across the bed. Slowly, deliberately, so he had no doubt as to her intentions, she wrapped one of the cuffs around his wrist. Chris felt a little faint as all of the blood in his body suddenly rushed to his cock. He'd engaged in light bondage before, but never in the sub-servient role. The idea of Julie on top of him, licking him, stroking him, fucking him, as he lay helpless to stop her, was, no doubt about it, the most erotic thing he could imagine.

Chris lay passively, allowing her to secure his other wrist. "Have your way with me, baby. I'm ready."

Julie bit her lip and smiled a sensual smile that made his toes curl. "I can see that," she said, eyeing his erection, which strained against the front of his boxer briefs. She stripped off her robe and, naked, knelt on the bed beside him.

The ripping sound of the Velcro as she adjusted the fit sent heat sizzling across every nerve, making him shift restlessly against the sheets.

"Hold still," she commanded as she looped the tether around the bars and fastened the clips on each end to the hoops on the wrist cuffs.

Her authoritative tone aroused him even more. "Bossy. I like that," he murmured. He tugged experimentally at the restraints. "I'm at your mercy. Now what are you gonna do?"

Julie ran her hand lightly across his chest, loving the way his muscles rippled and jumped at her touch.

"I'm not quite sure."

When she'd seen the cuffs, it had seemed the perfect opportunity to administer a little payback for Chris's dominance the night before. Now she wasn't exactly sure how to proceed. She took a moment to look at him and to drink him in. He was all lean muscle and burnished skin. And she could do whatever she wanted with him. A burst of wetness shot between her thighs.

She moved to straddle him, rubbing her slick mound against his straining cock. It seemed to be a step in the right direction, as Chris groaned and lifted his hips, grinding himself more fully against her. She leaned down as though to kiss him, but stopped just short of his lips. His moist breath mingled with hers as he strained towards her in an attempt to capture her mouth.

"Not yet," she whispered, bending her head to run her tongue between his firm pecs. His biceps bulged as he clenched and unclenched his hands, unconsciously pulling against the restraints.

Julie savored the heady sense of power at his impatience. She could really torture him if she wanted. The question was, how long could he hold out?

She scooted down until she knelt across his shins and hooked her fingers in the waistband of his boxers. His erection sprang free as though grateful to escape from the confines of his under-wear. His cock lay against his belly, thick and long, the en-gorged tip reaching up to brush his navel.

Julie uncapped the bottle of massage oil and poured a gener-ous amount in her hands. Starting at his feet, she kneaded his muscles with firm, smooth strokes, working her way up his calves and thighs. A light sheen of perspiration glowed on his skin, and the sharp, musky smell mingled with the hot scent of the cin-namon.

"How does this feel?" she asked. His toes curled and his thigh muscles rippled as her hands slicked against his skin.

"It feels great," Chris groaned, "but maybe you could rub up a little higher."

"Like this?" Julie slid up his body so her legs straddled his waist, and drizzled oil onto his chest. He let out a half laugh, half groan, as she lowered her torso so she could rub her breasts against him.

"Ooh, the cinnamon makes me hot," she said as the oil made her skin flush and tingle.

"You're already hot," he murmured. His hips moved under her, and she could feel him, hard and thick, rubbing against her inner thigh.

Julie pushed herself onto her knees, leaning over him so that her breasts dangled enticingly above his lips. "How do I taste?" she taunted, lowering so that he could just barely touch her nipple with his tongue. "Do I taste good?" She leaned down farther, and he obligingly sucked her nipple into his mouth with a pressure that elicited another burst of heat in her core.

"You taste sweet and spicy," he whispered between hungry suckles, "and hot. Unbelievably hot."

She pushed herself back to straddle his waist. He was like an erotic feast, and she couldn't decide what to savor first. He was straining against her thigh, growing harder by the second as he watched, anticipating her next move.

She picked up the massage oil and poured more into her hand, feeling a deep, languid sense of satisfaction as it trickled through her fingers and onto his skin. She rubbed her hands together, then brought them up to her breasts. She felt his hot blue gaze like a caress as it followed every movement of her fingers and palms as she cupped herself, rubbing the oil over her breasts and nipples.

Chris was afraid he was going to come right then, watching her. Her hands moved over her breasts, and he couldn't stifle a groan as she lightly pinched her nipples between her thumb and forefinger. His mouth watered for a taste of her hard, pink nipples. His fingers itched to feel the slick, muscular grip of her pussy closing around him. He shifted under her, rubbing his aching cock against the softness of her inner thigh.

"Jules, if you don't move this along, pretty soon you won't have much to work with."

Slowly she smoothed her hands down her with mock sternness. "I think my prisoner has forgotten who is in charge," she said, sliding herself down until she straddled his thighs. One small hand reached out to wrap around his erection. A thick bead of pre come appeared at the tip, and Chris groaned as she used her thumb to spread it around in a caress that made his balls tighten and his teeth clench.

"Please, Julie, I'm not kidding," he moaned.

"Neither am I," she said as she bent over him. He held his breath, every muscle taut as he anticipated the moment when her lips and tongue would close over him. It never came. Instead he felt the soft slide of smooth skin, the tingling heat of the cinnamon oil, as she rubbed her breasts against his cock. The sight of his thick shaft against her breasts nearly undid him. Several more pearly drops squeezed out to mix with the oil on her creamy skin.

He nearly burst out of his skin as she pressed her tits together, surrounding his cock with oil and come-slicked skin. His balls tightened, warning of his impending orgasm. "Stop, please," he pleaded breathlessly, then regretted it as she abruptly got up and walked away. "Where are you going?" he said, unable to keep the frantic note from his voice.

She disappeared into the bathroom. Chris shifted restlessly as he heard her rustle around, then sighed in relief when she reappeared seconds later.

She held up a foil packet.

"Thank God," he croaked.

But to his immense frustration, she merely placed the condom on the bedside table, making no move to sheath him. Instead she stretched out on top of him chest to chest, and let her thighs fall open around his hips.

"You're very impatient," she whispered before leaning down to kiss him. Chris sucked greedily at her lips and tongue, absorbing the taste of Julie tinged with cinnamon. Even though she maintained a façade of control, he could feel the faint tremor in her hands, feel how wet she was as she rubbed herself against his cock. He was certain that she wouldn't be able to hold out much longer either.

Julie hissed and sighed as she slid her open, wet, wet pussy against him, teasing him with her slickly aroused flesh. She pushed herself up and reached for the condom.

Chris grunted impatiently as she slowly unwrapped and slid the condom over him. "Jesus, are you trying to kill me?"

She shushed him and gave his cock a warning squeeze. "I've never put a condom on, and I want to make sure I do it right." He held back a curse, just as she unrolled the final inch onto his throbbing shaft.

"Ahh, that's better," she said. "All wrapped up like a present just for me." She held him in one hand and positioned his head against her core. She cried out, bracing herself against his chest as he thrust upward, entering her in one firm stroke.

\* \* \*

Julie began to move, spreading her knees so she could rub her clitoris against him with every stroke. She pushed herself up and leaned back so she could look at Chris, moving like an untamed animal beneath her. Sweat beaded off his oil-slicked skin. His chest heaved as he struggled for control. His biceps rippled as he strained against the ties, his hands curling around the bars of the headboard. And he was hers. All hers.

Her gaze traveled downward, to the place where they were joined, and she let out a soft cry. She could see her own flesh, glistening pink, drenched with arousal as she eagerly accepted his invasion. She watched his thick cock slide nearly all the way out, then disappear inside of her, and her body clenched around him. At that moment, she looked up, and saw Chris watching her watch them with a satisfied gleam in his eyes. Bracing his feet against the mattress, he ground himself against her. Julie arched her back and cried out as she felt him go impossibly deeper. Her orgasm hit her with such force she lost her breath, her body clenching helplessly around him.

Her hands on his shoulders supported her as she continued to move, up and down, drawing out the thick waves of her climax while driving him to his own. Within seconds he gave a shout, coming so hard Julie could feel every pulse and jerk of him inside of her.

"Goddamn, woman, you can boss me around anytime you want," Chris rumbled when he could finally speak again.

She loved the way he made her feel so safe, confident that she could try anything with him, sexually, and not worry about feeling embarrassed or inhibited. She could completely let herself go.

"Good. Because I think I like it." To her own amazement, she did. "Maybe it's all my years of letting everyone else control my life," she mused.

"Maybe," he said around a yawn as she snuggled against his chest. He was silent for several moments, and she was just about to doze off.

"Uh, Jules," he whispered.

"Hmm?"

"Mind untying me?"

*I'll leave after she goes to sleep,* Chris thought later as he lay in bed with Julie's head pillowed on his shoulder. It was still early, but her breath was already slowing and deepening. Chris knew his smile bore a self-satisfied edge. She'd exhausted herself.

His own eyelids grew heavy. He fought the urge to fall asleep. He needed to go home. Wanted to go home, in fact. He didn't like staying over with a woman. He needed his space, his privacy. Plus he never slept well with a woman in his bed. And with all the work he had with the wedding coming up, he really needed his sleep . . .

Julie snuggled closer to the hard, hairy chest at her back. She cracked open an eye at the gray morning light filtering through the blinds on the French doors. It was still early, not quite dawn. She smiled. Chris didn't have to be up for hours yet. She had plenty of time to savor the feel of him in her bed.

As if he read her thoughts, his muscled forearm tightened around her waist. She felt a taut, hair-roughened thigh slip between hers as he snuggled her hips more firmly into his pelvis.

She felt an immediate rush of heat at the feel of his erection throbbing against the cushion of her buttocks. She gently rubbed herself against him, gratified when he responded with a low, rumbling groan.

She caught her bottom lip in her teeth to stifle a moan as his fingers plucked and pinched at her nipples while he rained hot, open-mouthed kisses on her shoulder and neck. Amazing. One touch, one kiss, and already she was wet. She had never imagined that she was in possession of such an active libido.

She shifted to turn in his arms, but he tightened his arm around her, keeping her facing away.

"I want you like this," he whispered hotly against her neck, lifting her leg up and over his thigh. Julie could feel him, hard and probing at the entrance of her body. "This way I can touch you." He put his words into action, sliding his fingers between her legs, stroking her eager flesh. "I love feeling how much you want me," he said, reaching for a condom.

The sound of the packet ripping sent a shiver down her spine, and she tensed in anticipation as she felt his hand brush against her buttocks as he sheathed himself. Then he was sliding inside, slowly stretching her body as his fingers seemed to be everywhere, pinching her nipples, rubbing between her legs until she felt like she would explode. And he hadn't even moved.

"You make me so hard," he said, his voice a harsh whisper in her ear. "Can't believe how good it feels to fuck you."

His words, and the accompanying rock of his hips against her, sent a burst of heat to her core.

"Oh, my God, you feel so good," she moaned. Julie arched her back, pressing against his hand in front of her and his hips behind her, loving the way the position caused her to feel pressure and friction in new and interesting ways.

It didn't take long before she was panting and shuddering against him, her body squeezing and pulsing around him in release.

But he wasn't finished with her. Unlike last night, now he was in charge, and he would have *his* way. And Julie was more than willing to let him.

Rolling her onto her belly, he leaned back, pulling her up until she was on her knees. She fisted her hands in the sheets, moaning.

"You like being a bad girl, don't you?" he said, emphasizing his question with a hard thrust of his hips.

"Yes," she gasped, barely coherent as she rocked back to meet him.

His palm came down across her buttocks in a slap, startling a moan from her as her sex throbbed and clenched around him. "You like that, don't you? You like me to spank you like a bad girl." He smacked her again, the slight sting sending bolts of lightning to her nipples and between her legs. She couldn't answer, but couldn't stop herself from twitching her behind, trying to entice him into delivering more delicious smacks.

"Come with me, Julie," he commanded, alternating light smacks with deep, hard thrusts as he pumped inside of her. "I want you to come again."

She could hear the sound of his harsh breathing, the incredibly arousing sound of his palm hitting her ass. He pushed her harder, higher, until she teetered on the edge of pleasure so fierce she was afraid it would consume her. She clenched tight around him, moaned as he seemed to grow impossibly bigger, impossibly harder inside of her.

"Oh, God."

The force of her orgasm hit her like a physical blow. Wave after wave of ecstasy sizzled through her, racing across every nerve ending, starting at the top of her head, all the way down to the tips of her toes and fingers. She collapsed onto the pillow, weak, limp in his grasp. Vaguely she felt him shudder against her, heard the deep groan that ripped from his chest.

He collapsed against her back, then rolled to his side with her cuddled snugly against him.

Once the sexual bliss faded, Julie felt a vague sense of unease. Every time he touched her, every time they had sex, she felt like she was losing another part of herself to him. Back in college, she'd been half in love with him. Now she was afraid she'd fallen the rest of the way.

She was realistic and knew better than to let him in on her horrifying realization. Even if he were interested in more than a fling, he'd spent the last several years separating himself from his family and the D&D business. Getting tangled up in that mess was no doubt the last thing he wanted to do. And she was honest enough with herself to realize that part of the attraction to her was the novelty, to see what it was like to turn the perfect little princess into a bad girl.

A hot flush suffused her body as she remembered just how bad she'd been in the last twenty-four hours. But it wasn't just the sex. Spending time with him these last few days had made her remember all the reasons why she used to love spending time with him. Why he'd made such a great friend. He was funny and smart. He didn't judge her when she wanted to watch silly movies or brainless television. He never made her feel like she had to maintain some unattainable level of perfection. Being with him reminded her of how much she'd missed him when he left. A keen ache pierced her chest. This time when she left, she would miss him even more.

In just four days she would go back to San Francisco, while Chris would probably waste no time in filling any void Julie left in his bed. For all she knew, they might not even speak to each other ever again.

The thought was beyond depressing.

She seriously doubted he would be into any kind of a long distance relationship.

"Chris?"

"Yeah, Buttercup?"

Julie felt a reluctant smile tug at her lips at his use of the nickname. "Promise me something?"

Her stomach sank when she heard his hesitation. Thank God she wasn't going to ask him to promise to love her forever. She would have been *really* disappointed.

"What is it?" he asked, his hand flexing nervously against her belly.

She turned so she could face him, and brought her hand up to caress his stubbled cheek.

"Just promise that after this is over, you won't completely disappear again."

He smiled, and the relief in that gesture almost broke her heart.

"That's an easy one," he said. "Until I saw you again, I didn't realize I'd missed you these past few years. I'm not going to disappear."

It was so much more than what he usually offered to his lovers, she knew, and so much less than what she so foolishly wanted. But it would have to do.

# 11

Julie's words still rang in Chris's head two days later as he tried to concentrate on preparations for the wedding that was happening in exactly one week. *Promise me you won't disappear.* Jesus. She was the one leaving, in two days in fact. He should be relieved. He'd been having a hell of a time concentrating, and with her gone, maybe he could finally focus on the wedding from hell.

But he was sorely tempted to pack himself in her Louis Vuitton duffel bag and follow her back to San Francisco.

And earlier that morning, in bed, he'd been even more tempted to ask her to stay, so they could find out what was happening between them. But he knew her family—duty called. He could see it in the frown that puckered her brow as she stared off his balcony. With her vacation nearing its end, real life, and all its worries, was sinking its claws into Julie, pulling her away, back to her family and the world that didn't have room for him.

It didn't matter anyway, he reminded himself fiercely. It

wasn't like he was ready for a settling-down, rest-of-his-life kind of relationship, even with Julie.

So why was it that he craved her presence like nothing else? At first he'd tried to chalk it up to the fulfillment of a fantasy. After all, he'd been lusting after her for nearly a decade. A little indulgence was to be expected.

But it had been four days now. Four of the most amazing days of his shallow, emotionally bankrupt life, and he was starting to wonder what his existence would have to offer once she was gone.

He shook his head, trying to clear it of such ridiculous thoughts. He was sex drugged. That was all. The sex with Julie was just so much better than it had been in such a long time—okay, ever—with anyone that he was overcome by the novelty of it all. What if she did stay here with him? The sheen would wear off and eventually he wouldn't find himself obsessing about her thick blond curls and how they felt brushing against his thighs as she bent her head to—

"Earth to Chris!"

The crumpled ball of paper hit him square in his partially open mouth.

"You need to call the liquor supplier again," Carla said, waving an invoice in his face. "The price he quoted for the champagne is less than what he's billing us."

He shook his head in an attempt to clear it of any visions of Julie and her perfect, pink mouth.

"Sorry. I'm just a little distracted."

Carla rolled her eyes.

"That's because all of your blood is in your little head."

Chris grinned sheepishly but didn't argue. Carla was right, and this was getting to be a real problem. In the last four days, Chris had made a mistake on the catering order, messed up the bride's family's reservation so that the eight of them were scheduled to stay in a two-room villa instead of one of the mansions, and had accidentally copied the bride on an e-mail to Carla where he had called the bride a spoiled, tight-fisted wench.

Thank God Carla was able to clean up after him. Even so, if the wedding weren't a week away, Chris had no doubt the bride would be switching venues.

"This isn't like you," Carla said for the hundredth time this week. "You're usually so focused. I've never seen you so stupid over a woman."

Chris winced and focused on the invoices on his desk. This was exactly why he should be glad Julie was leaving in the morning. He was completely distracted at a time when he absolutely couldn't afford it. This wedding could either be a PR godsend or a disaster, and they were so short staffed both he and Carla needed to be one hundred percent focused on getting the event over and done with without a hitch.

Yet he'd spent the morning fighting the urge to blow off work and find Julie and drag her back to his place. He swallowed his resentment, that he had to waste one moment of her remaining days on the island at work, and focused on what Carla was saying.

"I didn't want to say anything," Carla continued, "because you actually seem happy, but I need you here, Chris. I can't pull this thing off by myself, and you know it."

"Right, I know. As of right now, I'm back, one hundred percent. Julie will—"

"I'll what?"

Chris felt his brain turn to mush as the cause of his distraction appeared in the doorway of the office. She looked delectable in her breezy floral-print sundress held up by fragile spaghetti straps. She wore impractical high-heeled flip-flops and his gaze caught the silvery glint of the ring encircling the pink polished middle toe of her right foot.

Chris felt an uncomfortable tightening in his groin as he remembered sucking on that toe just this morning, her foot propped on his shoulder as his cock burrowed into her pussy. Nice and slow, inch by inch, just the way she liked it . . .

"I'll what?" Julie repeated.

Chris glanced quickly at Carla, who wore a stern, expectant expression. Work. Right. Focus. Right.

"You'll understand that I have to cancel lunch so I can iron out some details about this wedding we're doing."

"The actress, right?" Julie asked, walking over to Chris's desk to peer over his shoulder.

Carla shot Chris a glare.

"You told her? Do you know how many times I've had my ass chewed by Dan the Dick over how important it is that no one finds out Jane is having her wedding here?" Dan the Dick was Carla's pet name for Jane's head of security. "I swear, if one press person shows up here, I'm going to kill you."

Julie jumped in before he could respond. "You have nothing to worry about." She held up her hand for emphasis. "Believe me, I understand the need for discretion."

Carla nodded and sat back in her chair, blowing out an exasperated breath.

"To be honest, part of me is tempted to leak it to the press so she'll cancel. She's being a total pain in the ass about everything," Carla said.

Before he could stop her, Julie picked up the invoice from the liquor distributor. Her brow furrowed adorably as she read it.

"You know they're overcharging you for these cases," Julie said.

"I know," Carla replied. "He quoted us at $350 a case but now he says since our quantity changed it's going to be $375—"

Julie cut her off with a harsh laugh. "No, I mean, he's really overcharging you. I've worked with these guys before, and I know they can give you a better rate."

Chris felt his hackles raise at the implication that he was too stupid to know when he was getting screwed. He knew what he was doing, damn it, and just because she spent her days flitting around the Winston's sales office didn't mean she had the first clue how to pull off an event like this.

"I think we have it taken care of," he snapped. "Is there something you needed to talk to me about?"

He pretended not to notice the wounded look she shot him. But it took all his self-restraint not to pull her into his lap and kiss her until she forgave him.

"I wanted to see if you wanted to have lunch," Julie said, "but obviously it's not a good time."

She turned to leave, but before she could, Carla asked, "So do you know someone at Kingsley's?"

"I've worked with them when I worked at the D&D property in St. Bart's," Julie said. "I could call them for you if you like."

"No—" Chris said.

"Why not," Carla said with a shrug. "Here's the number."

"I already know it," Julie said, perching on the side of Carla's desk as she dialed.

Chris and Carla watched and listened in shock and admiration. In the sweetest, most polite conversation Chris had ever heard, Julie had managed to negotiate their liquor supplier's price down another thirty percent.

"That was—" Carla started.

"Very impressive," Chris finished.

"Thanks," Julie said with a shrug. "Considering it's what I do for a living, it's nice to know that I'm good at my job."

"I thought—" Chris began, but Julie cut him off.

"I know exactly what you thought. You thought I was nothing more than a meaningless title, that because I was the boss's daughter, I never bothered really working."

\* \* \*

Julie took Chris's silence as agreement. She didn't know why it was such a surprise, or why it hurt so much, that he viewed her the same way as everyone else. Daddy's spoiled little princess, whose job was nothing more than a title on an elegantly embossed business card.

Sure, she enjoyed a very nice lifestyle, courtesy of her parents' wealth, but she also enjoyed her job as the special events director at the Winston, and worked her butt off to make sure the functions she planned surpassed their wildest expectation. Under her direction, the Winston had become *the* place in San Francisco to throw the swankiest of the swanky society parties.

She stifled the urge to list all of her accomplishments for him. She didn't have to justify herself to him. But it was a hard dose of reality, in the face of the idyllic week they'd spent together. While she was falling deeper in love by the second, he viewed her as a shallow, idle society girl. Not exactly a recipe for happily ever after.

Carla stared at Julie, a speculative look in her eye. "Chris, can I talk to you for a minute?" Carla stood and motioned him to the door.

Chris followed her out, leaving Julie to brood. Julie couldn't make out any of their conversation, just muffled whispers outside the door. Stifling the urge to eavesdrop, Julie maintained her position on Carla's desk.

After a few moments they returned, Carla looking eagerly self-satisfied, Chris looking distinctly uncomfortable.

"This is going to sound really unusual," Carla said, hands clasped in front of her, "and I would never dream of asking you this if you weren't such a close . . ." she paused and slanted a look at Chris, "*friend* of Chris's."

Julie propped herself against the edge of Carla's desk and nodded for her to continue.

"He probably told you how our catering manager quit

without notice about two weeks ago, and we've also lost some other staff—"

"Do you want my help with the wedding?" Julie cut in.

"We would appreciate it more than you can imagine," Carla said with a relieved smile.

Chris's expression was as grim as Carla's was pleased.

"I don't know, Carla. No offense, Julie, but it's one thing to make a phone call and use your name to get us a deal. It's another to manage the details of an event of this magnitude."

"Oh, really," Julie said, disdain dripping from every word. "And just how many 'events of this magnitude' have you managed?" she asked, fully knowing the answer was a big fat zero. "Because just last year, I was the wedding coordinator for Whitney Taylor." Even Chris, who had never paid attention to San Francisco society, recognized the name of the oil heiress. "A thousand people showed up, Chris. I think I can lend my hand to a wedding one-tenth of that size."

He didn't look completely convinced. She knew exactly what he was thinking. That her idea of coordinating the wedding was limited to picking out flowers and suggesting lobster for the entrée. Actions would have to speak louder than words. She relished the opportunity to prove him wrong, show him that there was more to her than met the eye.

"Fine," she said, "I'll make you a deal. Give me the rest of the afternoon to work with you. If I'm still just getting in the way and not adding any value, I'll go home Saturday as planned."

"Fine," Chris said curtly and set her up on the opposite side of his desk.

Two hours later, Julie had completely reorganized their files and come up with four different menus to satisfy Jane Bowden's incomprehensible preferences. Then she met with the chef and used every ounce of her adorable blond and blue-eyed charm to the point where he was only too happy to prepare all of the dishes for Jane Bowden to taste and approve once she arrived.

And to Carla's shock and unending gratitude, Julie had spoken to Dan the Dick and convinced him—with no shouting or cursing, to boot!—that there was really no reason to surround the island with yachts full of armored guards to keep the press at bay.

Finally, Chris pushed back from his desk, holding up his hands. "I concede. I'm sorry I underestimated you. If you're still willing, I would love it if you would stay and help with the wedding."

She knew she was smirking, but she couldn't help it. "I might be persuaded, depending on the offer."

He stretched his leg to brush hers under the desk. "I can offer great benefits," he said, wiggling his eyebrows.

Julie laughed, her earlier irritation fading under the force of his grin. Really, who could blame him for underestimating her? Even her own father had no idea how hard she worked, and he was her boss.

"We really do need the help," he said seriously. He folded his arms across his chest and slumped down in his desk chair.

"You don't have to sound so glum about it," Julie said.

"Think how you would feel, asking a guest who was paying a fortune to stay at a D&D resort for help at an event. It's embarrassing, to say the least."

Julie understood completely. She knew very well the pressure involved in attending to a guest's every whim with seeming effortlessness. Allowing anyone to see just how much work it took would ruin the illusion.

"I'm not just any guest, I'm your—" she snapped her mouth closed. Whoa, she'd almost referred to herself as his girlfriend. Now wouldn't that have sent him running for the hills. "I'm your friend," she began again, "and I *do* have a lot of experience with this sort of thing."

"You'll of course be refunded for your entire vacation," Carla said. She looked at a Chris for approval.

Carla moved over to her desk to look at her computer screen. Her brows drew down her forehead as she scrolled down the page.

"There's only one problem . . ." She clicked her mouse again, shaking her head. "This is so embarrassing . . ." She looked up at Julie, her face pulled into a tight grimace. "With the wedding, we'll be completely full as of this Saturday, including your villa. I know it's an imposition, but we have plenty of rooms in the help quarters available, and I'm sure we can fix something up."

"Julie will stay with me," Chris interjected.

"With you?" Carla said, not bothering to hide her surprise. "But no one *ever* stays with you. Even that time we were totally full and your best friend was visiting, you made him bunk with *me*—"

Julie felt her stomach clench hopefully. Maybe this was a sign, an indication that he wanted something more than just a fling. Maybe he actually had feelings for her that went beyond lust and friendship . . .

"Jesus, it's not a big deal!" Chris said, plowing his fingers through his hair. He looked from Julie to Carla. Then, in a much quieter tone, he repeated, "It's not a big deal."

Julie looked at her feet for several seconds, focusing on the bright pink of her toenails. If she blinked, the tears that were welling in her eyes would spill down her cheeks, and that would be beyond humiliating.

She'd always been good at hiding her emotions, never giving into tears of frustration or anger in front of anyone. And she certainly wasn't about to do it in front of Chris. So it was no big deal. Staying with him didn't mean anything special, any more than sleeping with him did. Hadn't she been telling herself that all along?

Julie spent the next two days working closely with Chris and Carla on the final arrangements for the wedding. Chris had insisted that she still have some fun, and made sure that she had plenty of pool and beach time with Amy, Jen, Kara, and Chrissy later that afternoon. They were leaving the following morning, and after that, Julie's time would be completely filled helping Chris and Carla with final preparations for the wedding the following week.

Even with Chris's insistence, she felt guilty taking the afternoon off. Part of her still chafed at Chris's initial doubt. She'd always felt like she had to work harder and longer than everyone else to prove to the other employees that pure nepotism wasn't the only thing that employed her. That pressure was multiplied now, and she wanted to prove to Chris how good she was at her job, that he could depend on her.

Still, it was good to get away from him for a few hours, clear her head and get a handle on emotions that were speeding out of control. This was a dangerous situation. While she had always liked him, enjoyed his friendship, the more time she spent with him, the more her admiration grew. She loved his intelligence, his keen business acumen, his ability to handle crises and continue to motivate an already overworked staff.

And she loved that he was beginning to trust her to do what she did best—managing the details and assuring that all parties involved in the event felt satisfied that everything was going to go off without a hitch. Already the mother of the bride had called Carla to compliment them on their new wedding coordinator.

"She's fabulous," Mrs. Bowden had gushed. "Of course, I knew you had it all well in hand," she quickly qualified, "but it's just so nice to know that Julie's looking after us."

"Quite an impression after just one phone call," Chris had said with a warm smile.

Remembering the approval in his eyes still had the power to send a tingle down her spine. It was silly, really. She knew she was great at her job. She didn't know why his admiration was so important, but it filled something inside her, knowing she was needed.

But her motives weren't all motivated by generosity and the desire to help Chris. Staying here served her needs too. Or her cowardice, depending on how one looked at it. She knew she was simply avoiding reality, delaying the inevitable confrontation that would happen when she returned home. Not for the first time, she wondered what she would do when she got there. Something had changed in her, and she didn't think she simply could go back to life as usual.

It wasn't just her romantic life that was no longer satisfactory. In the past few days, working with Chris, she couldn't help thinking of her career, or lack thereof. Sure, she had a job, and she was lucky enough to be passionate about it. But boss's daughter or not, she had to face the hard truth that she didn't have much of a career path at D&D. Unlike Chris, who was willing to trust her instincts and really listen to her ideas, her father usually blew her off with a proverbial pat on the head.

Chris was right, in a way. In her father's mind, her job was nothing more than a title on a business card. A way to keep her occupied and under his thumb until she married, had children, and quit working to raise the next generation of society princes and princesses.

And even if her father did have plans for her to move up in the organization, she wasn't sure she wanted that either. It would always be his company, his rules, his way.

Not to mention she would have to work with Brian, which didn't even bear thinking about. She wished she was more like Chris and had the courage to leave the family behind and strike out on her own. But she'd spent the past twenty-six years always doing the right thing, fulfilling her duty to her parents and the business. She couldn't just turn her back on all of her obligations.

She sighed, willing her jaw to unclench, reminding herself

now was not the time for self-analysis. Now was the time to enjoy the heat of the sun on her skin, the soft Caribbean breeze in her hair, the salty scent of the sea. If only she could stay here, in paradise, forever.

"Whatever he's doing to give you that look, I'm jealous."

Julie snapped her head around to look at Jen on the lounge chair next to her.

"Yeah," Amy said. "I thought my fiancé was good, but clearly Chris has skills beyond most mortal men."

"That's probably true," Julie grinned, "but I was actually thinking about how fun it is to work with him. We really complement each other."

"I'll just bet you do," Chrissy said with a giggle. "I bet he complements you all over the desk, all over the chair . . ."

"You have a dirty mind," Julie laughed.

But even as she protested her brain was flooded with images from yesterday afternoon. Even with all the wedding craziness, Chris had found time to play.

Carla had left to go talk to the chef. "I'll be back in twenty minutes," she said with a pointed look at both of them. "Got that? Twenty minutes."

Chris had nodded innocently at Carla's stern look. But the second Carla closed the door behind her, Chris was out of his chair and on Julie's side of the massive desk. Without a word, he'd jerked her chair out and lifted her bodily onto the slick surface of the desk.

"What are—"

He'd stifled her protest with his kiss and shoved his hand roughly up her skirt.

His urgency alone had sent an answering heat thrumming through her body. To know that he wanted her so much was enough to make her instantly ready. He'd let out a satisfied groan as he felt the moisture that so quickly saturated the silky fabric of her panties.

He'd wasted no time, quickly slipping on a condom he'd conveniently stashed in the pocket of his shorts. Stripping off her panties, he'd laid her across the desk and pumped urgently inside of her, driving as far inside as he could possibly get.

Julie felt her body clench in bliss as she remembered the way she'd come almost immediately. They'd finished with five minutes to spare, giving Julie enough time to run to the bathroom to clean herself up and splash cool water on her face in order to mitigate the orgasmic flush that stained her cheeks.

By the time Carla returned, Julie had resumed her position across the desk from Chris, and she was studying the latest revision of the flower arrangements. Julie was convinced they had gotten off scot-free. Even if Chris had refused to give back her panties, preferring to keep them in his pocket.

"For good luck," he said with a grin that curled her toes. But Carla didn't need to know that.

"You two are ridiculous," Carla said, and Julie caught the look of disgust on her face as she held the empty condom wrapper. "Trojan Magnum," Carla read the label. "Chris, you are such a show-off. Just tell me you didn't do it on my desk."

Julie stuttered her assurances and fought the urge to run from Carla's obvious disdain, while Chris, the jerk, just laughed uncontrollably as Carla checked her desk for evidence.

"You've got it *sooo* bad," Amy said in a sing-song voice. The other girls chimed in, making kissing noises.

"Julie and Chris, sittin' in a tree, f-u-c—" Jen sang.

"Don't say it, Jen," Chrissy said. "It's obvious they're makin' *loooooove.*"

"Would you guys shut up? I'm trying to enjoy our last day here, okay?" Kara snapped. "It's kind of hard to relax when you're acting like we're on the playground. So Chris is nailing Julie. Who gives a rat's ass?"

Julie had no idea how Kara had gotten her reputation as a

fun-loving party girl. Never in her life had she known someone so capable of sucking all of the fun out of a moment. But suddenly the Caribbean sun felt overbearingly hot, the breeze was blowing sand into her nose, and her mouth tasted brackish from her earlier swim. Even though she had a couple of hours before Chris and Carla were expecting her, she gathered up her stuff.

"Don't go, Jules," Amy pleaded. "It's our last day, and I want to hang out with you."

"Yeah—don't mind her." Jen didn't bother to look up from her book as she nodded her head in Kara's direction. "She's just pissed she's not getting any, and if we're too loud, the island has lots of places where she can go to be alone."

Kara took her iPod out of her bag, and with a pointed glare, slipped on the headphones.

"It's okay," Julie said, gathering up her beach bag. "I should be going."

"Oh, come on," Jen said, "You can hang out for a little while longer. We'll have a drink, and you can tell us more about the supersecret wedding plans."

Julie laughed. "No way am I falling for that one." The girls had been trying to trip her up and spill information on the bride and groom all day. They swore up and down they'd keep the secret, but Julie knew damn well it would be too juicy not to share with someone. Even she was having a hard time resisting the urge to call Wendy—Jane Bowden was one of Wendy's favorite actresses.

"I promise I'll knock off early and have dinner with you," Julie said with a little wave, ignoring the girls' good-natured protests.

"Hey, Julie!"

Julie smiled. The girls wouldn't miss her for long. Mike, Brad, Greg, and Dan were all making their way down the beach. She took a moment to admire the mouthwatering display of tanned flesh over lean muscle. None of them could hold a candle to Chris, of course, but she wasn't dead.

Amy was right. She had it bad. Really, really bad. And working with Chris was only making it worse, creating a snowball effect. The more time she spent with him, the more she craved his company. Not to mention the sex. That too seemed to feed on itself. Instead of dissipating, her desire for him grew more intense every time they made love.

At one point, Julie had thought herself in love with Brian. Now she knew she had never even been close. The mild affection and passing attraction she felt for Chris's older brother was nothing compared to what she felt now. But there was no reason Chris needed to know any of that. As far as he was concerned, she was having a good time with an old friend, fulfilling a long standing crush. And if, when the time came for her to leave, she went home with a bruised and battered heart, well, that was her own damn fault.

# 12

Chris did his best to appear engrossed in what the supermodel was saying, but his attention was riveted on Julie where she sat with Amy and her friends and the diver guys. He also noticed, will no small amount of relief, that Mike was very well occupied with Chrissy perched in his lap.

Since it was the last night for several guests, including both the bachelorette and diving party, Chris was duty bound to socialize and mingle before heading to dinner with Julie. What he really wanted to do was hole up at his place with her as he'd already done several times in the past week.

Which was crazy, considering he was also spending several hours a day with her in the office working on the wedding. But he found that after they quit for the day, the idea of taking Julie out to one of the resort's three restaurants held very little appeal. Most nights he just wanted to order room service and spend the evening watching their favorite movies and making love.

And just this afternoon she had moved all of her stuff over to his place so that her villa could be taken over by wedding guests tomorrow morning. He'd stood there, watching her unpack, putting her clothes in the drawers next to his, placing her razor carefully on the edge of the shower. The whole thing should have made him feel utterly claustrophobic, but instead it made him feel oddly content.

It was getting out of hand. All of his misgivings about getting involved with Julie were coming to pass. She'd always been the one girl he couldn't forget, the sweet, sexy, good girl who'd driven him crazy. He'd put her on a pedestal, forced himself to keep his hands off, afraid that one taste of her, one touch, would never be enough.

Damn, he hated being right. When she'd first arrived at Holley Cay, he'd convinced himself she'd changed over the years. That the sweet, funny, surprisingly smart girl he'd nursed a secret crush for in college didn't exist anymore, if she ever had. That girl would have never married Brian. Nor would she have used Chris for revenge sex on her wedding night. He'd deliberately misled himself, he realized, thinking he could keep his distance and give her what they both wanted—a no-strings-attached fling that would satisfy their mutual taste for the forbidden.

He was such an idiot. From the second he'd seen her at her rehearsal dinner and had that strange, uncontrolled, falling-off-a-cliff feeling, he'd known he needed to stay away from her or risk getting burned. Now, he was royally fucked. Because in the brief time she'd spent here, she'd shown Chris that she *was* everything he'd built her up to be, and more. Working beside her every day, he fell more and more under her spell. He could all too easily imagine her here, in his life. As his partner, his lover.

He watched her across the crowded bar, his chest tightening as she flashed a smile at another guest. He'd been tempted, more than once, in the past two days to ask her to stay. Screw going home, screw her life back in San Francisco. Just stay here with him and see where this thing went. But despite the amazing connection between them, he didn't really know where he stood. Obviously she liked him, liked being with him, and he had no question that she enjoyed the sex.

But he was no idiot. He knew a big part of the reason she came here was to escape the chaos at home, and she was extending her stay to avoid the same. But when it came down to it, she wasn't ready—if she ever would be—to turn her back on her family and start a new life with him.

"We can't wait to come back with Nicole and her boyfriend, but you have to promise not to leak it to the press," Nadia was saying.

"Of course," Chris replied, forcing himself to focus on his conversation and not on his ambiguous relationship with Julie. "We're known here for our discretion."

"Discretion? I guess that only applies to your guests and not to yourself."

Chris turned at the sound of the voice. Kara was standing so close that when he turned around, he couldn't possibly avoid the brush of her ample breasts. And just in case Chris didn't notice the deep cleavage displayed by her halter-style dress, Kara subtly squeezed her arms against the sides of her breasts until they threatened to spill from the confines of her dress.

Under other circumstances, Chris would have appreciated the lush display of feminine flesh. But it was disconcertingly easy to focus on Kara's face as he said, "I'm not sure what you mean."

"You and Julie," Kara replied, as she exchanged her flirty smile for a sullen pout. "The way you two are groping each other, I'm sure the press would love to hear about how she went from one brother to the other."

He tensed. "I don't know how they would find out," he said in a warning tone.

"Don't look at me," Kara said in mock innocence. "I don't need to give the press any more reason to bother me."

Chris snorted, well aware of her reputation. "You'd go to the opening of an envelope if you thought the paparazzi might be there."

Her smile tightened around the corners and her green eyes took on a flinty edge. "In any case, I don't need the competition for column space," she said, glancing derisively at Julie. "Not that I have much to worry about." She ran her fingers seductively down Chris's forearm. "Listen, after Miss Priss goes home, if you find yourself in need of a real woman, give me a call. Daddy's jet is on 24-hour standby."

He resisted the urge to wipe away her touch. Before he could respond he felt a familiar warm presence behind him. Julie. He didn't even need to turn around to know that she was there. He could smell her soft, flowery perfume and the clean scent of her shampoo.

Relieved, he turned and caught her with an arm around her waist, pulling her snugly against his side. "Hey, Buttercup," he leaned down and placed a lusty kiss on her mouth.

Her expression softened, but she shot a wary glance at Kara, who seemed determined to pretend she didn't exist. "Everyone's headed to the restaurant," Julie said with a bright smile for Kara. "Amy wanted me to come tell you."

Kara gave Chris one last, sultry look before she turned and strutted away.

"That is one woman I will not miss," Julie said fiercely.

Chris chuckled. "Feeling a little bit territorial, are we?"

"Do you have a problem with that?" Her chin tilted in challenge.

"Absolutely not," he grinned, cupping that stubborn little chin in his hand. And he didn't, which was really scary. Usually when a woman started acting jealous, it was high time that he put a little distance between them. "I like it that you're jealous."

"Good," she whispered and leaned up to kiss him on the

neck, right in the spot guaranteed to make his cock spring firmly to attention. Simultaneously, she pressed something into his hand.

"What's this?" he managed.

"Just a reminder."

Chris felt himself grow even harder as he looked down at the wad of silky material he held in his fist. Her panties. Her pale pink, silk and lace thong panties. He groaned even as he smiled. Never in a million years would he have ever imagined Julie Driscoll giving him her panties in the middle of a restaurant. This was another surprising side to her that he loved, the surprisingly sensual, sexually confident woman who'd come to life in his bed. He remembered back to their first time, only weeks ago, but it felt like years. He'd been so worried, holding himself back, not wanting to shock her with the full force of his hunger for her.

But since that night that started on the beach and ended on the bed, she'd let go of her inhibitions. He'd given his lust free rein, knowing she could take it all and give it right back. To his great delight, he'd discovered behind those wide, innocent-looking eyes lay a dirty little mind.

"A reminder?" he asked, his eyes scanning the bar for the fastest escape route. Screw mingling with guests. He needed to get Julie somewhere private before he injured himself or someone else with the massive hard-on he was suddenly sporting.

"A reminder of what's waiting for you." Julie laughed and trailed her fingers down his forearm in a mockery of Kara's earlier caress. But instead of repulsing him like the other woman's had, Julie's light touch sent splinters of heat along his nerve endings. His hand slid down her back, to her hip, giving the ripe curve a squeeze as he pulled her more firmly against him.

"I'll see you at dinner," Julie whispered, slipping out of his arms. Another soft kiss on his neck, and she was gone.

Leaving him alone, aching, as he willed his erection to subside. He turned his body toward the bar, hoping that no one noticed that his shorts were unnaturally tight around his butt.

Julie slid into the booth next to Greg with a self-satisfied smirk. Mission accomplished, and with such finesse if she did say so herself. Julie had always been a good negotiator. She never lost her cool or allowed the situation to grow antagonistic. Who would have thought her skills would come in so handy in the dating world?

Kara was glaring daggers at her, but Julie smiled serenely in return. The expression on Chris's face when she'd handed him her panties . . . If nothing else, it was nice to know his attention wasn't waning. And it gave her an unreasonable thrill to know that she, who up until very recently had had a decidedly vanilla sex life, was now capable of bringing a sexual athlete like Chris to his knees.

She excused herself to go to the bathroom while they were waiting for their appetizers.

She had just finished and was opening the door when it flew open, sending her stumbling, startled, into the corridor. Before she could recover, she was being shoved back into the bathroom by a pair of large, tan hands.

"What are you—"

Chris looked down at her with a grin that was decidedly feral. "You think you can just hand me your panties and go off on your merry little way?" He backed her up so that she was sitting on the counter next to the sink. "You need to learn not to play dangerous games, Buttercup."

"What if someone comes in? Don't you have guests to take care of?" she sputtered. But then she fell silent as the look in his eyes made her instantly wet.

"You're right, we better block the door."

Moving so fast it made her head spin, Chris lifted her off the counter and braced her against the door. His hands shoved her skirt to her waist while she eagerly unfastened his shorts and shoved them down his hips.

"You make me so crazy," he groaned against her neck, shuddering in bliss as she circled her fingers around his erection. "The thought of you, naked and wet," he slid two fingers against her cleft as though to prove his point, "and I forget everything."

Abruptly he let her go and grabbed her purse, grunting in satisfaction when he found a condom. Within seconds he had sheathed himself. Bending his knees, he forced Julie up against the bathroom door as he drove inside her. "You're such a dirty little girl, giving me your panties like that." He bit at her bare shoulder.

Julie muffled her moans against his shoulder, wrapping her legs around his waist. A bead of sweat rolled down his flushed cheek.

"All I can think of is you, making you come," he growled. "You make me forget about everything except getting inside of you, as deep and hard as I can."

His words, combined with the feel of him so hard and heavy inside of her, were enough to send her shooting over the edge. His hands gripped her butt in a hold that should have hurt. Julie clung helplessly as he continued to piston his hips against her. He sucked her tongue into his mouth, muffling his groan as he came with such intensity his knees buckled.

"I think if we're not careful we're going to kill each other," Chris grumbled as he did his best to regain his composure.

Right then, voices sounded outside the door. Julie grunted as the door opened a couple of inches, only to be blocked by the back of her head.

"Just a second," Chris growled.

Julie giggled helplessly as she caught their reflection in the mirror. Forget the fact that her skirt was up under her armpits and Chris's shorts were around his ankles. Disheveled clothing aside, there was no mistaking exactly what had gone on in here.

Julie's face was flushed deep pink, and her hair stuck to her cheeks in sweaty tendrils. The skin around her mouth was abraded by his five o'clock shadow. She looked up at Chris, who braced himself with both hands against the wall. Sweat streaked his face and he was panting like he'd just run a fast mile.

"This is going to look really bad," he murmured with a reluctant chuckle.

Julie looped her arms around his neck and gave his chin a quick kiss. "Nonsense. Holley Cay has a reputation for being sexy. What's wrong with the owner taking advantage?"

"Sexy is one thing. Trashy is another."

Julie slapped his shoulder in mock offense. "Just because I have sex in public bathrooms doesn't mean I'm trashy." At least, she didn't like to think it did.

"You could never be trashy," Chris said, pushing away from her so that he could pull up his shorts. "You're too classy."

"But sexy-classy, right? Not classy-uptight?" Julie's tone was light, but she was mildly concerned. She'd done her best to show Chris there was more to her than a spoiled good girl princess this past week, and she thought she'd made some progress.

"Definitely sexy-classy," he reassured her as he helped her straighten her dress. "So sexy that if we don't get out of here soon, whoever's waiting outside will end up in the men's room."

By the time they joined the group for dinner, Chris was feeling the kind of relaxation that only came with immense sexual satisfaction. But amazingly, one touch of her hand on his thigh and his cock twitched hopefully to life. Fortunately the tablecloth hid any action going on below his waist. He took full advantage, sliding his hand up Julie's smoothly muscled leg, under the silky fabric of her skirt so he could feel the slick, smooth heat of her pussy, completely bare to his touch.

Kara slanted them a dirty look, as though she knew exactly what had gone on in the time between Julie's trip to the bathroom and her return with Chris on her arm. Chris shot her a smug grin. A real woman, Kara had called herself. She had no idea that a sex goddess hid beneath the prim and proper image Julie was so careful to cultivate. He couldn't believe it had taken him so long to figure it out.

And he couldn't believe he had so little time left to enjoy it.

His stomach clenched, and the exquisitely grilled mahimahi he was chewing suddenly tasted like dirt. He moved his hand back down to rest on Julie's knee.

As though reading his thoughts, Jen asked, "So Julie, when will you be back home?"

"Next Saturday," Julie said. Chris was heartened that she at least sounded a little bummed out about it.

"You'll have to call me as soon as you get home," Amy said. "You can come visit me at the winery. And, of course, you *have* to come to my wedding next month."

"That's so sweet of you," Julie said.

"Chris, maybe you could join her?"

The smile fled from Julie's face, and Chris found himself waiting tensely for her response.

"I'm sure Chris has too much to do here," Julie said breezily, making it sound like a ridiculous idea.

"Unfortunately, we're booked solid. I couldn't leave Carla high and dry like that," Chris replied, acting as though he wasn't tempted to follow her home to San Francisco like some pitiful damn puppy.

"Besides," Kara said snidely, "it's not like she can parade her new lover around the country club without sending the society mavens running for their OxyContin."

Though her comment was meant to be derisive, Chris couldn't deny Kara's dead on assessment of the situation. Newfound sexual prowess or no, Julie still wasn't the type to openly flaunt an affair with her husband's brother.

Julie sat back from the table, pinning Kara with a frosty stare. "It must be so sad," Julie said, "to know that the only way you get attention is by being known as the world's biggest bitch, and that you've taken that attention-getting act so far that even your real friends don't like you anymore."

A loud laugh burst from Jen's mouth, followed swiftly by a muffled giggle from Chrissy. Kara gasped in outrage and looked to Amy for support. Amy avoided her gaze, shaking her head slowly as her cheeks flushed.

"You push too far, Kara. It's not fun anymore," Jen said.

Kara stood and glared at each person in turn. But through the haughty disgust, Chris could see the last vestiges of vulnerability. For a moment, he thought he caught a glimpse of a little girl, screaming for someone, anyone, to pay her some attention, and in that split second he felt a little sorry for her. But the little girl was quickly hidden by a superior smirk.

"I may be a bitch, but no one ever forgets my name." She stalked off with a toss of her thick brown hair.

"Well done," Jen said, raising her glass in a toast to Julie. "It's nice to see the sweet little kitten baring her claws."

Everyone else followed suit, toasting Julie for standing up to one of the biggest bitches in the known universe. In the few weeks since they'd reconnected, this funny, sexy, surprisingly tough woman had surprised him at every turn. Not for the first time, he wondered how the hell he was going to find it in him to let her go.

# 13

The next morning, Jane Bowden, the uncontested queen of prime-time television, arrived with her wedding party in tow. The chaos that ensued would forever be remembered on Holley Cay as "Hurricane Jane."

"Typical Hollywood nouveau riche," Carla muttered several hours later as she and Julie rearranged the table arrangement for the fifth time.

"Now, Carla, let's not be snobby," Julie chided, although she herself was more than a little annoyed. The rehearsal for the ceremony was in less than an hour, but instead of making sure the catering was in order for tonight's dinner, Julie and Carla were stuck, with the rest of the staff, sweating and laboring under the tropical sun.

Jane had taken one look under the gauzy tent at the table configuration for tomorrow's reception and had declared it immediately unacceptable. No amount of cajoling from Julie, Jane's mother, or even the groom could convince Jane that there were other, more important things to focus on.

"Mom, you don't know anything, so just be quiet, okay?"

Jane snapped. "We have to arrange it so that everyone has a view." Jane insisted that the entire table setup be reconfigured to face the beach. Until she realized that when arranged like that, the late afternoon sun would blind each and every guest before the cake was served. Then she had them change it back.

"I have to go," Jane snapped. "I have a manicure and pedicure appointment. With the way things are going so far, I'll probably end up with a fungus."

Jane's mother, a sweet-faced woman in her forties who was as softly plump as her daughter was aggressively bony, offered Julie and Carla an apologetic smile before jogging off after her daughter.

"Look on the bright side," Julie said as she heaved two folding chairs over her shoulder. "She could have done this tomorrow, right before the ceremony. And at least she won't have time to change the menu."

"Not for tonight," Carla agreed, "but I'll bet you five bucks she tries to change the menu for the reception." Carla's head snapped as Dan, Jane's head bodyguard, called her name. "Please, spare me," Carla muttered as she gathered up her clipboard and notes. "If he asks to go over 'possible infiltration points' one more time, I'm going to slit my wrists."

"Come on, Carla," Julie teased, "he's kinda cute."

"Yeah," Carla snorted, "if you like the beefy, linebacker, muscle-bound meathead type." Which, if the shimmy of her hips as she walked over to Dan was any indication, Carla most certainly did. Despite their acrimonious phone relationship, even the most casual observer couldn't miss the sexual tension that shimmered between those two like heat lightning. She predicted that by the time the wedding party left the island, he and Carla would hook up. That is if they didn't kill each other first.

Right now though, she had bigger problems to deal with than Carla's potential sex life. Namely, a bride who seemed to have gone off her meds and was headed for manic land.

Julie was anything but surprised later that evening when Chris pulled her aside. "We have a problem," he said.

Julie did her best to concentrate on what he was saying, although it was difficult with the way he was casually rubbing his thumb over the soft skin of her inner elbow.

"Jane has decided that we can't possibly serve snapper, because that's what Sarah Michelle Gellar had at her wedding."

Julie rolled her eyes, bracing herself.

"So she wants Chilean sea bass instead."

"But that's twice as expensive, not to mention totally politically incorrect."

Chris plowed his fingers through his hair. "Yeah, I know, I tried to tell her that. You'd think after all the trouble she gave us over the budget . . ." His jaw flexed and a vein appeared in his left temple.

Rising up on tiptoes, Julie planted a soft kiss on his mouth, hoping to dispel a little of his tension. It worked a little, judging by the way his mouth opened eagerly over hers. Tearing herself away, she whispered, "Don't worry, I'll take care of it."

She turned, but before she could leave he caught her hand and pulled her back into his arms.

"It's really great having you here, helping me," his words were punctuated by the way he pulled her flush against his body in a warm squeeze. "I don't know what we would do without you."

"I can't wait for you to show me how grateful you are," she said teasingly, relishing the sensation of his powerful back muscles beneath the fabric of his shirt. She breathed in the salty, soapy fragrance emanating from the skin of his chest. It was all she could do not to blow off Jane and her menu concerns and drag Chris off somewhere private. "But I guess we better wait until later for you to thank me," she said, reluctantly pulling out of his arms.

"Later," he said with a wolfish smile. Julie noted with satisfaction that the only frustration he seemed to feel now was of a sexual nature.

"Later," she echoed.

Chris continued to be amazed at the way Julie smoothly handled every crisis. She easily solved the fish fiasco by gently reminding Jane of the PR nightmare that would ensue should the press get wind of the fact that she served an endangered species at her wedding reception.

Wedding dress that "shrunk" in the process of being pressed? Julie tracked down a maid who just happened to be an expert seamstress and was willing and able to make the alterations even without the bonus Julie promised.

"Shrunk, my ass. She needs to lay off the carbs," Carla cracked as they watched Amalie, a chambermaid, put the final stitches in Jane's now perfectly fitted gown. "You can't starve yourself your whole life and not expect to bulk up after that first scone."

Julie emitted a tired giggle, but immediately smothered it when Jane shot them both a glare.

Drunken best man? Julie managed to lure him aside and sober him up enough to get through the toast.

Guests pairing off and having sex on the beach? Julie alerted the wait staff to watch out, as sand on the dance floor could make it a bit slick.

Now she was standing on the edge of the dance floor, watching the bride and groom gyrate wildly to "Brick House." Miraculously, Jane was smiling. Even Dan the security guy had cracked a smile at something Carla was saying.

Chris came up behind Julie and slipped his arm around her waist. "Look at her," he whispered, nuzzling into the blond curls surrounding her ear. "She's practically glowing."

Julie sighed. Chris curved his head so he could look into her face. For the first time he noticed the strange sad expression she wore.

"What's wrong? You managed to turn the biggest bridezilla in Hollywood into the epitome of the blushing bride. You should be really proud of yourself."

"Thanks," Julie said with a small, fleeting smile. "They look very happy," Julie sighed.

"You don't look too happy for them." He jostled her arm in an attempt to shake her out of her blues.

"I am. I'm happy for anyone who manages to find the right person."

Chris's arm tensed around her midriff. "You're thinking of Brian." He couldn't stop the resentful tone that crept into his voice.

"Yes. No." She turned to face him. "It's just hard to look at them and know that I was weak enough to marry someone just because he was the 'right' person, according to my parents."

She looked up at him with eyes full of self-derision, glowing blue in the light of the torches. Any resentment Chris felt towards his brother was overcome by his need to comfort her.

"Don't think about him," he said, pulling her against him as his hands kneaded the tension from her shoulders.

"You're right," she said, nuzzling her face into the open collar of his shirt. "We only have two more days, and I don't want Brian in between us."

The band started up a slow, romantic ballad. "Come on," Chris said, leading her out onto the dance floor. He swayed against her, molding her body against his. She felt so good, her head tucked under his chin, the feel of her slender back and waist against his palms. He didn't want to think about her leaving. Instead he focused on here, now, and the way she fit so perfectly in his arms.

Julie wrapped her hands around Chris's waist, snuggling closer as they moved to the music in perfect unison. She nestled even closer, her skin tingling as Chris slid his palms over the skin of her shoulders, left bare by the thin straps of her silk chiffon dress. Heat emanated from him in waves, his warm, oceany smell enveloping her.

She loved him. There was no getting past it now. She'd tried to fight it, telling herself that she was caught up in the fantasy of finally fulfilling her adolescent crush. That she was taking a little revenge on Brian by finally having the affair she'd always wanted with his bad boy younger brother.

She'd always had a crush on him, from the first second she laid eyes on him. But she'd always known he would never be the right kind of guy for her. He was too wild, too antagonistic toward the world she grew up in. Besides, he had never even shown the slightest bit of interest in her.

But what she felt now, this was beyond any teenage crush. This was deep, and it was real. It wasn't just the amazing sex. Julie might be less experienced, but she wasn't stupid. And she would have to be stupid to not acknowledge the intense connection she felt to Chris, one that went far beyond the bedroom.

His hands moved to the small of her back. Julie sighed as she felt the warm glow of arousal gathering between her thighs.

He made her feel so . . . good. There was no other word for it. Beautiful and sexy. But also smart and capable. His praise at how she handled Jane's wedding and all of the challenges that went with it meant more to Julie than he could ever understand.

She herself hadn't understood it until tonight, when he'd told her he couldn't have done it without her. When was the last time she'd actually felt indispensable, like what she did was important? Her father had always watched her with a critical eye, to the point that she worked herself to the bone just to elicit one word of praise. No matter that her coworkers constantly told her how good she was. She was always striving for that elusive compliment from Grant Driscoll.

And Brian? When had Brian ever treated her like anything other than an empty-headed ornament? According to him, Julie's position as special events manager at the Winston was nothing more than a hobby designed to keep her busy between their social engagements. To think, she'd been stupid enough to actually marry him, simply so she could finally feel like she'd done something right in her father's hypercritical eyes.

Funny, but the short time she'd spent out from under the watchful gaze of her family had done wonders for her self-esteem. She couldn't remember the last time she'd felt so confident, so capable, and so appreciated. For once she wasn't constantly looking over her shoulder, worrying that someone would catch her in a mistake. She wasn't second guessing herself, waiting for someone (namely, her father or Brian) to question her decision. Chris and Carla had shown complete confidence in her and her abilities, giving her seemingly boundless energy and enthusiasm to tackle even the toughest bride.

If only work were like this at home. Snuggling closer to Chris as they swayed to the music, she wondered if maybe what she needed was a long-term change of scenery. Maybe, like Chris, she needed to get out of the nest for once to see what she was really capable of. If only she could stay here. She quickly banished the thought. Chris hadn't even hinted at anything long-term, and newfound confidence or not, she wasn't about to risk her heart and her pride by asking him if she could stay on here at Holley Cay.

Still, she was resolved to make big changes, and as soon as she got home, she was going to ask her father to transfer her to another D&D resort for a while. He would have to agree—even her father would understand why Julie wouldn't want to work in the same office as Brian. Maybe she'd move to New York, or even London. *Or St. Bart's. Then you'd at least be in the same geographic region,* a sly little voice suggested. Julie mentally smacked the thought aside. Foolishly tempting though the idea was, she wasn't about to sit pining away in the Caribbean on the off chance Chris would decide he wanted her as his girlfriend.

She looked up at him, feeling a quiver at the now familiar heat in his midnight eyes. His lips were full, slightly parted in an expression she'd come to recognize in the past two weeks.

He wanted her. If nothing else, she had that.

"If you keep looking at me like that, we're never going to make it through the bouquet tossing," he teased.

Julie chuckled as the last strains of the ballad faded, pulling Chris close for one last, tight squeeze. "I wish we could go home, but I suppose that would be unprofessional."

A surprised look crossed Chris's face, an expression so fleeting Julie thought maybe she'd imagined it. Then she realized what she'd said. She'd called Chris's place "home." A minor slip, and understandable. Completely insignificant, right?

Apparently not, if the strain on Chris's face was anything to go by.

Desperate to prevent any further weirdness, Julie placed a quick kiss on Chris's jaw and stepped out of his embrace.

"I need to tell the servers to pass out the champagne for the cake cutting," she said. "Hopefully, she won't smash it in his face."

# 14

"C'mon, let's go." Chris watched impatiently as Julie pulled on a pair of shorts and a tank top over her shiny coral bikini.

"I'm coming," she said grumpily. "But I don't see what the rush is. It's only eight-thirty."

Chris could forgive her the bad mood. It had been almost two o'clock before the wedding revelers finally moved the party from the beach to one of the larger villas. And, Chris thought with a smirk, he and Julie hadn't exactly gone to sleep right away.

But today was special, and he wanted it to start as quickly as possible. He was going to have Julie to himself, all alone, all day. No interruptions. Who could blame him for his impatience?

"I have sunblock in my bag," Chris called as Julie rummaged around his bathroom.

"I know. I'm getting my lip balm," she snapped, grabbing the tube from where she had very carefully placed it on the bathroom counter. Right in between her face scrub and her moisturizer.

For some stupid reason, the placement of her toiletries

brought a smile to his face. He remembered that from college, the way she put every cosmetic, every piece of clothing, in a precise location, and always put it back after use. She was no different now. When she moved her stuff to his place, Chris had gotten a strange thrill watching her carefully make room for her things among his clutter.

But he didn't want to dwell on how right it felt to have her shampoo next to his in the shower. Right now he wanted to get her alone and show her an amazing day.

He'd planned this day in part as a thank-you for all of her help with the wedding. Julie deserved a reward for giving up her vacation to help him and Carla. And God knew there was no way they would have survived without her. To say that they had been unprepared for what the wedding of a demanding Hollywood starlet would entail was an extreme understatement.

*Note to self: The next time you try something new to expand the resort business, start a little smaller.* But that had never been his style. Chris was always a go big or don't show up at all kind of guy, and the first high-profile wedding at Holley Cay was no exception. And apparently his luck hadn't run out yet, because it had delivered Julie just in the nick of time to save his ass.

So a sailing trip around the neighboring islands and deserted cays was the least he could do.

And conveniently, he could service his own selfish needs in the process.

He grinned as Julie grumbled her way down the beach, holding her hat to her head with one hand to prevent it from being blown off by the morning offshore breeze.

"Are we all set?" Chris called as they reached the dock.

"Good to go, Chris." Nathan, a native islander who worked as a deck hand on the resort's boats, flashed a white smile against his dark skin. "She's all gassed up and the freshwater reservoir is full—enough for you to take showers if you need to. And I picked up the cooler from the kitchen like you asked."

A slow smile spread across Julie's face as she took in *Holley's Pleasure,* a fifty foot Beneteau 505. It was remarkably similar to one owned by Chris's father, the one Julie and Chris had raced together out of the San Francisco Yacht club his senior year at Berkeley. From the way her eyes crinkled behind the lenses of her lavender tinted sunglasses, it was clear Julie remembered.

"Chris," she squealed, her normally composed demeanor having fled in her excitement. "It's a Beneteau 505. I didn't even know it was in the fleet."

"I know. It's not part of the resort fleet—it's for my own private use. I usually keep it dry-docked over on Tortola, but I had Nathan and Ricky go pick it up. I thought you might like to sail instead of motor the entire time."

Julie practically glowed in the bright sunlight that reflected off the water. "I would love it. I haven't sailed in . . . God, not since you left."

Chris felt his smile slip a little at that.

How could he have been such an idiot? Maybe if he'd bothered to call, hell, send her an e-mail in the past five years, maybe she'd never have hooked up with Brian. Maybe Chris would have actually had a chance if he'd fought for her.

Chris stumbled as he boarded *Holley's Pleasure,* nearly sending his backpack into the bay. What was he thinking, that they would have been together? Even if she had been willing to leave the protective cocoon of her family—and that was a gargantuan if—he knew himself, knew how he was in relationships. No, if they'd gotten together back then, he would have gotten bored and dumped her, just as he had done with every other woman he'd ever dated. Just like if he tried to make this into something more now, it was doomed to fail.

At least that's what he told himself, because that was easier to deal with than the idea that he might have blown his chance with a woman he could have spent the rest of his life with.

Julie didn't seem to notice his emotional distress as she eagerly clambered aboard and set about inspecting every square inch of the deck before heading down below to see what the cabin had to offer.

He went over the checklist with Nathan with half his brain, the other half firmly focused on Julie, and the frightening, unfamiliar feelings of attachment she elicited. Would he really have gotten bored with Julie? He'd never tired of their friendship in school. And after two weeks of her near-constant company—not to mention nonstop sex—he still wasn't even the slightest bit bored.

Could Julie possibly be the one? The one woman who he would never tire of, the woman he could wake up next to for the rest of his life?

It was a thought so frightening it actually made him light-headed.

But that would mean he had to believe in "the one," which he didn't. He was pretty sure about that, after watching the messes his parents, hell, even Julie herself, had made in pursuit of that ideal.

He forced a smile as Julie popped her head out of the hatch and helped him fend off the dock as he backed out of the slip. He felt his smile grow more natural as he responded to her contagious enthusiasm.

His unusual attachment to Julie was a product of pent up desire, combined with the genuine affection of friendship. He'd lusted after her for, Christ, almost ten years, so it made sense that it would take longer than normal to get her out of his system, sexually speaking.

"It's such a beautiful day," she crowed. "Although I guess every day is a beautiful day here."

He carefully steered them around the reef and headed off toward a clump of small islands that stood out like bright emerald swells in the turquoise horizon. "You wouldn't be saying that during hurricane season."

Julie's mouth twisted wryly. She tilted her face up to the sun, and his breath caught at the way the bright glow caught the curve of her cheek and highlighted the golden skin of her breasts, swelling above the scoop neck of her tank top. "This is just like old times."

"Not exactly," Chris said.

"What do you mean?"

"I never did to you on my father's boat what I plan to do today."

Her breath caught, and she sidled up behind him, sliding her hand seductively down his abs. Her fingertips rested just inside the waistband of his board shorts. "Oh yeah, and what's that?" Her breasts nestled deliciously against his back as she rose up on tiptoe to place a nipping kiss on his shoulder.

"A few more inches lower and you'll have a very good idea of exactly what I have planned," he murmured.

"Mmm, is that so?"

Heat pulsed through him as she obligingly slid her hand lower, teasing him to full hardness, gently cupping the weight of his testicles.

Reluctantly he reached down and grabbed her hand. "But first you need to handle the mainsail so we can get out of here." They were still in full view of the dock, where several wedding guests had gathered for a morning cruise.

With a mock pout, she sashayed away and took up her post. Chris couldn't keep the grin from his face.

"What?" she said defensively when she noticed his expression.

"Little Julie Driscoll just practically gave me a hand job in front of the mother of the bride."

Julie's cheeks were still burning when Chris maneuvered the boat into a cove on the south side of Sandy Cay, a deserted islet several miles from Holley Cay. She'd been totally unaware of the group gathering at the dock, oblivious to the fact that it would be obvious what she was doing only fifty yards offshore.

A steady wind blew, and they were able to sail most of the distance to Sandy Cay. In efficient motions Julie lowered the sails while Chris dropped the anchor. Julie retrieved a bottle of water from the well-stocked cooler and took a long drink, savoring the sun, the sea, and most especially, the gorgeous man she was with.

She stared unabashedly through the lenses of her sunglasses. It still blew her mind, how unbelievably sexy he was. He'd doffed his shirt quickly after they'd set out, leaving him in only his red, knee length board shorts. His skin gleamed bronze in the sun. Muscles rippled in his back as he tied off a line, and Julie unconsciously licked her lips at the sight of his large, long fingered hands. So big, big enough to span the width of her back, but always so sensitive to her every need.

She sighed audibly and took another deep gulp of the icy water. She was starting to understand what Brian might have been talking about when he claimed to be a sex addict.

But Julie wasn't addicted to sex. She was addicted to Chris.

She sighed again.

"Something wrong?" Chris asked, dusting his hands on his shorts as he finished tying off the lines. He looked like the ultimate beach fantasy, with his dark hair streaked with gold and red, his Ray-Bans the perfect frame for his wide, cocky smile.

"Just a little warm," Julie said, sidling over and wrapping her arms around his waist.

"You have too many clothes on," he said, removing her tank top in one smooth motion.

She tilted her head back and smiled up at him. "I don't know, I'm still pretty hot."

His hands swiftly pushed her shorts down her legs, leaving her covered by four coral fabric triangles of varying sizes. "Unbelievably hot," he said.

Her fingers threaded through the thick waves of his hair, and she tilted her head to meet his kiss. But instead of the deep, carnal kiss she expected, his mouth was surprisingly gentle as he gently teased her lips and tongue with light, feathery caresses.

She felt a tug at her bikini top, and shivered as it loosened. One more tug, and Chris was tossing the top on one of the bench seats.

His hand slid down her bare back, under the waistband of her bikini bottoms, and a rush of wetness surged between her thighs at the hot touch of his fingers on the bare skin of her butt. Before she could decide whether she wanted to protest, Chris had untied the side ties that kept her bottoms up, and she was completely naked on a boat in the bright sunlight.

Self-consciousness momentarily outweighed desire as she pulled away, groping for something to cover herself.

He would have none of it. "There's no one around for miles," he said in a hot whisper that sent sparks running along all her nerve endings. "We're completely alone," he said, tracing his fingers deliciously along the underside of her breast, "and you didn't have a problem sunbathing topless before."

"But I—I'm naked," she said, knowing how stupid she sounded.

"All the better to work on your tanlines, my dear." His hands splayed across her back as he pulled her against his chest, and she moaned against his mouth at the rasp of chest hair against her nipples.

Her nimble fingers made quick work of the snap of his shorts, and within seconds her hands were pushing them down his tanned, muscular legs. Her hand reached out to stroke him. Creamy warmth erupted between her thighs as she anticipated that thick, hard length inside of her.

In one smooth motion, Chris swept his arms under her legs,

and Julie closed her eyes, letting a little fantasy play in her head. He was a pirate, and she was the maiden he was carrying off to ravish . . .

"AIEEEEEE!" She was free-falling through the air, her scream abruptly cut off as she hit the water, butt first.

She broke the surface, sputtering, just in time to nearly be clobbered by Chris who cannonballed into the sea only inches from her.

"You stupid jerk," she yelled as she used her palm to sweep a wall of water right into Chris's face.

Chris flipped his hair back from his face, howling with laughter. "You should have seen your face when you fell—"

"I didn't fall, you threw me."

"I was just trying to help." His smile reeked of false apology.

With a screech she launched herself at him, trying to climb on top of his head and force it underwater. He easily deflected her, immobilizing her with a leg wrapped around hers and his arms flattening her own against her torso. They bobbed and splashed, until Julie managed to get free and make a break for shore.

Chris caught up with her easily, tackling her in knee-deep water as she staggered and laughed her way up the beach. He rolled over until he was seated with her on his lap, the water gently lapping at their chests.

Breathless, Julie pushed heavy hanks of hair from her face. "I think I'm cooled down now," she said with a raspy giggle. She squirmed to get into a more comfortable position against him, and felt his still very evident erection pressing against her hip. "But I think you could get me hot again pretty quickly."

He pulled her to lean back against him more fully. Her cross-legged position left her open to the gentle assault of his hand as it slid over the top of her thigh to tease in between her legs. "You're already wet," he murmured, "but let's see if we can get you hot."

Julie gasped and tipped her head back against his shoulder. His mouth captured the whimpering sounds she made as his fingers slid against her cleft, opening her, exposing the hard bud of her desire to his gentle onslaught.

One finger slid inside the entrance of her body, circling as it withdrew, spreading her own rich moisture to mingle with the warm salty water of the Caribbean.

She moaned as he stroked her first gently, then with increasing pressure. Unconsciously her hand stole down to grasp the wrist of his other hand wrapped firmly around her waist. Tugging at it, she drew his hand upwards until his palm enveloped her breast.

"What do you want me to do?" he whispered, his tongue flicking hotly at her earlobe.

The words stuck in her throat. Odd, that after all they'd shared she could still feel embarrassment. But it was so decadent, being out here, in the bright light of day.

"Tell me," he said, at the same time arresting his strokes between her legs.

Her other hand grabbed his wrist and held it between her thighs. "Don't stop." Any lingering sense of modesty was no match for the intensity of her desire.

"Tell me how you want me to touch you," he repeated.

She swallowed heavily. Then, in a voice so soft she could barely hear herself, "Touch my nipples."

The fingers of his left hand lightly circled her left nipple, teasing, flicking, in a caress that only fueled her frustration.

"Like that?"

"No."

"How then?"

She closed her eyes against the bright sun, against the embarrassment that threatened to overwhelm the urge to tell him exactly what she wanted, and how. "Pinch them," she murmured. Then in a firmer voice, "Pinch my—" Her voice broke off in a gratified groan as he obliged her, firmly plucking at the hard little bud.

"Is that all?"

"Touch me . . ." she moaned, "between my legs, like you were before." She covered the back of his hand where it rested between her thighs, pushing down until he exerted the pressure she craved. "Oh, just like that," she murmured as his fingers slid against her slippery flesh. "Inside," she coaxed, crying out as she felt the delicious stretch of his entry. "Deeper."

She writhed against him, continuing to gasp words of encouragement. His fingers dipped and plunged as his palm ground against her mound. One last, firm stroke, and she was gone, shuddering against him. He held her against him, steadying her with one arm while his other hand stroked her until he'd wrung every last tremor from her body.

Julie sighed and relaxed back against him, feeling rather proud of herself. For a woman who had spent most of her life trying to please others, she certainly had a knack for demanding her own pleasure.

For several moments, she rested there, reclining in his arms. She felt safe, enveloped in his warmth, his scent.

"You are so sweet," he whispered, his lips brushing the tender skin of her shoulder.

Julie turned her head, nuzzling her cheek against the firmness of his jaw.

Chris shifted underneath her, trying to stretch his leg into a more comfortable position. Immediately she became aware of his straining erection throbbing insistently against the small of her back.

She turned to straddle him so that his hardness was nestled into the wet heat of her still pulsing sex.

"Don't," he groaned as she wriggled. Every motion caused him to rub deliciously against her moist core. "The condoms are back on the boat," he protested as he halfheartedly tried to lift her from his lap.

"We don't need them," Julie said, leaning in for a kiss. "Stand up."

# 15

---

Chris watched Julie as she scooted off his lap and knelt before him as he got to his feet. He felt lightheaded for a second, a sensation that wasn't helped as Julie rose up on her knees and cupped her palms around the firm muscles of his calves.

He caught his breath at the sensation of her soft breasts pressing against his thighs and his erection strained, desperate for the feel of her mouth, only millimeters away from his throbbing head.

A low groan rumbled from his chest as she skimmed her palms up the backs of his thighs, drawing him so close he could feel the heat of her breath on his hypersensitive skin. His eyes drifted closed as she leaned forward.

But instead of taking him into her mouth as he had expected, she placed a kiss, first on one hipbone, then on the other. "I love how soft your skin is here," she whispered, her tongue swirling against the hairless patch right next to his hipbone.

He exhaled on a ragged sigh. "God, please, Julie," he gasped, snagging his fingers in the damp curls framing her flushed face.

"And I love how hard you are here." She raised heavy-lidded blue eyes up to meet his gaze, licking her lips as though she couldn't wait to taste him. "I love knowing how much I turn you on. Even though I just came, I feel like I could come again just from looking at you."

He didn't think anything could turn him on more than having Julie beg him to pinch her nipples and to tell him to slide his fingers inside her sweet pussy. He was wrong. Having her kneel in front of him, so close he could feel her hot breath on his cock, was making him so hard he hurt. He groaned, his hands fisting in her hair as she took his erection in her hand, gently squeezing and stroking him in her firm grip.

Her tongue, delicate and pink, stole out to taste the bead of moisture that clung to the tip of his cock. It swirled around the head, flicking first gently, then more firmly along the sensitive underside.

Then he let out a shout, his head falling back as her lips closed over him, enveloping him in the hot, wet suction of her mouth. She had gone down on him before, but not with this kind of single-minded purpose, this kind of . . . relish.

She was solely focused on pleasuring him with her lips and tongue. As though reading his mind, she whispered, "I love sucking your cock." The frank, carnal words coming out of that sweet mouth was almost enough to make him come right then.

Her hand matched the strokes of her mouth as she took him as deeply as she could, then released him, inch by tantalizing inch, lavishing attention on the swollen, plum shaped head.

Chris fought the urge to grab her head and force her to take him deeply into her throat. Instead he stood complacent as she set the pace, kissing, licking, sucking, savoring him.

He could feel his balls tightening up, and he fought the impending climax, bearing down on him like a freight train. He wanted to absorb every detail of this moment. The wet heat of her mouth and tongue, her beautiful blue eyes that looked up knowingly as she watched his pleasure, the soft weight of her breasts, bobbing gently as the water swirled and lapped around her.

One hand stole between his legs, gently cradling his balls, rolling them around in her palm as she suckled him hungrily.

She moaned, low in her throat, and he felt the vibration in every cell.

He wasn't sure if he wanted to come this way, wasn't sure if she wanted him to. His eyes focused on her full, wet mouth, sliding up and down his shaft, thick and glistening. He held her head in his hands, stilling her movements. "You need to stop," he groaned, "I'm too close."

Her tongue circled him lustily. "I want to taste your come in my mouth." Breaking free of his hold, she sucked him deep into her throat.

White stars appeared behind his eyelids as he came, pulsing thickly against the back of her throat. His back bowed as she continued her firm suction, until she had milked him of every last drop of come.

His knees buckled with the force of it, and he sank into the water, gathering her into his arms. He marveled at the faint tremor in his hands. How could she do that to him?

"Do what?" Julie asked, a tentative note in her voice.

Chris hadn't even realized he'd spoken the words.

He gathered her closer, trying to free his brain from the soft pink mushy feelings that threatened to overwhelm him.

"Do what?" she repeated, trying to push out of his embrace. "Did I do something wrong?"

He tightened his arms around her, pulling her so she sat facing him, her legs wrapped around his waist. "God, no," he whispered, burying his head in the soft curve of her neck, drinking in the warm scented flesh, tasting her in a soft nipping kiss when scent was not enough.

"Then what did I do?" Julie pressed, her voice muffled by the flesh of his shoulder muscle.

What could he say? That she made him come harder than he ever had in his life? That she, a relative novice when it came to sex, constantly surprised and amazed him every time they made love? That he felt like he could make love to her forever, and never stop wanting her, and that the thought of that scared him to death?

"I just can't believe how you make me feel," he said finally.

"How do I make you feel?" She pushed herself back, capturing his face in her hands so she could look into his eyes.

His hand came up to cradle her cheek, and he rubbed his thumb across the fullness of her mouth. "Amazing," he said softly. "You make me feel absolutely amazing."

Julie stared back at Chris, but she couldn't read the emotion behind his intense midnight gaze. A thousand questions roiled through her brain. Having never brought Chris to climax this way before, Julie was of course gratified by his response. However, maybe his look of overwhelming exhaustion was typical.

*Amazing.* Amazing like, I love you, you're so amazing; or I always feel amazing after a really good blow job?

But nothing in his expression of satiation indicated any deeper emotion, so Julie kept her questions to herself. Instead she just leaned forward and kissed him softly, trying to convey all the tenderness she felt with that one caress.

"You make me feel amazing, too."

Something flashed in his eyes then, something burning and intense, but it was gone before Julie could identify it. Then, without warning, Chris stood up, barely catching Julie before she toppled over backwards into the knee-deep water.

"I'm hungry," he said quickly. "Are you hungry? There's a ton of food back on the boat." He dove cleanly into the waves, his dark brown head bobbing up sleekly several yards away.

With a leisurely, graceful stroke he made his way back to the boat.

She needed to keep it together, if only until she got on that ferry tomorrow. She was starting to see things that weren't there. Like for a minute, she could have sworn she saw something close to love in Chris's eyes, before he had started a lazy crawl stroke back to the boat. Just because she wanted to see it, didn't make it real.

She was going home the day after tomorrow and that was it. She would put in for that transfer, and armed with her newfound knowledge and experience, try to be the strong, independent woman she knew was lurking somewhere inside her.

And with her life firmly back in perspective, she would see her affair with Chris for what it was. A momentary blip on the radar screen of her love life, a passionate interlude that would help jumpstart her new life as a sexy, single, independent woman who was in control of her life.

*It was not,* she told herself firmly as she ducked under the water, *love.* Not the real kind anyway, that grew into marriage and babies and rubbing Bengay on each other's arthritic knuckles.

*Remember who Chris is.* Brian's brother. David Dennison's son. Like father like son, like brother like brother. He'd never given her any indication he wanted anything more than this. She may have fallen in love with him, but she was not so dumb as to believe Chris was the kind of man a woman could pin her hopes on.

Julie pulled herself up the ladder and was immediately wrapped up in a huge, thick beach towel. She looked up to see Chris smiling down at her with a look so tender she promptly forgot everything she'd just told herself.

Even though he'd always been something of a bad boy, a black sheep, he was generous with his friends and family. He was thoughtful. This day was evidence of that.

More than that, he was smart, responsible, and resourceful. It took an extraordinary person to start something from scratch and turn it into a well regarded, not to mention profitable, business in just five short years, but that's exactly what Chris had done with Holley Cay.

Not for the first time, Julie thought that her father and Chris's father had chosen poorly in grooming Brian to eventually take over the D&D business. Brian might dress and act the part of the savvy executive, but at heart he was a spoiled child who cared only for the power his position could afford.

Her eyes stung with the combination of seawater and tears as she contemplated her own stupidity. She herself had been blinded by Brian's act, and even when she had suspected the truth of his nature, she had willingly deluded herself in deference to her parents' wishes.

And all this time, she'd been focused on the wrong brother.

From the beginning, she'd always loved Chris. Loved him with every inch of her swollen, aching heart.

Her eyes tracked him hungrily as he gathered up a picnic basket, lounge chairs, and a huge beach blanket and loaded them into the little motorized dinghy to take them to shore.

But love him or not, it didn't make a difference. He was not about to change his ways or change his life just because Julie had fallen in love with him. And Julie wasn't prepared to turn her back on her family obligations for something that wasn't real.

She wiped her face and went to retrieve her bathing suit and shorts from where Chris had discarded them. All she had to do was keep it together until she left and make sure that Chris never guessed the truth about how she really felt.

Easier said than done, Julie thought later as she helped Chris spread out a huge beach blanket on the sand and unfolded two chaise longues. The entire day seemed designed to seduce. The sailing, the private beach, the ridiculously elaborate picnic complete with chilled lobster and wine . . .

As though he needed any help. She felt a new surge of lust as she admired his bare torso while he laid out their lunch buffet. He flashed her a cocky grin when he caught her staring, as though he knew exactly what she was thinking.

"Lunch first, then dessert," he said, pulling her down on the blanket beside him.

She lay back and pulled him down on top of her. Wrapping her arms around the back of his neck, she pulled his mouth down to hers for a deep, leisurely kiss.

He responded enthusiastically, one palm sliding under the hem of the tank top she'd put back on along with her shorts. Julie wriggled and sighed at the feel of his warm, heated palm against her stomach. Releasing her lips, he rained soft kisses on her forehead, cheeks, nose. Julie nuzzled her face against his mouth, her heart swelling at the tenderness in his caress.

Her hands traced the sleek muscles of his back, reveling in the way they rippled under his hot, smooth skin. She drew one leg up against his hip, cradling his pelvis in the soft curve of her belly.

His mouth came back to hers, gently nipping at her bottom lip, then soothing with a flick of his tongue. He pulled back a moment and gazed down at her. His blue eyes gleamed with lust, and something more. It was as though in that moment, he felt as overwhelmed as Julie by the sheer pleasure of being there with her. As though he, too, felt like he was the luckiest person on the planet to be on that beach making love to her.

God, she loved this man. But the only sound she emitted was a soft moan as she pulled his head back down to hers, trying to convey every bit of emotion in her kiss.

Maybe it was the harsh midday sunlight, maybe it was the knowledge that this was one of the last times she would ever make love to him, but suddenly everything became more acute, more intense. Her body became a mass of uncontrollable sensation, enveloped in the heat of the sun, the gentle caress of the breeze, the sound and smell of the ocean.

And Chris, the texture of his skin, hair roughened in some places and smooth as a baby in others. His scent, warm, musky, flooded her senses. She wanted to touch him, taste him everywhere, memorize every square inch of his body and absorb it into her own.

Her caresses grew more frenzied as the throbbing ache between her thighs intensified. "Please, Chris, I need you inside of me," she whispered. She wanted him so much she was physically aching for him.

But he wouldn't let her increase the pace. "Slow down, Buttercup. We have all day, and this time I want to take it slow."

She moaned as he stripped off her tank top, the cotton fabric abrading her already ultra-sensitive nipples. The warmth of the sun made them pucker even tighter, until they were like tiny little points demanding to be kissed and sucked.

She sighed in relief as he bent his head. But instead of giving her the firm suction she craved, he circled her areolas with his tongue, first one, then the other, his mouth coming within a hairsbreadth of where she needed him but not quite touching.

"Don't tease me," she murmured with a sharp tug on his hair to emphasize her point. He left her breasts all together to trail soft kisses across the smooth skin of her belly. She decided to try a different tack.

Releasing his hair, she reached down in between them, firmly rubbing his erection through the heavy nylon of his shorts. "I want this, Chris, inside me, now."

Rather than following her directions, he chuckled softly and easily captured her hand, and pulled it away from his fly.

"Patience, Jules. Just be patient, and I promise it will be worth the wait."

She opened her mouth to protest as he captured her other hand and held her wrists pinned above her head. Her words of protest died on her lips as he settled more firmly against her, his chest gently crushing her breasts as his steely erection settled against her hot, melting core.

"This time I want to touch you everywhere," he whispered, his tongue thrusting against hers in a deep, familiar rhythm.

She moaned and squirmed against him, already at the edge of climax and he hadn't even taken off her shorts. It was as though their earlier sex play hadn't even occurred. Chris had awoken an ache inside her that would never be truly satisfied.

His mouth slid down her throat, across her collarbone, and finally, *yes*, his mouth closed over her nipple with a firm pull that sent her arching off the blanket. She rubbed herself against him, straining against his hold on her wrists, her breath coming in harsh pants.

He released her wrists, and she immediately thrust her fingers into his hair to hold him to her. He used his fingers to tease the other stiff peak, biting and pinching her nipples until she went nearly out of her mind with the pleasure and pain of it.

Her legs entwined with his, the sole of her foot rubbing encouragingly up and down the back of his calf as her hands kneaded the muscles of his back and shoulders. His skin was warm, slick with sweat, and she smelled his arousal rolling off of him in waves.

"Oh, yeah," she sighed in pleasurable anticipation as Chris trailed hot, wet kisses down her belly. He slid her shorts and her bikini bottom down her legs in one move.

His hands slid up the insides of her thighs, his mouth following his progress. She quivered as the heat of his breath touched her, like the softest of kisses against her sex. Her already highly aroused flesh engorged even more as her body strained, yearning for the touch of his lips and tongue.

"Do have any idea how much I love going down on you?" he whispered. His tongue delicately traced her cleft as his fingers parted her, opening her even more fully to his eyes and his touch. "You taste so amazing." His tongue swirled around the hard knot of her clitoris. "And when you come against my mouth, I imagine how you'll feel when I'm inside you, all pulsing and slick and snug around my cock."

He buried his mouth against her in earnest, his tongue swirling and thrusting, his lips sucking. She was already so primed she came within seconds, crying out his name.

"Ouch!"

Julie looked down at Chris with slightly bleary eyes. How odd that after only two weeks it seemed perfectly normal to see his dark head buried between her thighs.

It was then that she noticed her hands, fisted so tightly in his hair that it had to hurt. "Oh, I'm so sorry," she gasped.

"It's okay," he laughed. He rubbed his chin against her belly. "I take it as a compliment that you were trying to keep me down here."

She swatted at his head, giggling as she tried to close her legs against him. But he wouldn't budge, and held her hips firmly in place as he rained kisses on her belly.

Her laughter faded as she hugged him to her. How could she possibly leave him, leave this? The thought brought such pain that tears welled in her. She quickly blinked them away before he could see.

Because what choice did she have?

Instead she focused on the tenderness with which he touched her. He was so amazingly sensitive, paying attention to what she liked in order to give her maximum pleasure. She'd always thought it was a cliché when she'd read it in romance novels, but Chris actually did know her body better than she did herself.

He put that skill to good use now, as his fingers teased at the entrance of her body, then slid in with firm thrusts, reawakening her desire, her anticipation for the moment he would bury his cock deep, deeper than any man had ever gone.

"I need you inside me," she whispered against his neck. She needed to feel that joining, that melding, even more than she needed physical relief. She needed the memories to savor, memories of those brief moments when Chris was actually a part of her.

"Say the words," he teased, holding himself away.

She bit back a smile. He loved getting her to talk dirty. "Fuck me, Chris. Slide your cock deep inside me."

He stemmed her words with a nearly savage kiss, groaning into her mouth as he quickly sheathed himself. Within seconds the thick, blunt head of his erection was squeezing its way inside, rasping deliciously against slick, pulsing flesh. She arched herself against him, taking him deep as she used her muscles to draw him even further.

Her arms and legs wrapped around him as she arched up to meet his every thrust. *I love you.* She buried her open mouth against his shoulder to keep herself from saying the words aloud. *I love you,* her mind screamed as she came, clenching around him in rippling waves, giving him everything, her heart, her soul, as her orgasm sizzled through her.

*I love you,* she whispered silently as she watched him follow her over the edge. His eyes burned into hers, inviting her to share in his surrender to the intense, overwhelming sensation. With a low groan he collapsed heavily against her, his face cushioned in the soft flesh of her breasts.

Pulling him against her, she closed her eyes, trying to etch every detail of this moment into her brain. She couldn't have forever, but she could have right now. And right now was pretty damn perfect.

The morning sun hit Chris square in the face. He squinted as his eyes adjusted to the brightness. He smiled at the sight of tumbled blonde curls spread across his bare chest. After they'd cleaned up and put their clothes back on, he and Julie had enjoyed a decadent picnic of lobster tail, white wine, and fresh fruit. After a nap in the shade they went for another skinny dip. Chris had insisted on reapplying Julie's sunscreen very thoroughly, which led to him making love to her again.

Eventually they'd made it back to the boat, planning to head back to Holley Cay. But then Julie had pointed out that sunset was only a couple of hours away, and wouldn't it be wonderful to watch it from the yacht? Chris had agreed wholeheartedly, and decided that, as they had plenty of food and fresh water, they might as well spend the night on the boat.

The night was so perfect and clear, he had made a makeshift pallet with bench cushions and bedding taken from one of the berths.

"Why spend the night below when we have all this?" Julie had said, stretching luxuriously as she gazed up at the star-filled sky.

She'd looked so gorgeous with the light of the nearly full moon highlighting every curve, Chris had been forced to make love to her again.

Now it was morning, and they really should be heading back. He needed to get back to work, and she needed to pack.

Because she was leaving tomorrow.

His arms tightened involuntarily around her. She shifted in her sleep, making a small sound of protest.

He really, really didn't want to think about her leaving.

He closed his eyes, for once not forcing away the very dangerous ideas floating across his brain.

What if she didn't leave? The whole point of this trip was to make some changes, right? And what could shake up her life more than leaving San Francisco all together? God knew he and Carla needed the help running the resort. It was perfect. She would have a job ready-made for her, she could move into his place . . .

His heart skipped a beat, then started to pound. He had never in his life considered living with a woman, and he felt a flurry of panic that he was even entertaining the idea.

But even stronger than the panic was a voice telling him that it was definitely a great idea. A perfect idea even . . .

She shifted against him, and he opened his eyes. She was staring at him intently, and for a crazy second Chris thought maybe she knew exactly what he was thinking.

She stared silently, her blue eyes blazing turquoise against the golden tan of her skin. Her mouth was pink and blurred-looking, swollen from his kisses. Tiny freckles dotted her nose, and he could see every individual eyelash that curled up, long enough to almost touch her eyebrows. She was so damn adorable it made his chest hurt.

He watched as one corner of her mouth lifted in a tiny, inquisitive smile. "What?"

*Ask her. Ask her, you pussy. Tell her you don't want her to leave, that you want her to stay here with you and find out whether or not you're really in love with her.*

"Nothing. Just thinking how beautiful you are."

*Coward.*

She smiled wider and pulled him down on top of her. *I'll ask her later, when the opportunity presents itself. You don't just spring something like this on a woman when she first wakes up.*

Her leg looped around his waist and her tongue slid inside

his mouth. *And you don't interrupt a woman when she clearly has other things on her mind.*

He'd wait for the opening he was looking for, and then he'd ask her to stay, to take a chance on him, a chance on them. Heat coursed through him as her small hand closed over his quickly hardening cock. But later. Much later.

# 16

The opportunity presented itself as they were sailing home.

Julie leaned back against Chris's chest, his arms wrapped around her waist as she steered. She tilted her head back and smiled at him.

He kissed her, savoring the taste of her mouth. This was so perfect, so right. Why had he been such a coward up until now? He had never considered himself a fearful person. He'd always gone after what he wanted. Julie was the only exception. He wanted her, more than anything he'd ever wanted in his life. Because of that, he'd convinced himself they could never work, that she would never turn her back on her family. But right here, right now, the way she was kissing him and putting what felt like her whole heart and soul behind it, how could he doubt she felt about him the way he did about her?

She ended the kiss with a sigh and said, "I wish I never had to leave."

He couldn't have asked for a better opening if he'd written her a script.

"What if you didn't go home tomorrow?"

She stiffened in his arms and turned to face him. "Why wouldn't I go home tomorrow?"

"What's the rush? You could stay here . . ."

"Chris, I have a job, I have a life that I need to get back to."

Chris fumbled for a moment. He'd expected her to jump at the chance. "We need help here," he said, in a foolish attempt to salvage some semblance of pride.

"Are you saying you want to hire me?" Her eyes clouded with hurt, and he experienced another surge of hope.

"No, I mean, yes, but there are . . . I want you to stay for us." Chris dragged a hand through his hair. Jesus, he felt like a thirteen-year-old asking a girl to dance. Where the hell had his smooth moves gone? He took the wheel as they approached the dock at Holley Cay.

But her face softened, finally, and her smile sent warmth trickling through his belly. "Really?"

He felt a smile curving his own lips. He opened his mouth to reply, but as he steered the boat into the slip, he became aware of several other, unfamiliar boats anchored off the beach. A little Zodiac sped by, its passenger snapping photographs as it passed.

"What the fuck?"

Chris and Julie quickly tied off the boat, gathered their things, and climbed onto the dock. Dozens of people milled around, shouting, jostling, and it looked like the local island police were attempting to hustle several people onto the resort's ferry.

A man sprinted over to them, shouting incomprehensibly. Julie flinched as he shoved something in her face, and Chris instinctively pulled her to him. Holy shit, were those paparazzi? Within seconds, others had surrounded them, answering his question.

Somehow, Carla and Dan broke through the throng, followed by several policemen who managed to hold the photographers at bay so they could make their escape.

"Thank God, you're back!" Carla said. "They showed up last night, after you left. I have no idea how they found out—"

"Because there was a leak," Dan broke in, his voice tight.

Chris met Julie's troubled gaze. It didn't take a brain surgeon to figure out who'd tipped off the press.

"Kara," they said in unison.

Carla's fists clenched in frustration. "Jane and her husband had left already, and it's not like they were able to photograph the wedding." Dan didn't look impressed.

"This isn't the worst of it though," Carla said. "It wasn't Jane Bowden who set off this mess, it was—" She broke off, interrupted by two men who had appeared behind her. "Julie, there are some people here to see you."

Chris heard her gasp, and he wasn't sure if it was from his suddenly tight grip on her shoulder or from the shock of recognition.

His brother Brian and Julie's father glared at them over Carla's curly dark head.

Julie felt Chris's body go completely stiff, felt the chill as he released her shoulder and stepped away.

Brian stepped forward, fists clenched, chest out. "What the hell do you think you're doing with my wife?"

Never one to back down from a challenge, Chris glared down at his older brother from his superior height. "As far as I'm concerned, if you couldn't appreciate her when you had her, all bets are off. Not to mention," he stepped forward menacingly and poked Brian hard in the chest, "she's not your wife anymore."

"Actually, he hasn't signed the annulment," Julie said, darting nervous glances between her father and Brian. "Yet."

Chris's eyes filled with confusion and anger, but before she could try to explain, her father grabbed her by the arm.

"We are not going to do this here," he said. He turned to Julie, his low voice making up in menace for what it lacked in volume. "You'll notice that every sleazy tabloid reporter in the country is either on that dock or in the water snapping pictures as we speak."

The bottom dropped out of her stomach, and she felt all the blood draining from her face. Within hours, minutes even, their pictures would be broadcast to every gossip site on the Internet. Her picture and story would be fodder for the rags for weeks to come. How could she have been so foolish? And now she'd dragged Chris and his reputation down into the muck with her. But if she had her way, she'd be here to work tooth and nail to pull him and Holley Cay right back up. "You're right," she said around the thick lump in her throat. "Let's go somewhere private."

She started towards the main building, thinking to go to the office.

"Julie." Chris's voice cut through the roaring of dread in her brain. His face was set in tight lines. "You don't have to go with them."

But she did. She needed to explain to her father and Brian what exactly she would and would not do with her life and her time. And if they didn't like it . . . oddly enough, for once in her life she could truly say she didn't care. "I have to," she said. "Trust me, this is for the best."

Once in the office, Julie whirled on Brian, who looked taken aback at her assertiveness. "Why haven't you signed the annulment?"

"Because there's not going to be an annulment," her father said. Grant Driscoll's short, stocky frame was clothed in Bermuda shorts and a white golf shirt that already bore perspiration stains under the arms. He was a stark contrast to Brian, who, despite his heated temper, had barely broken a sweat in the intense Caribbean heat.

"Of course there will," Julie practically shouted, gratified at the surprised look on her father's face. She had never challenged him before. But it felt really good. "I can't believe you want me to stay married to a man who would cheat on me repeatedly, including on my own wedding day."

Grant sighed and raked his fingers through his short, graying blond hair. "You don't have to stay married to him forever. Just a year, maybe two, until this entire thing blows over. Then you can quietly go your separate ways."

Julie's jaw nearly hit her chest in shock. "Are you kidding me?"

"You need to come home and clean up the mess you made."

"The mess *I* made?" Julie gestured helplessly at Brian, who displayed not the slightest bit of shame for his own behavior. "He's the one who—"

"It doesn't matter who started it," Grant cut her off. "You're the one who made the scene."

"And you're the one who ran off with my brother," Brian interjected.

"—and the resulting negative press we've received has been devastating to the company," Grant finished. "And now with this fiasco," he gestured out the window toward the dock, where what seemed like legions of reporters were boarding the ferry, whether they wanted to or not, "we'll be even more of a laughingstock. We have to put up a united front even if it's temporary."

The knot in Julie's stomach expanded until it nearly choked her. "You call two years temporary? We're talking about my life." She hated the way her voice cracked, hated the way her father looked at her like she was the biggest disappointment of the century. Most of all, she hated that she was tempted to do exactly what he said, if only to wipe the horrible look from his face.

But she wouldn't, because she had finally accepted the truth. This wasn't about her or her happiness. It was about the bottom line, and it always had been.

"How did you find me?" she asked.

"That bitch Wendy was no help," Brian said.

Julie shook her head in disbelief. Had she really ever felt anything even approaching affection for this spoiled dickhead?

"A woman, Kara something or other, was more than happy to call us shortly after she alerted the media."

"And yet no one seems to care that you were humping your assistant and then took her to Fiji on what was supposed to be our honeymoon," Julie said snidely.

Brian at least had the grace to blush.

"Both of you acted with incredible stupidity," Grant said. "But there is only one solution. The fact is, this catastrophe of a marriage has our investors worried about a potential rift between me and David. In this kind of market, we have to do everything we can to make sure investors know that our company won't fall apart."

"You mean, *I* have to do everything," Julie spat. It was unbelievable. It was ludicrous. D&D's rapidly expanding revenues would more than make up for any scandal she might have helped cause. The stock would rebound in no time.

This was all about her father's ego. He hated to lose, despised any setback of any kind. This was his way of forcing a situation so that he wouldn't have to admit that he was wrong in encouraging Julie and Brian's marriage.

"I'm sorry, Dad, but this is impossible." Julie was proud of her delivery. Her voice was steady and strong, without the barest hint of a quaver.

"What?" Brian and Grant burst in unison, their eyes practically bulging in shock.

"I'm not doing it. I'll come home, but only long enough to get the annulment finalized. Then I'm getting out of San Francisco for a while." Back to Holley Cay, in fact, and hopefully for the rest of her life.

Grant's mouth opened and closed like a carp hurled onto dry land. "You will do as I say, or you can consider yourself disowned and disinherited," he boomed.

Julie felt a sharp, stabbing pain somewhere in the region of her chest. So this was it. This is what it came down to. What she had always feared, but never wanted to fully acknowledge. At the end of the day, business was the most important thing to her father. Not her happiness. Julie only mattered to Grant insomuch as she could help maintain the squeaky-clean, upper-class image of the D&D empire.

"I can't believe you would do this."

"Believe it, missy," Grant said, pointing a finger at her nose for emphasis. "You're reserved on a flight out of St. Thomas tonight. You better be on it."

Chris was swarmed with upset guests and concerned employees as soon as Julie walked away with her father and her—it made him a little sick even to think it—husband. He did his best to address his guests who were pissed—deservedly so—at having their privacy breached. Most of the press had been chased off by the resort's security and the island police, but, really, what could he do but allow them to check out early and refund a portion of their stay? Though paparazzi had come specifically in search of Julie, he couldn't guarantee they wouldn't distribute other pictures.

So much for Holley Cay's reputation as one of the few resorts that could offer complete privacy. Sure, Kara's leak to the press was an anomaly, but potential guests wouldn't see it as such. He ran a frustrated hand through his hair and started down the dock, back to his place. He'd been on such a high after the success of Jane Bowden's wedding, and now he was facing the worst setback of his career.

But that wasn't what made him feel as though he was being eaten from the inside out. No, as upset as he was about the future prospects of Holley Cay, it was Julie who was twisting his gut in knots. *This is for the best.* Five little words, delivered in her low, sweet voice, were enough to bring him to his knees.

She'd turned away from him, run back to Daddy as soon as he quirked his finger. Chris wasn't surprised. He'd known all along that's what would happen.

But he *was* pissed. Mostly at himself, for being the world's biggest fucking idiot and actually believing it was different this time, for thinking for one second Julie would stay here with him and live happily ever after. And pissed at Julie, for being exactly the girl he'd always known her to be.

He got back to his villa, relieved to see she wasn't there yet. Grabbing a beer, he went out on the deck and toyed with the idea of taking off before she came back to pack. No. He wasn't a coward. He'd known what he was getting into from the very beginning, and if he didn't want to get hurt, he should have stayed the hell away from Julie Driscoll. Now it was time to face her like a man when she told him good-bye. It *was* all for the best, just like she said. The sooner she left, the sooner he could get to work salvaging what was left of Holley Cay's reputation.

"Chris?" Every fiber went taut at the sound of her voice. After a few moments, she found him on the deck. With her hair a tousled mop, her eyes puffy and nose red from crying, she looked like a sad, lost little girl. He gripped the arms of his teak lounger to keep from going to her and wrapping her in his arms.

She came and sat on the edge of his chaise, placing a tentative hand on his arm. "I'm so sorry about all of this. I'll do whatever I can to—"

He stopped her mid-sentence. "Why didn't you tell me he wasn't signing the annulment papers?"

She jerked back as though startled. "It didn't matter—it was just a technicality."

"Just a technicality?" The bitterness searing his throat erupted like bile. "You didn't think I would care that I was fucking my brother's wife?"

"You didn't seem to care on our wedding night," she snapped.

Okay, she had him there. "Let me guess—he won't be giving you an annulment any time soon."

"Can you believe that? Daddy wants me to stay married to Brian for a year or two." She stood and paced angrily across the deck. "As though that's nothing."

"And you'll do it, won't you?" he all but sneered.

She stopped pacing and looked at Chris, her shoulders slumping. "Dad says if I don't, he'll disinherit me. Take away my trust fund, my allowance, everything."

Well, that sealed it then. Julie was too used to a life of comfort and luxury to risk losing her inheritance. Even more importantly, money was the defining symbol of her father's approval. If Grant Driscoll took that from her, he took everything. Chris didn't stand a chance, not that he ever had.

"You're leaving soon then?"

"Tonight," she sighed. "But only for a little while, just until I get everything straightened out and pack up my apartment. Then I'll come back."

His heart skipped, and for about a nanosecond he let himself hope, let himself believe that she'd actually endure being disowned by her family just to be with him. Loved her so much he *wanted* to believe it more than he'd ever wanted anything. But he knew better than most that *wanting* someone to love you enough to make sacrifices wasn't enough. Her willingness to go running home at her father's bidding was a sharp dose of reality, reminding him that in their eyes—in Julie's eyes—he would always be the "bad" brother. Always on the outside looking in on their perfect little world. Even if she did come back to him and kept the charade going for a while longer, eventually she'd realize her mistake. He'd be doing them both a favor by making a clean cut now, and not dragging this thing on to its inevitably messy end.

"Why would you bother coming back?" Chris's mild, almost emotionless question froze her heart in her chest. It started beating again, thudding hard in apprehension.

"What do you mean? Earlier we talked about me staying on here, with you. Just because I have to go back to San Francisco for a little while doesn't mean that can't happen." She tried to tone down the hysteria creeping into her voice. Had she completely misunderstood him in those few minutes before they'd been sidetracked by the pandemonium here at Holley Cay? He had asked her to stay, hadn't he? He had said he wanted to be with her?

"It was a stupid idea," he said dismissively.

Her voice pushed past the icy fist that gripped her throat. "But what about us?" A noncommittal shrug was his only answer. Desperate, she tried a different tack. "You said yourself you needed help. After this week, you know how good I am—"

"And how long do you think you could live on the salary I could afford to pay you?" he snapped. "How long before you're running back to Daddy, begging for your trust fund back and leaving me in the lurch?"

"I wouldn't do that!" She would do fine on what he could pay her—whatever that was.

"Come on, Julie, it's one thing to play at working girl for a week, but an entirely different thing to have to actually work to pay your bills. And frankly, right now all my money is in this place, and I don't have any extra lying around to take care of you."

"What about us?" she asked again, knowing the answer with every beat of her bruised heart, but needing to hear the words.

Needing to hear him say it, so there was no ambiguity. She was afraid she might vomit when she saw the pitying expression on Chris's face.

"Jules, we knew this had to end eventually. This just forces our hand."

Something cracked at the sight of his condescending smile.

She couldn't believe this was the same man who had worked beside her, made love to her with such passion and tenderness for the past weeks. That man had looked at her with admiration and respect. That man had made her feel cared for.

The gorgeous man staring at her, unblinking, was a stranger. The world fell away, and suddenly Julie saw everything in keen, cold, clarity. She was a fool. She'd let herself be swept away by the fantasy, the fairy tale where Chris was the Prince Charming who finally saw her for the smart, capable woman she really was. But he was just like everyone else. He looked at her, and he saw the spoiled little princess. A shallow piece of fluff, incapable of taking care of herself. She'd thought she'd shown him this past week, but even that hadn't been enough.

"Fine," she said, her voice sounding old and weary even to her own ears. "I'm so tired of trying to prove myself to everybody. I know what I can do, I know what I'm capable of, but I'm not going to kill myself trying to change your mind." Her eyes ran over him, memorizing every line of his gorgeous face, every muscular curve of his tightly hewn body.

"Just remember this," she said, surprised at how calm and steady her voice was. "When you look back and you miss what we could have had, remember that you did this. This was your call. I was ready to take the risk and go all in, and you're the one who gave up."

Five hours later, she sat at the gate in St. Thomas waiting for the departure of flight 95, service to Miami. There she would hop her connecting flight back to San Francisco. She didn't want to go home, but her brain was so numb she couldn't think of any other options. For now she was focused on getting Wendy's help to end this sham of a marriage. Then she'd tackle bigger things, like what the hell she was going to do with her life.

Her father and Brian had left earlier in the day, thank God. Evidently they were so convinced of her obedience that they didn't see the need to escort her home personally.

Despite herself, she glanced up every five minutes, part of her fully expecting Chris to appear and whisk her back to Holley Cay.

Chris hadn't paid any attention to her "you're gonna miss me when I'm gone" tirade. Still, she was glad she'd said it. She needed him to know where she stood, needed him to know what she was willing to give up, regardless of what he'd thought of her.

He either hadn't believed her or hadn't cared, because he'd barely waved to her as she boarded the ferry, not even waiting for it to leave the dock before walking away.

Surprisingly, she didn't feel like crying. A blanket of numbness had mercifully settled over her as she'd packed, and she was clutching it to her for all she was worth. She'd grieve later, she knew, but for now it was nice to give intense emotions that had been her constant companions of late a well deserved rest.

Her flight was called. Her lungs seized and her heart began to race. Was she having a heart attack? She gasped for air as a wave of panic washed over her, dark and unrelenting. She didn't know what was happening, but something inside her, a voice emanating from her very bones, screamed at her not to get on that plane. If she did, she was ruined. Her entire future flashed before her eyes. An image of herself smiling politely at Brian at a social gathering, forced to endure his company in the name of "keeping up appearances" for the sake of the company. Working her butt off for her father, knowing all the while that he was willing to sacrifice his only daughter on the altar of public image.

She grabbed her carry-on bag and made a beeline for the main terminal. No way in hell was she getting on that plane. As she made the decision, her heart rate slowed, her breathing eased, and she felt, if not calm, at least not like she was about to have a coronary.

*I don't have any extra lying around to take care of you.* Chris's words echoed in her brain, offensive for all their truth. He was right. He had no reason to expect she could take care of herself financially or otherwise—she had been taken care of by others for most of her life. But as far as she could tell, they hadn't done a very good job of it. She might as well give it a try—she doubted she could treat herself any worse.

# 17

Chris stared blankly out the window of his office. The afternoon sun reflected off the water of the bay, obscuring his vision so that he couldn't see the ferry arriving with the latest round of guests.

He didn't need to see it to know it was approaching. He glanced at his watch. Three twenty-four. Max, the ferry captain, had said they would be there at three twenty-five, and Max was always on time.

"Ready to go?" Carla put a hand on his shoulder, and gently prodded him.

Chris sighed heavily and did his best to put on his game face, just as he'd done every week for the past two months. He schooled his face into a polite, welcoming mask, went down to the dock and greeted the newest group of the world's wealthiest looking for the epitome of luxurious vacations.

And every week, he watched each guest disembark with unwavering intensity. Every so often he would catch a glimpse of a slender, petite figure, a curly mop of blond curls, and his heart would leap in a moment of sickening hope.

And every single time, it was someone else. He knew how ridiculous it was to hope that Julie would tell her father and Brian to take a flying leap. It was even more unlikely that she would then hop on a plane and come back here.

Still, a day didn't go by when her parting words didn't replay in his mind. When he didn't wonder if his decision to push her away was the worst mistake of his life.

"Chris, come on. Try not to look like someone just killed your puppy, okay?" Carla said, her tone gentle despite her words. "These people are expecting paradise, and paradise isn't run by some grumpy, lovesick loser."

"I'm not lovesick."

Carla snorted. "Moping around? Hermiting up in your house every night? Showing not even a smidgen of interest in the many single female guests we've had in the past two months? If that's not lovesick, I don't know what is."

Chris glared at Carla, unable to argue with her painfully accurate assessment of his behavior.

"And if anyone knows about lovesick, it's you, right?" Chris felt like an ass, throwing Carla's own painful past breakup in her face, but he couldn't seem to stop himself.

"Damn right I do," she snapped. "And now I realize how annoying I must have been. So just call her, tell her you love her, and get it over with." She paused to put some papers in a file. "In any case, it's affecting your work, and we have too much to do for you to be distracted."

They had Julie to thank for their increased workload. Despite her tantrums and complaints, Jane Bowden had raved to all of her friends, including some in the press, about her amazing, wonderful wedding at Holley Cay. Since she'd left before the paparazzi had descended like locusts, she miraculously didn't have a single bad thing to say about Chris, Carla, and the entire staff at the resort.

Thanks to her, Carla had already booked two more weddings in as many months and Chris was actively courting a crown princess of Sweden who was scouting several locations in the Caribbean. Not bad, considering they had hosted their first wedding only two months ago. If only Julie was here to help, he thought ruefully.

But her hospitality management skills were far from the biggest reason he missed her.

He was in love with her, no question, and his heart got sorer every day that he wasn't with her.

He'd realized he loved Julie about five minutes after she left. That wasn't the problem.

"She would never defy her father that way."

"What is this, the feudal system? Julie loves you. If you asked her to come back, she'd do it in a heartbeat."

Chris envied the conviction in Carla's voice. "She's always done everything her parents told her. She always does the right thing. It's just the way she is."

"Clearly she's trying to change that, or she would have never crawled into bed with you."

He thought about that for a moment, and for a minute he savored the slight tang of hope. But even if Julie did love him, she'd still left, hadn't she? *Only after you practically kicked her out the door,* a harsh voice reminded him.

*But for good reason,* he reminded himself. Women like Julie didn't walk away from the tight grip of their families—not to mention a mega trust fund—in the name of love. She might have grown up some, but underneath it all she was still the same college girl who didn't even want her father to know they were friends.

"You don't understand how it is with her family. She's lived her whole life under Daddy's thumb, doing everything he says without question. That's not going to change in the course of a couple of weeks."

Carla fixed him with an analytical stare. "You know what I

think?" she said after several moments. Chris wasn't sure he did, but he knew better than to say so. "I think you severely underestimate her. I may not know her as well as you think you do, but she was happy here. Maybe you're right. Maybe she would have given it all up in a couple of months and gone running back to Daddy, but I really don't think so. I think you're looking for excuses because you're too much of a coward to put your heart on the line. Inside, you're still that angry teenager who was rejected by his father and everyone in his world."

"Thanks for the analysis, Dr. Freud," he snapped, standing from his desk chair with enough force to knock it to the ground. "If you're done with your bullshitting, we need to go greet the guests."

They walked down to the dock in tense silence. Chris greeted the guests, doing his best to be cordial and welcoming, despite the internal storm Carla's comments had ignited. She was wrong. He wasn't afraid, he was practical. What was the use of putting himself and Julie through the emotional torture when he could already foresee the outcome, clear as day?

*Unless you're wrong.*

*I was ready to take the risk. I was ready to go all in.*

A lump lodged in his throat as he remembered Julie's face, the defeated, resigned look in her beautiful blue eyes. He'd done that. Broken her. Even when she'd come back to his villa after talking to her father, she'd had fight left in her. But when Chris had forced himself to tell her to go, that had been the killing blow.

It made him sick now to think about it. He didn't want to remember her looking at him with defeated resignation. He wanted to remember her smiling at him, looking at him with the heat of passion when he'd slid inside the giving heat of her body. Looking at him with love.

He'd thrown it all away. Pain cut through him like a white-hot blade. Carla was right. He was an idiot. He was a coward.

That day at his villa, Julie had been ready to fight, ready to take on her father, Brian, all the people who sought to control her. All she'd wanted was his support, and instead he'd given into his fear of being hurt, his fucking cowardice, and pushed her away.

Something of his thoughts must have shown on his face, because Carla said, "She loves you, you know. And unlike me, she's not a vindictive bitch. I bet if you beg her forgiveness, she'll give you another shot."

He managed a half smile and draped his arm over Carla's shoulder, praying she was right. "You think it'll be that easy?"

"Your pride may sting a little, but yeah, I'll lay odds that Julie wants to forgive you. Now let's get back to the office so you can call her. Beg and plead, but get her back here. I need her help with the princess."

Chris followed Carla, a genuine smile spreading across his face for the first time in two months. Julie. If he called her today, she could be on a plane tonight, and back in his arms by morning.

If only it were that easy. After hurrying back to the office, he'd dialed Julie's number in San Francisco, only to be greeted by a message that the number was no longer in service. No forwarding information was provided.

Her coworker at the Winston, whom he contacted next, informed him that Julie no longer worked there and, no, she had no information of her current whereabouts.

Chris broke down and called Brian.

"We don't know where she is," Brian said. "Grant got an e-mail that said she wasn't coming back to San Francisco, but it didn't say where she was."

His brother's indifference made Chris's rage move from a simmer to a boil. Brian had laughed in a way that made Chris wish he could commit fratricide over the phone line. "Honestly, I assumed she was still with you. I don't expect she got very far without her credit cards and her padded bank account."

"So Grant cut her off?" Chris asked, pressing his thumb and middle finger against his eye sockets to stave off the impending headache.

"Yep. Completely and totally. It about gave him a heart attack when Julie wasn't on that plane. But you know how he is—he never lets anyone call his bluff. Not even Julie."

Chris hung up the phone, a ball of sick rage roiling in his stomach. God, Julie was alone somewhere, with no money and apparently her own father didn't even care. Contrary to what he'd thought, Julie didn't need anyone's support to stand up to her domineering father. Worry, pride, and regret formed a tight ball in his gut. Carla was right. He'd underestimated her. The realization re-doubled his determination to find her and use whatever means necessary to convince her to take him back.

Finally in a last ditch effort to locate her, Chris searched through his past reservations lists, cursing himself again for not taking the time to key the guest information into his searchable database. After sorting through what seemed like hundreds of pages and handwritten notes, he finally located the number of her best friend, Wendy.

Chris sighed impatiently as Wendy's phone rang a third time. Crap. He was going to get sent to voicemail. Maybe he should just book a flight to visit her in person—

"Hello?" Wendy's voice was slightly breathless.

"Wendy, this is Chris Dennison."

"What the hell do you want?"

Chris held out the handset, surprised that icicles hadn't formed. "I'm looking for Julie," he began.

"Look, I'll tell you what I told her father. Julie is fine. She's taking care of herself. You don't need to worry about her. Now do her a favor and leave her alone."

"But I lo—"

"No, you listen," Wendy raged. "Julie is one of the best people I've ever known, and you pushed her around and broke her heart. She finally has the chance to figure out her life, and I won't let you mess it up."

Chris swallowed heavily. "Is she happy?"

"She's working on it," Wendy replied.

"Will you tell her—" The click of the connection being broken cut him off before he could finish: "That I love her."

He impatiently hit redial, cursing when he rang into voice mail. Who the hell did Wendy think she was, coming between him and the woman he loved? Still, he managed to temper his anger enough to leave a civil message. No sense antagonizing the only person who seemed to know where Julie was.

"Wendy, I know you have no reason to trust me. I don't blame you for trying to protect Julie. I know you think I'm an ass, and you're probably right. But you should also know this. I love her. I've loved her since she was sixteen years old. I love her more than I ever thought I'd love anyone. All I want is the chance to tell her in person. So please call me back and tell me where she is so I can—" a sharp beep cut him off, telling him he'd reached the time limit for his message. "Shit," he murmured as he hung up. Now all he could do was stare at the phone like some lovesick teenager, praying Julie's best friend would call him back.

". . . and you can either have the reception out here by the pool," Julie gestured to the expansive pool deck, currently occupied by several lounge chairs, "or we can set up tents and a temporary dance floor on the beach."

Christina, the crown princess of Sweden, looked around the grounds of the Ritz-Carlton St. Thomas with a critical eye. "I like your ideas, but we will review additional properties in the area before I make a decision."

Julie smiled, nodded politely. "I hope your search is successful. Of course, we would be thrilled if you chose the Ritz, and we will do our very best to accommodate your every whim."

Julie knew better than to press Christina to make a decision before she was ready.

Even though a royal wedding would be quite a coup, it wasn't as though they needed the business. In the two months since she'd become the special events director here at the Ritz, she'd already successfully overseen half a dozen nuptials of varying sizes.

As if that weren't enough, she was currently working on a plan to sell wedding packages for couples with smaller ceremonies, while hosting the larger events at the same time. If her numbers were right, they stood to make several hundred thousand in additional revenue per year.

She headed back to the sales office to prepare for a meeting with the catering manager. Not bad for a woman who couldn't even get a recommendation from her former employer.

She didn't even bother asking her father for a reference for fear he'd a) try to sabotage her, or b) fly down here to personally escort her back to San Francisco. Fortunately her resume spoke for itself, and several of her former colleagues had given her glowing reviews, and promised to keep her whereabouts secret from her family.

It still seemed a little surreal. Here she was again, working in another hotel. But this time, no one could accuse her of getting her job through nepotism. And she was finding that when it came to her client's parties the sky was still the limit, her personal budget had a much lower ceiling compared to what she'd been used to.

When she left the airport that day she'd taken a cab to a hotel, only to find out that her credit card was refused for non-payment. She had just enough money left in her checking account to cover a few nights' lodging. Desperate, she'd called Wendy, who as usual had a perfect solution.

Luckily for her, her six carat diamond engagement ring was of such high quality (she had to give Brian credit—the man certainly knew his jewelry), the jeweler was willing to provide a substantial, if not full, refund. Under other circumstances, Julie might have felt guilty about using the proceeds from the ring, but she had taken the money Wendy wired her and set up a checking account in St. Thomas with nary a twinge of regret. It was the least Brian could do, after all this.

Once her credit card and other bills were paid off, she had just enough to tide her over until she found gainful employment. Fortunately, the Ritz had an opening that was right up her alley.

It didn't pay a huge salary, but for the first time in her life, Julie was confident that she'd been hired because her employers believed in her ability and her willingness to work hard. The position was a perfect fit—challenging, fun, and it even included room and board at one of the most beautiful resorts in the Caribbean.

Still, work wasn't quite enough to keep her spirits up all the time. As she headed back to her little studio apartment for the evening, a familiar heaviness settled in her chest.

She looked around the single room, with its big bed, utilitarian kitchenette, a single chair in front of the desk, and felt the crushing weight of her loneliness crash down around her.

She missed her friends in San Francisco, especially Wendy. It was still too early to call her—Wendy would still be at work.

But homesickness was the least of her problems.

She missed Chris. God, how she missed him! Everything reminded her of him. The smell of the ocean reminded her of the scent of his tan skin. Every well-built guy with sun-streaked brown hair turned her head. But only for about a millisecond, until her brain kicked back in to remind her that Chris was at Holley Cay. And that he didn't deserve her moping, not when he'd kicked her out so coldly, dismissing her as no more than a spoiled, useless society princess. He was so convinced he knew her, he hadn't bothered to look beyond the surface.

It never failed to bring tears to her eyes, the memory of his parting words. The way he'd let her go without a fight, as though she wasn't even worth the effort.

She should hate him, she told herself for the thousandth time. Or at the very least, be very, very angry with him. How could she love someone who had no faith in her? Was he really any better than her father or Brian? Like them, Chris fully expected her to tuck her tail between her legs and trot obediently home.

She poured herself a bowl of cereal. Not the world's best dinner, but it was all she had in her apartment. If only Chris could see her now. This was hardly the pampered life he no doubt thought she'd returned to. That is, if he bothered to think of her at all.

That depressing thought was nearly enough to make her lose her appetite. But she crunched resolutely and gave herself the same pep talk she'd given herself last night, and the night before, and the night before that. *I'm going to get over him. And once I do, I'll meet someone new. Someone who will love me and appreciate me for the smart, capable, independent woman that I am.*

Her slightly bolstered spirits stayed up for precisely forty-four minutes, until she came across *Blue Lagoon* as she flicked through the stations. The sight of the two lovers cavorting on the beach and in the water reminded her so much of her last day with Chris that she burst into tears.

Her phone rang, and she took a deep breath and blew her nose before answering.

"Hello?" she said, her voice cracking.

"Jules, my God, are you okay?"

Wendy's concerned voice on the other end elicited a fresh wave of sobs.

"I'm f-fine," she sputtered, just so Wendy wouldn't think anyone had died or anything.

"I just wanted to check up on you. I guess you're not doing so good?"

"I'm fine," Julie repeated, and this time her voice only trembled a little. She poured herself a glass of ice water to wash away the sticky, salty taste of tears. "I just—it's so stupid—I'm watching *Blue Lagoon*, and I just can't stop thinking of Chris." Julie strove to get a handle on herself. "I know it's silly, I mean, I've kept it together this entire time." Privately, at least. As far as Wendy knew, Chris was yet another guy who had screwed Julie over, and Julie was relieved to be rid of him.

The truth was, Julie was embarrassed to admit, even to Wendy, that she'd been stupid enough to fall in love with him.

"Jules, you were in love with him, and the guy broke your heart," Wendy said.

Julie drew herself up, surprised. "I'm not in love with him," she said, her voice sorely lacking in conviction.

Wendy chuckled wearily. "I know you're trying to put on this tough act for everyone, but remember who you're talking to."

Julie flopped down on her loveseat and exchanged *Blue Lagoon* for MTV.

"I'm that transparent, huh?"

"To me, yeah."

"I don't know why I can't get over him. What ever happened to that theory that it takes twice as long to get over a relationship as the relationship lasted? Or is it half as long as the relationship lasted? Either way, it's been two months! I should be over him by now, not falling apart every time I see a couple rolling around on the beach." At least the self-directed anger felt better than self-pity. "And I just can't get over the way he let me leave. As far as he knew, I was getting back together with Brian, and he didn't even care."

Wendy murmured some comforting words and was silent for a few moments. Then, "Actually, that gets to my other reason for calling. I thought about not telling you at all, but then I realized I would be no better than your parents, doing what I thought was best for you, rather than letting you decide for yourself."

Tiny hairs prickled up on the back of Julie's neck. "Let's hear it, then."

"Yesterday, I got a call from Chris. I would have called you before now, but with the time change I decided to wait until you were out of the office."

Julie's heart jerked in her chest, then started pounding so hard she could feel the vibration in her fingers and toes. Ruthlessly reminding herself not to get her hopes up, she asked, "What did he want?"

"He was trying to get in touch with you. He'd tried you at your old number and at the Winston. He even called Brian. He finally called me as a last resort."

"Did you tell him where I am?" In the split second it took for Wendy to answer, Julie sent out a fervent prayer. What if he tried to contact her? What would she do? Worse, what if he did know, and hadn't tried to get in touch with her, and had no intention of doing so?

"No."

Julie's eyes closed as the breath she'd been holding whooshed out of her lungs. But her relief was immediately followed by anger at Wendy's next words.

"I told him you were fine, but that if he cared about you at all, he should stay out of your life."

"Why would you tell him that?"

"Because I thought that was right. But then he called back and left a message and . . . now I'm not so sure."

"What did he say?"

"Stuff." Wendy was holding out on her, and so obviously not trying to hide it.

"Why won't you just tell me what he said?"

"Because he said things that are best said in person. I didn't want to give him your information without asking you, but I think you should call him. He seemed really worried when he found out you'd been cut off."

"Great, he's worried. Probably still thinks I'm barely surviving without Daddy's bank account. He was probably calling for his own peace of mind." Despite her harsh words, Julie couldn't entirely squelch the sensation of hope, pushing its way free of the knot of confusion in her gut.

"I think it's more than that," Wendy said, still evasive. "You really should call him and find out. Or better yet, go visit." As though it were that simple.

"Two months ago you were telling me good riddance, that I was better off without him. Why do you think it's such a good idea for me to go chasing after him now?"

Wendy paused, mulling it over. "Let's just say I think he's realized his mistake." Wendy paused, then chuckled. "I'm lucky I'm not in the same room with you, aren't I?"

Julie looked down at her clenched fist. Wendy was right. If she were there in person Julie might have punched her by now.

"What if he sends me away again?" Despite the seed of hope that Wendy was right, the raw wound inflicted by Chris's casual dismissal was far from healed. What if Wendy was wrong? She didn't know if she could handle another crushing rejection from Chris.

"You were tough enough to get back on your feet—and quickly I might add—when your dad pulled the rug out from under you. I think you can handle Chris and whatever happens after that. Besides, I think chances are good this will end the way you want it to."

"Thanks, Wen. I love you."

"Love you, too, girlfriend. Now go get him."

# 18

"She's having the wedding where?" Chris asked Carla over a plate of coconut banana crepes they'd had sent up for a working breakfast.

"The Ritz St. Thomas," Carla said, drenching a crepe in warm maple syrup.

"But that's so, so," Chris searched for the right phrase. "Pedestrian," he said finally.

Carla arched an eyebrow.

Chris winced at his own snobbishness. "Jesus, I sound like my father."

"Pedestrian or no, Christina's assistant said that her highness was particularly impressed with the woman in charge of their events department. Said she felt more confident about their ability to meet the princess's standards."

A flush of anger stole up Chris's face. "What, like this is Motel 6?"

"She did say that in terms of sheer beauty, Holley Cay was far superior, but in the end she and her staff thought the Ritz was more capable of hosting the event."

Chris swore loudly.

"Face it, Chris, we need someone who really knows how to manage these things. We've done okay so far, mostly through dumb luck. But we can't seem to figure out how to do one of these big events without shorting the other guests, and that's just not fair."

Chris tugged at his lower lip, thinking. "You said it was the events person at the Ritz who sold them?"

Carla nodded.

Without a word Chris jumped up and grabbed his wallet. "Call Max and tell him I need a ride over to St. Thomas, ASAP."

"What are you doing?"

"Poaching from the competition."


"Thank you. We're very excited at the opportunity to host her highness's nuptials. I'll send you some figures next week, and we can begin ironing out the details."

Julie hung up, then stared at her phone. She hadn't called Chris the night before. She'd gone to their Web site, found the main number for Holley Cay, and had the phone in her hand before she stopped herself.

The office would be closed, and she didn't know Chris's private number. And what were the chances that he would be at home at nine in the evening? Most likely he was mingling with the guests, making sure everything was perfect in the fantasy world he'd built for them.

Even worse, maybe he was having dinner with a beautiful, single vacationer, one who didn't come with enough family baggage to sink the *Titanic*.

Once that depressing thought had taken root in her mind, she'd decided to put off her call until this morning, when he would be in his office, alone. At least for the time being.

She shook off the negative thought. If she was going to do

this, she needed to have faith, if only for a few minutes, that maybe, just maybe, Chris was pining away for her, too.

*Call him,* the voice inside her head screamed.

Julie snatched up the phone and dialed before she could think about it.

"Good afternoon, Holley Cay Resort, how may I direct your call?"

Julie requested Chris's office and closed her eyes, heart pounding. She took several deep, calming breaths and focused on the light reggae hold music chirping out of the phone. A little cheesy. Chris should really change that.

*Hi Chris, it's Julie. I heard you were trying to get in touch with me.*

Too impersonal.

*Chris, it's Julie. I can't stop thinking about you and I want to see you as soon as possible.*

Truthful, but too needy.

*Chris, I've loved you since I was eighteen and I wish you'd never left so I could have married you and had your babies and never ended up in this awful mess with Brian.*

Also truthful, but borderline crazy. And, to be fair, putting a bit too much of the blame on Chris. Sure, he'd left, but she was the one who never told Chris how she felt, and taken up with Brian in the first place.

*Chris, I love you. I want to be with you, and I'm hoping we can take what we had and make it into something real and lasting.* The line clicked and Julie braced herself to say the words out loud.

"Chris Dennison's office, Carla speaking."

It took a moment for Julie to compose herself. "Carla, hi, it's Julie Driscoll. I really need to talk to Chris."

"Dang, he just left, like, an hour ago. It was the weirdest thing. He said something about the competition and took off. I have no idea where he went."

"Do you know when he'll be back?"

"No clue. Want to leave a number in case he calls in?"

"No, I'll just try back later." Chris would know immediately that the number was from a location in the Virgin Islands. Julie wanted to tell him herself that she was still in the Caribbean. Needed to see his reaction. Or hear it, as it were.

Julie shuffled through her paperwork. After the adrenaline rush she'd experienced while dialing the phone wore off, she felt completely deflated.

Suddenly her assistant burst in. "Julie, I'm sorry to interrupt, but there's this guy here to see you. He won't tell me—"

Julie looked up in time to see a large, tan hand push the door all the way open. A tall, well-built man pushed his way past Julie's assistant.

Her pen slipped from her numb fingers and her stomach did a triple flip with a twist as she looked up into those achingly familiar midnight blue eyes.

"I'm sorry to bother you but . . ." Chris's voice trailed off as he recognized the woman gaping at him from her seat behind the massive desk. He shook his head. It couldn't possibly be—

Julie snapped her mouth closed and tried to look composed, but Chris didn't even try to stop himself from flying across the room and gathering her in his arms. Julie. Chris buried his nose in her hair, wrapped his arms around her, and lifted her off the ground. Her fresh, flowery scent fogged his brain, and the familiar weight of her felt so good that for a moment he couldn't even speak.

Julie wasn't suffering from the same affliction.

"What are you doing here?" she asked, trying to pull away. He tightened his arms around her, not about to let her break free. "How did you find me? Wendy said she didn't tell you where I was—"

He cut her off, wrapping his hand around the back of her head to hold her still for his all-consuming kiss. He thrust his tongue against hers, savored her sweet salty taste. He would answer all of her questions later. Right now he wanted to savor his impossibly good luck at finding her again. He knew this time, he would never let her go.

She returned his kiss with fevered impatience, sucking at his tongue, sinking against his chest like she wanted to crawl inside his body. Helpless little whimpers emitted from the back of her throat, sending a jolt of lust straight to his groin.

"Um, Julie, is everything okay?" Chris heard the assistant's voice. It sounded like it was coming from the bottom of a well, barely cutting through the lust-filled haze in his brain.

She pulled away from his embrace. Reluctantly he released her and smiled as he watched her smooth the front of her sleeveless blouse and run a hand over her hair.

"Yes, Meg, everything is fine. Chris is an old friend." Only someone who knew her very well would detect the slight tremor in her voice. That was Julie, polished and professional.

Meg backed through the door, and shut it behind her.

He immediately pulled her back against him.

"I can't believe you're really here," she said, running her hands up and down his back as though proving to herself he was really here. "How did you find me?"

"I didn't. I mean, I didn't know you were working here." He felt her stiffen, and he tightened his arms around her so she couldn't escape.

"Then why are you here?"

"I wanted to find out who the crown princess of Sweden liked so much that she decided to have her wedding here." He flashed a smile, which faded when Julie didn't smile back. "And I wanted to hire her for myself."

Julie put her hands against his chest and tried to push away. "You came here to offer me a job?"

"No, well, yes, but not you specifically. I had no idea you were my competition."

She turned her face away, but not so fast that he missed the tremble in her full lower lip.

"I thought you were happy to see me."

Julie let out a ragged little sigh. "For a minute I thought . . ." She shook her head.

"What?" He asked, capturing her chin in his hand and forcing her gaze back to his. He couldn't resist. He pulled her towards him and his tongue stole out, tracing the plump curve of her bottom lip. "Tell me what's wrong, Buttercup, so I can make it better."

Julie let out a ragged little sigh and pushed his head away. "I'm disappointed, okay? I had this stupid little fantasy that maybe you tracked me down and came here to tell me . . ."

"Tell you what?"

Julie just shook her head. "Never mind. By the way, Wendy told me you called, that you were worried."

His mouth set in grim lines. "Is that all she said?" He remembered saying quite a bit more in his follow up message. Either Wendy hadn't repeated it, or Julie didn't give a flying fuck. He hoped like hell it was the former.

"I think that was the gist of it. Behold." She spread her arms, sarcastically showcasing her small office. "Despite what you thought, it appears that silly, spoiled Julie can actually take care of herself."

Chris looked around the office. "I think you've proven that beyond a doubt, as well as proving that I'm the biggest idiot that ever lived."

"No argument there," she muttered, but he could see the faintest twitch of a smile.

"Look, I know I was an asshole. I should have had faith in you, but I didn't." Chris cupped her cheek, fingered a strand of her hair, marveling at the fact that she was here, she was real, and finally he had the chance to do something right. "I missed you so much, it made me crazy," he admitted.

Julie's eyes lit up.

"You don't have to look so happy about it. I've been miserable."

"Then why didn't you try to find me sooner?"

"I wouldn't let myself believe you'd actually turn your back on everything just to be with me."

Her eyes clouded and she looked away, and again he was hit with the full force of his own stupidity. He didn't want to do it, but he was going to have to do some serious begging. What the hell. Julie was worth it.

"I was an idiot," he repeated.

"I think we've established that."

He chuckled and reached for her hand, toying with her fingers. "This is going to sound corny as hell, but from the time I first met you, I wanted you. And I think everyone knew it, except you. But everyone was very quick to tell me to stay the hell away from you. That I may be half Dennison, that didn't make me good enough to lay so much as a finger on you."

Her delicate brows knit in a frown. "Didn't I have some choice in the matter?"

"Come on, Julie, you knew it, too. Even in college, you made sure your parents never knew we hung out. Sure, I knew we could have a fling, but when it came down to it you'd never fight your family for me." Though his tone wasn't accusatory, merely honest, she winced at hearing the truth.

"You're probably right," she grudgingly admitted. "I would like to say I've come a long way from that spineless eighteen-year-old, but up until a few months ago, I was a spineless twenty-six-year-old willing to marry your brother to make my father happy. It's not exactly a shock that you thought I'd eventually run home with my tail between my legs." The defeated slump in her shoulders broke his heart.

He gripped her hand tighter. "You're wrong. I was a coward. I should have trusted you, believed you when you said you were ready to risk it all." He sat down in a leather armchair she used for guests, pulling her into his lap. "I'm ready to risk it, too, and, if you give me another chance, I swear I'll never let you regret it."

Julie kissed him, melting into him with a sigh as a surge of love and lust crashed through her. Part of her wondered if she should play harder to get, give him a worse time before giving in so completely. But he was here, he wanted her, and she wasn't about to waste any more time holding back her forgiveness. Of course, that wouldn't stop her from milking his guilt for all it was worth.

"Don't think this means you'll be able to hire me away without a fight."

"I can offer you a very competitive position," he murmured between kisses. "Not to mention the extra benefits. I wish I'd known you were here," he whispered against her lips, "because I could have put together a better package."

"I have no complaints about the package," she said, sliding her hand down between them to press against the erection threatening to burst out of his fly.

He half laughed, half groaned. "It's still incomplete. For one thing, I don't have a ring."

That froze her where she sat. Her heart started to race when he gently lifted her from his lap, took her shaking fingers in his, and sank to his knees in front of her.

He took her hands in his again, slowly bringing each one up to his lips. "The two weeks we spent together made me realize something I've known for a long time. I love you, Julie, more than I've ever loved anyone, more than I ever thought it possible to love anyone."

Her breath caught on a sob as she sank to her knees, too. "I love you, too, so much," she murmured, threading her fingers through his hair and pulling his mouth to hers.

Amazingly, his dark blue eyes sparked with tears, his Adam's apple bobbed before he continued. "I know it's probably too soon, since you just got out of one marriage, but do you think you can handle being Julie Dennison again?"

Julie choked on a sob and threw her arms around his neck. "It's not too soon, so if you're asking, I'm saying yes."

# Epilogue

She was without a doubt the most beautiful, sexiest bride that had ever lived. Chris's heart was so full, he was afraid it was going to burst through his chest as Julie walked toward him. Her silk dress showed off her sweet curves, making his hands itch to take it off her. Her gold-streaked hair tumbled around her shoulders, the soft curls brushing against her lightly tanned shoulders. No veil obscured her hair, but she'd tucked a single, fluffy white flower behind her right ear. Her mouth was stretched in a smile so wide, it nearly took up the bottom half of her face, and pure, unadulterated happiness radiated from her blue eyes.

His breath grew tight as she approached, his heart pounding so hard he was sure she could see it through the fine linen of his shirt. With his heart in his throat, he took her outstretched hand, and suddenly the raging storm inside him turned perfectly calm. This was it. He was holding everything he'd ever wanted in life in his hand.

"Where is he? It's time to cut the cake?" Carla asked Julie.

Julie put a soothing hand on her arm. "Don't worry. He's

right over there, talking to Drew," she indicated Chris's friend from high school.

"This is so much more fun than your last wedding." Wendy, once again Julie's maid of honor, sidled up next to Julie and wrapped her arm around Julie's waist.

She briefly laid her head on Wendy's shoulder. "I agree. Of course that could be due to the fact that I'm actually marrying the right guy this time." Across the dance floor, her gaze met Chris's. The heavy-lidded look he shot her was so full of heat it put the blazing Caribbean sun to shame. Noticing Chris's distraction, his best man turned around and smiled, saluting the women with his drink.

Her gaze slid back to Chris. She couldn't wait to get him alone. It had been hard, the last few months, shuttling back and forth from St. Thomas. Julie hadn't felt right about leaving the Ritz in a lurch and had stayed on until Princess Christina's wedding. At first Chris had been disappointed, but ultimately he understood her sense of responsibility, and he loved her all the more for it. So for four months he'd paid Max overtime to ferry them both back and forth to St. Thomas.

The last month had been particularly torturous, as Julie had insisted that they abstain from sex in order to make their wedding night more special. Unconsciously Julie licked her lips at the prospect of getting him naked. Oh yeah, the fifteen seconds that she would last would be very special indeed.

"I'll say you got the right guy," Wendy sighed. "I don't think any man has ever looked at me like that."

"I don't know, I think Chris's friend Drew is definitely checking you out."

Wendy snuck a peek at Chris's best man. Sure enough, he was looking back at her, his green eyes gleaming under dark arching eyebrows.

"Hmm. He seems like a cocky bastard."

Julie looked up at Wendy, surprised. "I thought that was your type."

Wendy frowned. "Not anymore." Then she released Julie's waist to chase down the waiter with the champagne.

It was amazing how different this wedding was from her last. Unlike her last over-engineered dress, this time she wore a simple sleeveless ivory satin gown. Its lingerie-like design skimmed her curves, and the ankle-length hemline offered glimpses of her feet, completely bare except for a platinum toe ring set with a tiny diamond. It was a gift from Chris, specially made to match the gorgeously simple three carat solitaire that decorated her left hand.

A small party of friends and relatives gathered at the beach bar under a tent. Even her parents seemed to be enjoying themselves. Shortly after Chris had proposed, Julie had called her mother, who showed surprising assertiveness in her efforts to get Julie and her father to reconcile. Though she doubted they would ever be close, Julie and her father had formed an ever-strengthening truce in the past several months. Ironically, he seemed more impressed by her newfound independence than he ever was with her endless efforts to please him.

She felt Chris's presence even before he touched her. She leaned back against his chest, turning to nuzzle the warm skin of his throat bared by his open collar. He was so gorgeous in his black linen trousers and white dress shirt. Unlike her, he did wear shoes—black leather flip-flops.

They watched Carla as she bustled around, directing waiters, instructing the band on what song to play while they cut the cake.

"It's really nice having someone else take care of everything for a change," Julie said as she burrowed against him.

"Yeah, remind me to send Carla on a vacation," Chris said,

nuzzling her curls. His fingers dislodged the gardenia blossom she'd tucked behind her ear, and she felt the petals caress her cheek and shoulder as it fell.

"How soon do you think we can sneak off?" Chris's hot breath caressed her ear before his teeth closed over the lobe in a teasing nip.

Julie's nipples beaded against the silky fabric of her dress. That was the problem with the tropics. There was no way to hide your arousal by claiming to be cold. "We should probably stay a bit longer . . ." Dampness soaked the silk of her ivory La Perla thong panties as she felt the hard length of Chris's erection growing against her belly. "But I know of a certain ladies restroom that could be put to good use . . ."

And this time, when Julie Driscoll Dennison's groom was caught in flagrante delicto, it was with the bride's full and vocal approval.

Turn the page
as Jody Lynn Copeland
shows us some
BODY MOVES!

On sale now from Aphrodisia!

# 1

---

Jordan Cameron sank back in his office chair and glared at the reflection of his father's profile in the eighth-story window of the New York City investment firm. For the first time in over a decade, John Cameron wore no beard, and every trace of gray in his hair had been covered with dark blond. He looked more like Jordan's older brother than his father. It wasn't right and, clearly, neither was his father's state of mind.

Jordan swiveled in the chair, curling his fingers around a brochure for the medical tourism resort his father returned from three weeks ago and had yet to stop talking about. He respected his father and never questioned his choices aloud. However, this latest decision wouldn't allow him to bottle his exasperation. "Jesus, Dad, think about what you're doing. It's a passing fad at best."

Inspecting himself in the golf green–etched mirror hanging on the wall kitty-corner from Jordan's desk, John rubbed his first finger and thumb along his clean-shaven chin. "Oh, I think about it. Every time your mother sneaks up and pinches my ass. I forgot how strong my sex drive was until I spent a week at

Private Indulgence. Thanks to that 'fad,' our marriage and love life are stronger than ever."

Jordan sighed. From the way his father talked, you would think the resort staff had restructured his entire reason for being and not just his underdeveloped chin.

"Fine. Let's say this place is the real deal and will be around for years to come; that still doesn't explain why you feel the need to sink your entire life savings in it." Not when he'd spent the last five years refusing Jordan's investment advice because he claimed the only safe place for his money was in the bank. "Split the money. Let me put seventy percent of it into annuities."

Barking out a laugh, John looked over. "Back in the day, we considered a split to be fifty-fifty."

Back in the day, there wasn't an endless supply of lowlifes coming up with every scheme under the sun in the hopes of getting their hands on an old man's money. Jordan had heard the buzz on the medical resorts—Private Indulgence had never been among those said to be taking off. Even those resorts that claimed to be doing well had yet to provide convincing proof of their longevity. "At least give me some time to check this place out. You got to know too many of the staff to view it objectively."

"Not to mention I was strung out on Percocet ninety percent of the time I was down there."

"Exactly."

His father crossed to the twin tan leather chairs opposite Jordan's desk and slammed his hand down on the back of one. "By God, son, you've gotten so stiff, you don't even recognize sarcasm anymore."

"Oh, I recognize it. I just don't find it humorous when it mixes my father with habit-forming drugs."

John closed his eyes and pinched the bridge of his nose—a habit Jordan had picked up from him. Opening his eyes, he let his hands fall at his sides. "All right. You've got four weeks. Only because I want to see you away from this damned desk for more than a few hours at a time. This place is sucking you dry, stealing your zest for life—"

"And worrying Mom sick she'll never have grandkids," Jordan finished dryly. He'd been through this song and dance too many times to count. Sorry to say for his parents, he wasn't one of those kids who lived to please only them. "She'll get her grandkids when I'm ready. Right now, I'm enjoying the zest for life you seem to think I've lost by dating whatever women appeal to me."

His father snorted. "Whichever ones are willing to come in second to your career is more like it."

"Dad . . ." Jordan warned.

"I'm leaving." John went to the door, turning back when he reached it. "Four weeks. If I don't hear convincing evidence against the resort by then, I'll be on the first flight to the Caribbean to share my investment decision with Dr. Crosby."

With the *snick* of the office door, Jordan turned his attention to his laptop. He clicked on the bookmarked resort informational page for Danica Crosby, MD, the plastic surgeon cum owner of Private Indulgence who'd somehow convinced his father to sink his money into her resort.

Calling the plain-looking, glasses-wearing redhead who appeared on his screen a surgeon was pushing it, considering she was barely out of her residency. The sudden ache in Jordan's gut told him that calling her business dealings with his father *reputable* would be pushing it even further, and in less than four weeks he would prove it.

"What in Hi'iaka's name are you doing?"

With her friend and assistant's question, Danica Crosby released her death grip on the alarm clock radio and set it on her desk. Lena stood in the doorway of Danica's office, eyeing her as if she'd lost her mind. For now, her sanity was intact. God only knew what would happen in the next few minutes.

Danica pushed aside one of several wayward envelopes and grabbed a chocolate-covered almond from the starfish-shaped candy dish on her desk. She popped the nut into her mouth, letting its soothing taste and texture work their magic on her tension before giving the alarm clock's red digital readout another glance. "Waiting. Three minutes from now, something bad is going to happen."

Lena's brown eyes flashed with hope. "You became psychic last night?"

"Wouldn't you have felt some sort of psychic friends' connection if I had?" Lena gave the expected dry laugh, and Danica continued soberly, "I grabbed my morning Pepsi out of the refrigerator this morning, only to discover there was no Pepsi to grab, even though I know there was one last night. An hour later, I almost cut my nipple off shaving."

Day-Glo pink and lime-green hula-girl earrings—what Lena claimed to be her twin talismans, since her supposed visionary powers began the day she'd put them on—swayed with the scrunching of her nose. "Ew. Your breasts are hairy? I just thought you'd given up on dating because you realized you were a lesbian and were afraid to come out of the closet."

"Not everyone's a date addict like you." Probably because not everyone had Lena's cute build, which had only gotten cuter with the recent chopping of all but the last couple inches of her hair and subsequent dye job that turned her locks from near black to dirty blond with fuchsia streaks.

"I prefer 'serial dater.'"

"Whatever. I'm not one. I also don't have hairy breasts. I was shaving my underarm and fumbled the razor. It nicked my nipple on its way down." Danica winced. The memory hurt almost as much as the real thing.

Lena frowned. "A nipple ouchy tells you something bad's going to happen in three minutes?"

Danica gave the alarm clock a glance. Her stomach tightened forebodingly, so she popped another almond. "One minute now, and yes. Haven't you ever heard bad things happen in sets of three?"

"Sure, but I never knew there was a timetable."

"Well, there is. In fifty seconds, mine's due up." Judging by the fact that last almond didn't even touch her anxiety, whatever happened at the end of those seconds was bound to be a doozy.

Lena studied her so long and thoroughly, Danica thought another of her friend's questionable visions was about to strike, but then she just smiled, calling out the exceedingly cute dimple in her right cheek. "You know, most of the time you're as boringly normal as they come, and then you go and say something totally whacked like this and I remember there's hope for you yet."

The alarm clock rolled over to ten o'clock. Any amusement Danica might have found in Lena's words was forgotten in the wake of her heightened unease. "Time's up."

She looked around the office, half expecting the overflowing bookcase to fall on her, or the chaos on her desk to blow up in her face, or the bay window behind her to shatter, or . . . She swiveled in her chair, praying her customized golf cart hadn't gone up in flames.

Nope. Still there, parked two stories below.

"Looks like your timetable's off—Strike that." Lena inhaled audibly. "Trouble's headed this way. Don't look like no cowboy, but I'd know the smell of Stetson anywhere."

Danica swiveled back in her chair in time to see her friend exit her office as an unfamiliar man entered it, bringing with him the mouthwateringly spicy tang of cologne. Her belly did a slow warming, her inner thighs mimicking the intimate response as she took in the newcomer.

Lena was right. With his black power suit, which was completely inappropriate for the humid island weather, and polished Kenneth Coles, he didn't look like a cowboy. Danica still had the urge to climb up his long legs and take him for a ride.

Wow! Where had *that* come from?

She never thought of sex while on the clock and nearly as seldom while off it. It wasn't because she lacked Lena's perfectly cute everything and the natural tan complexion of her friend's Hawaiian heritage—Danica liked her fair complexion just fine. It was that she had too many other, more important, things to fill her days, namely seeing Private Indulgence, the elective surgery medical tourism resort she'd started up three years ago, continue to thrive in a way that would eventually allow for expansion into nonelective areas.

The guy moved into her office, assessing each inch before moving on to the next one. His measuring gaze landed on her. "Interesting place you have here."

Holy killer eyes! They matched the turquoise waters of the Caribbean Sea right down to the sparkle.

The way Danica's sex grew moist with the striking shade suggested his walking through her door might well be the third bad thing to happen to her this morning—by making her focus on something other than work. Even if she did have time for dating and he lived locally—doubtful, given his attire—and showed an interest, things would never work.

From his carefully styled dark blond hair and neatly trimmed mustache to the perfectly symmetrical dimple in the knot of his gray silk tie, there was an order about him that his delectable appearance wouldn't allow her to look past. Danica and order went together like Lena and celibacy—both would be happening the same time pigs sprouted wings.

She relaxed with the knowledge they wouldn't be having sex. All but her churning stomach relaxed anyway. It was a little too coincidental he'd shown up right at ten. "May I help you?"

"I have a meeting with Dr. Crosby. I was told at the front desk that you're her."

"You *do*?" Pepsi withdrawal had to be playing hell with her memory. She didn't do visual order, but her mind usually had a firm grasp on things.

Danica stood, offering her hand over the top of her desk, along with an apologetic smile. "Sorry, this week has been hectic. I recall it now, Mr. . . . ?" Shoot. So much for correcting her oversight.

His lips twitched as his gaze slid the length of her, eyeing her in a penetrating way that renewed the wetness between her thighs and made her want to squirm.

His gaze returned to hers, and he took her hand in a firm shake. "Jordan Cantrell."

She made it a point to personally greet as many resort guests as possible, shaking dozens of hands each week, many of them male. Not one of them rendered visions of strong, warm hands sliding over her aroused, nude body the way Jordan's did. Her jean skirt would allow easy access. The thin barrier of her panties barely an obstacle. She glanced at his fingers—ringless and long like the rest of him. Able to easily slide between her thighs and deep inside her slick pussy.

The increased twitching of his lips broke through Danica's reverie. Heat flooded her face and undoubtedly flushed her fair skin with the reality of where her mind had traveled. As if her thoughts weren't bad enough, he was silently laughing at her. *Mocking* would be the better word.

Damn it, she'd worked hard to see the resort gain a foothold in the fast-growing medical tourism industry and come far in the time since its launch. Too far to be made to feel incompetent by a man who didn't know her from the Easter Bunny. Yet incompetent was exactly how she felt.

"I'm here to check out the resort for potential surgery," Jordan supplied, his derisive tone making it clear how unimpressed he was so far.

She wanted to give him a tone of her own. Or forget the tone and tell him off outright. For the sake of the resort's reputation, she refrained. "Of course you are." Ignoring her damp panties, she forced a smile and rounded her desk. "Let me grab your file from my assistant and we'll get started."

Danica entered Lena's next-door office as her friend stood from behind a desk that was so efficiently organized it made Danica feel dysfunctional by comparison. Lena flashed a smart-ass grin. "So, is he here to repossess your villa, or tell you an active volcano was discovered in the resort's backyard?"

"Neither. He's a potential patient." *And not even close to a gentleman.* Danica ran a hand over her belly. God, she needed an almond, or maybe a handful of them. "He says he has an appointment with me this morning."

"If he's J. Cantrell, he has a ten-fifteen. He took over a late cancellation spot a few weeks ago. I was about to pull his file when you walked in." She went to the rear wall, which was lined floor to ceiling with shelves of patient files, and pulled a thin manila one from the Cs. Halfway back to her desk, she stopped on an indrawn breath and gasped out a "Whoa!" that in Lena-talk meant she'd had a vision.

She crossed the rest of the way to Danica, handing her the file and sitting down without a word. Completely unlike Lena, who compensated for her small stature by being as vocal as possible. "Well? What was it about?" Danica prompted.

Lena didn't look up. "You don't want to know."

"I asked, didn't I?"

She looked up, her lips curving in an impish smile. "A Pepsiaholic with one hairy armpit because she was too afraid to go back and finish the job."

"Cute, Lena. Very cute." Despite her follow-up groan, the friendly jab eased Danica's tension—until she returned to her own office to find Mr. Hot, Blond, and Oppressive waiting in front of her desk.

Jordan happened to walk in right at ten—fifteen minutes early for his appointment—and made her have sexual thoughts for the first time ever while on the job, but that didn't mean he was trouble. He could just be a pain in the ass.

She sat down on her side of the desk, popping two chocolate-covered almonds into her mouth before opening and quickly reviewing his file—all one and a half mostly blank pages of it. She looked up at him. Damned if a bolt of lust didn't shoot through her with the brilliance of his eyes. "There's nothing listed on what you would like to have done."

"I didn't say."

"The facilities vary a great deal depending on the type of procedure you're considering. Showing you the entire resort would require hours, possibly days."

"It's a"—he glanced down—"sensitive matter."

"A sensitive . . ." Danica's gaze landed on his crotch. For an instant, as she thought about the anatomy behind his zipper, the heated state of her body returned. Then his meaning settled and she barely subdued her gasp.

She didn't exactly like the guy, but there was no denying he was a stunning specimen of masculinity. Was it possible he could be equipped with an undersized penis?

Of course it was possible. She'd scrubbed in on several phalloplasty surgeries where the patient was bigger bodywise than Jordan yet minuscule below the belt.

The irritation in her belly let up some, knowing he was here because of body issues beyond his control—something she could relate to well. "I understand. The facility for that surgery is quite a distance from here. If you don't mind going for a ride in the open air, we can use my golf cart to take a shortcut."

"You golf?" He sounded impressed.

"Actually, I bought the cart because I live only a half mile from here and figured it a more economical choice than a car." Technically, her rationale had been the more she saved on auto expenses, the more she would have to invest in the resort. Since he actually looked impressed now, she kept that tidbit to herself. Not that she was trying to impress him. Even if she could get past the whole "order" thing, he probably had performance-anxiety issues.

How small could he be?

Her gaze strayed back to his crotch, lingering for a few seconds before intelligence caught up with her Pepsi-starved brain. "I do golf, when time allows for it."

"Same here. It's been a while since time has allowed for it," Jordan admitted, perhaps a bit grudgingly.

Danica closed his file and pushed her chair back from her desk. "Work has a way of taking over."

"That it does."

"Having a job you love helps."

He gave a noncommittal murmur. She took it to mean he wasn't comfortable with the conversation any longer. While the casual talk had lifted his oppressive air and mostly relaxed her stomach, it was time to get on with the tour.

She gestured to the door, then pointedly led him to the elevator and out into the parking lot so she wouldn't be tempted to peek at his ass.

"Have you tried a natural approach?" Danica asked as she slid into the driver's side of her golf cart.

After climbing into the cart, Jordan looked over with a frown. "Natural?"

The breeze wreaked havoc on his previously flawless hair.

The sun baking through the roof of the cart already had perspiration gathering on his forehead. He should look like an imbecile for how warmly he was dressed. Not to mention completely unappealing with that frown. Instead he looked sexy and sweaty, and he smelled downright appetizing.

It was a good thing he probably had performance issues, because Danica was aching to let passion rule her in a way she hadn't allowed in ages.

"Have you tried exercising your..." She sent a covert glance at his groin. "The area in question?"

"Yeah. Sure. Didn't work."

She started the golf cart. "What about pills?"

"Didn't do a thing."

"There are a lot of placebos being illegally marketed as the real deal. It's an easy mistake to make."

Jordan wanted to view the words as an insult. The reassurance in Danica's greenish gray eyes when she told him it was an easy mistake made that hard to do.

She wasn't what he'd expected. For one thing, she didn't wear glasses—not at present anyway—and for another she did play golf. Her behavior skirted from strange to skilled to sexual. She kept staring at his crotch. No way in hell could he be imagining it, his dick would know the difference and not be in the process of tenting his pants. Then there was her appearance.

The Internet hadn't done her justice. In person, her layered, shoulder-length hair was more fiery copper than dull red, her nose narrow and straight with a charming bump and even more charming freckles near the tip. Her mouth was soft pink, lush, and wide, and he had more than one idea of how she might use it on him.

Danica reached across to a small compartment in front of him. The back of her hand brushed against his knees, jetting frissons of heat up his thighs to his stimulated groin. On a sharp inhale, Jordan retracted his body into the seat. He was acting like a pubescent teen, but he didn't want to like her, and he sure as hell didn't want to want her.

"Sorry." With a sympathetic smile, she lifted a pair of wire-framed glasses from the compartment. "You don't want to ride with me when I'm not wearing my glasses."

As it turned out, Jordan didn't want to ride with her when she had her glasses on either. The golf cart had clearly been modified to go beyond traditional speed. Twice, on the mile or so ride, he'd been certain she was going to need to call 911 to come scrape his remains off the ground.

Danica halted the cart in front of a wooden footbridge surrounded by tropical underbrush and trees. "It's easier to walk from here."

He jumped out and hoofed it across the bridge, wanting the hell away from the psycho driver who had overtaken her body. The bridge opened up on the other side to reveal a number of pale gray and slate blue villas detailed in sky blue and separated from one another by a good-sized yard and towering palms. A three-story, mostly glass building loomed past the villas. He headed in that direction, guessing it to be the facility she planned to show him.

She surprised him by sprinting past, the developed muscles of her bare legs constricting enticingly. His gaze lifted to a high, round ass cloaked in a short jean skirt, and his blood heated. She could owe her body to faithful jogging. More likely, her muscles and the ample breasts filling her knit pink tank top were the result of implantation.

"In a hurry?" Jordan called after her.

"I thought you were." Danica dropped back to match his reduced pace and gave him an openmouthed smile. "I'm all yours till noon, so anything you want to know"—she looked at his crotch—"don't be shy about asking."

The glimpse of her moist pink tongue and the suggestive

words would have been enough to have his shaft hardening again after the hellish ride's deflating effect. The continued ogling of his groin had his cock stiff as a board.

He considered stripping away his suit coat and dress shirt under the pretense he was roasting his ass off—technically not a pretense but a reality he owed to the airport for losing his luggage during flight transfer—and seeing how she responded. Learning she slept with prospective patients in the hopes of ensuring their patronage would be as good of a way to start unveiling the resort as a bad investment as any.

"We have a fully equipped hospital," Danica said in a voice that sounded both professional and proud, "but the majority of our surgeries are done in ambulatory facilities, which are housed in the same building as the surgeons' offices for the associated procedure. Using these facilities is one of the ways we're able to keep our costs substantially lower than most public practices."

"Should I be worried *ambulatory* and *ambulance* sound remarkably similar?"

Her throaty laugh was as unexpected as her appearance—totally enticing, totally dangerous to his mission. "Not at all. *Ambulatory* means you arrive and leave the facility on the same day. Your phalloplasty surgery . . ." She sent him another of those damned apologetic looks that made it difficult to remember she was the bad guy, or rather woman. "I didn't mean to put it into words."

Jordan sent a pointed look around. The closest person lounged on the front porch chaise of a villa over a hundred feet away. "I don't think anyone heard."

"I'll still be more careful."

"You said same-day facilities are one of the ways the resort's able to keep costs down," he rushed out, needing to get the apologetic look off her face. "What are the others?"

"Unlike a lot of the islands around us, we're not governed by the United States."

Now they were getting somewhere. "In other words, you're able to avoid licensing fees and training staff in the latest procedures."

Danica stopped walking to shoot him a frosty glare. "All of Private Indulgence's facilities and staff are accredited and operate under international standards, Mr. Cantrell." The icy look softened, along with her tone. "The cost of living is simply lower here, which allows us to charge less overall while providing first-rate, state-of-the-art services by top-notch specialists. Many of our procedures are discounted seventy to eighty percent as compared with the national average."

Well, fuck. Instead of uncovering a skeleton in the resort's figurative closet, he felt impressed for the second time since meeting her. He couldn't stop his smile. "I'd prefer you to call me Jordan."

"Like the almond." Cheeks gone rosy, she leaned close to release another of those dangerously enticing laughs. "That probably sounded odd." Her eyes warmed as she confided in a husky whisper, "It's just that I have a nut fetish."